LEAF & SCALE
3

THE SPECTRAL ORCHID

TILLY WALLACE

Cover by Malice and Mayhem

Version 04122025

To be the first to hear about new releases, sign up at:

https://www.tillywallace.com/newsletter

A MOMENT PLEASE...

This book is written in British English, with the odd Kiwi idiom—if I can sneak them in without my wonderful editor noticing!

You cannot offer me enough coffee to prise that extra 'u' or 'l' from me. Nor will jam & cream scones served the correct way (jam first) persuade me to insert a 'z' when 's' does an entirely satisfactory job.

These books are based in England, Scotland, or New Zealand—where we speak British English. As the old saying goes... *when in Rome....*

CHAPTER 1

Drake's Bend, early summer

Fern slipped through the wrought-iron gates of Wyndham Hall with her thoughts in as much turmoil as when she entered. That was probably why she never saw the bat that slammed into her face, its claws tangling in her hair.

"Ugh!" she cried out as wings covering her eyes momentarily blocked her vision.

Reaching up, she was about to fling the confused nocturnal creature away when her brain registered that bats weren't usually covered in looping purple scales. Nor did they excitedly puff warmed air.

"Squib?" Fern held the small creature far enough away from her face to get a better look at it.

The pixie dragon trilled and snorted a quick burst of air at her nose.

"Let's see if we can get the claw out." With care, Fern

unhooked his wing claw that had twisted in her hair. "What are you doing so far from the village on your own?"

Once free, she placed Squib on her shoulder, where he trilled and bounced up and down.

"Fern! Fern!" Millie called from along the shady road. The writer held up vibrant blue skirts with one hand, her other steadying her bonnet as she hurried towards them.

"Millie! I didn't hear you." Fern's thoughts had been in a shadowy room lined with dragon skeletons, remembering a heated kiss that even now she could still feel on her skin.

"I was calling your name, but you seemed a thousand miles away. Squib took it upon himself to attract your attention." Millie dropped her skirts and fanned herself with both hands.

"Sorry. My mind was somewhere else." About a mile up the driveway of Wyndham Hall. "What brings you out to this end of Drake's Bend? You're not leaving us to walk back to Warrington Manor, are you?"

Millie blanched, the rosy pink draining from her cheeks, and her eyes widened. "Oh. No." She swallowed as though her mouth had gone suddenly dry. "I...I...wanted to explore a little."

Squib fluttered to his mistress and nestled under her straw bonnet.

Mentally, Fern chided herself for not having thought to ask if Millie wanted to ramble over the countryside surrounding Drake's Bend. "I am sorry, Millie. Recent events have distracted me, rather like Squib's claw in my hair. I should have offered to take you out on some walks."

Millie rested one hand on the pixie dragon as she chewed

her lower lip. "We have both been busy. And it has taken me some time to realise the cottage won't disappear when I walk out the front door. It's just that I used to love roaming the countryside as a girl. When Father died, Bertie said it wasn't seemly, and he forbade me from leaving the immediate garden. Although I rather suspect he thought I'd run off and do something *unseemly*."

Fern's heart ached for her friend, who had been confined to her family estate. Her brother didn't want his sister to embarrass him with her wild flights of fancy. She threaded her arm through Millie's. "No one is going to stop you now. I will join you if you tell me what direction you had in mind?"

A brief smile crossed the other woman's features, and the worry lines eased. "I wanted to see the cemetery. I was told it's out this way? I find them peaceful and inspiring."

"Perfect. That is exactly where I am going." Fern guided the other woman along the road and towards a gap in the trees. The passage of many feet, horses, and carriages over the years had worn a dipped path in the earth. "I was on my way to talk to my parents, as I have much to tell them. But I am curious, how is a graveyard inspiring?" Fern asked as they entered the tunnel created by the foliage of the closely growing trees.

"Cemeteries are libraries of souls," Millie said in a hushed, reverent tone as they emerged from the tunnel into the picturesque meadow bathed golden by the sun.

They paused, and Fern saw the little graveyard through her friend's eyes. With its enclosing boundary of ancient trees, the weathered stone church at one end, and wildflowers scrambling among the tombs, it created a restful and peaceful place.

"A library of souls? I've never thought of it that way before." Fern and Millie walked along the main path that led from the tunnel to the church. The grass was interspersed with cobblestones to stop anyone slipping in the worst of the winter rain.

Millie paused and rested her hand on a gravestone. The etched words had turned green with moss. "A tombstone is like the title of a book. It is but a hint of what lies beneath. Each of these graves holds a story. Some are grand romances, others are adventures, and some are quiet tales of hardship and endurance."

They moved on and stopped at the small grave of a child enclosed by an ankle-high railing. Both of them fell silent as they considered a life snatched before the youngster had ever learned to walk.

"Some stories are tragically short," Millie whispered as she read the dates that began and ended in the same year. "Everyone here took the lead in their tale, and I like to sit among them and see if I can hear what they have to say. You probably think I'm silly."

Fern swallowed a lump that had formed in her throat. "No. On the contrary. I think that is a beautiful way to view a cemetery. My parents had a grand romance, with a dash of adventure if half the stories my Uncle Ambrose tells are true. Then it ended in tragedy, with both of them taken too early."

Millie leaned close to peer at Fern and abruptly changed the direction of the conversation. "Why do you keep touching your lip? Is something wrong?"

"Um..." Fern stared at her raised hand, unaware she had been rubbing her lip. "I might have...kissed Lord Drakeman."

"What? No wonder you were so distracted earlier." Millie grabbed both her hands and pulled her down onto the grass. "You must tell me everything!"

"There's not really that much to tell. I kissed him, and I should probably go back and apologise." Fern crossed her legs and plucked a blade of grass. She seemed to make rather a number of apologies to the lord of Wyndham Hall. There was something about being around him that made her more impulsive than usual. Perhaps the Moray sisters could create an amulet to shield her from his dragon gaze.

"Why do you need to apologise? Oh, Fern..." Millie's eyes widened. "Did you make an unwelcome advance?"

Squib, unlike his mistress, narrowed his gaze and huffed at Fern in disapproval of her actions.

Had the kiss been unwelcome? There had been a crackle in the air between them, as though someone had been frantically turning the crank on a galvanism machine. As she recalled, *he* had leaned closer to her first.

"I...well...he kissed me back." Fern replayed the moment over again.

Lord Drakeman had remained still for the first heartbeat of their kiss. Then his hands had cupped her nape as, rather enthusiastically in her opinion, he took control of events. It had been Fern who had broken away.

Millie huffed and shared a long look with Squib. "His lordship's response is not quite the same as having permission beforehand. What happened next?"

Fern threw herself back on the grass and stared at the

fluffy clouds above. She couldn't face either her friend or the pixie dragon when she said the next bit. "I ran off."

The huffy chortle of a tiny dragon joined Millie's tinkling laughter. "You don't strike me as the sort to take flight because of a kiss you started."

"It wasn't the kiss that bothered me." Fern heaved a sigh and glanced at her friend, who appeared to be sucking on her lips to contain either laughter or more questions. "It was what might have come next if we continued that made me need fresh air." It had been a thrilling kiss. Even now, she curled her toes as she remembered how her body had reacted.

"Did you desperately want him to ravish you on his desk?" Amusement sparkled in Millie's warm gaze.

"Desk? No, it was a rather substantial table." In her mind, Lord Drakeman swept the surface clear in the heat of their passion as their entwined bodies tumbled to the wood...No. Wait. He couldn't do that because of..."Dragons!"

Fern shot bolt upright and grabbed hold of Millie's hands. She shook them up and down as excitement tingled along her veins for an entirely different reason. "Lord Drakeman is studying the decline in dragon numbers. That's why he wanted the one I found by the odd kelmsgale."

"Gosh." Millie drew the word out like a sigh. "The reader learns an unexpected revelation about the brooding lord that may explain his withdrawal from society. Does he eschew all good company in his single-minded pursuit of a way to save dragonkind?" The writer disentangled one hand from Fern's and searched her pockets for the ever-present notebook and pencil.

"Before your quill turns him into a horribly misunderstood character who is actually softer than melted butter on the inside, we don't know why he is investigating the decline in dragon numbers yet. Maybe he wants their pieces for his experiments." Not that she genuinely believed that of him anymore. Not after how he had reacted when she accused him of grinding up a dragon's bones to make bread or some other baked good. But thinking badly of him dampened the swirl of heat his kiss had provoked.

Having located her notebook and scribbled a few sentences, Millie paused and tapped the tiny pencil against her bottom lip. "I need to meet him. Only then can I accurately portray his tortured soul in my story."

"Why don't you write to him and say you require an introduction as research? Unfortunately, the terms of my employment strictly prohibit the use of human assistants. I'm only allowed to take Riddy." Although now she thought about it, Fern would love to see how Quint would react to the dramatic writer. But if he yelled at her and gave her a fright, Fern would never forgive him. No, better not to risk it. Not unless both men could promise to behave. So Millie would most likely never get to see the inside of Wyndham Hall.

"I shall do just that! My story also requires a tour of the Hall so that I can discover what is kept in the attic and behind the locked doors of shut-up rooms." Millie added another note in the little book before snapping it shut and sliding the pencil back along the spine.

"Now, if you don't mind, I'd like to spend a little time with my parents." Fern stood and brushed out her skirts. Today, a dress suited her mood more than practical trousers.

The swirl of fabric against her legs reminded her of walking in the ocean and slowed her thoughts.

"Of course. We'll not intrude. Squib and I will get acquainted with the souls here." Millie smiled at the rows of carved headstones as though they were much-loved guests at a family dinner she couldn't wait to talk to.

While Millie wandered among the graves, Fern sat with her parents at their resting place in the dappled shade of the trees. Now she could spill forth her excitement at how the kelmsgale seeds were germinated. "A dragon, Father! No wonder we failed in our attempts. They had to pass through a dragon's stomach. I wondered if any sort of animal would do, but we don't see kelmsgales growing where cattle or sheep might have eaten them. Or other birds, for that matter." Now that Fern had a direction, she could study what happened if other creatures ingested the metal-like seeds.

After she caught her father up on all the gardening news, she turned her attention to her mother. Curling her fingers into the warm soil, Fern conjured her mother's face in her mind. "Oh, Mother, I kissed Lord Drakeman, and I haven't felt such a kiss since..." Her words trailed away. The last man who had muddled her thoughts with a kiss had led her down a ruinous path.

She recalled a saying that George often repeated. Fool me once, shame on you. Fool me twice, shame on me.

Could her body's reaction be a warning not to tangle with the dragon lord? Of its own volition, her hand raised to trace the line of her bottom lip. Then she dropped it to place both hands on the grass. Staring at her mother's etched name, Fern whispered, "I've never felt such a kiss."

Thinking about past events and how her unguarded heart led her to make unwise choices, Fern sat a little taller. She was older, wiser, and no longer easily swayed. "But I am no fool, Mother. Whatever I decide to do, I will do so with my eyes wide open and after careful consideration of all the consequences."

Having said the words aloud solidified another decision for Fern. She would return to the Hall, apologise for kissing his lordship, and ask him to forget all about it. Yes. That was the best course of action. Then she could return to her work in the conservatory and hope that one day soon, Eurydice would test her wings from the balcony.

After placing a kiss on the granite headstone, Fern cast around the meadow to find Millie and Squib. The pair were standing at a grave marked by an open book. The pages were so weathered and worn that most of the words had been erased from the stone, and only a few letters were legible.

Fern joined her friend. "You have found Mr Leggett. He died when the Moray sisters were young girls. From what I recollect, he was also a writer."

"Oh, how marvellous. That would explain the book. What a shame that time has erased his story. I shall learn all I can about him and see if I can fill the page again." Millie patted the carved sheet that curled as though caught by a faint breeze.

"I have to check on the orchid before we leave." Fern gestured to the miniature greenhouse.

The two women wandered through the graves and back to the central path. In the middle, the path split in two to curl around the glass construction that sheltered the spectral orchid. Fern knelt down to open the door. Today, the lump on the side of the stem had grown and taken on the distinctive oval shape of a bud and not some other type of growth. "Look, it's going to flower soon."

Millie peered over her shoulder. "A spirit has a tale to tell."

Both women glanced around, half expecting to see a restless soul hovering above a grave.

"The flower itself will offer a direction, but to know exactly who it is among the souls at rest here will require the help of the Moray sisters." Fern would let the old women know that a spirit would soon make itself known. They brewed a concoction she would mist into the air (rather like spraying roses with vinegar to protect against mould) that would identify the grave from which the soul had emerged.

"We had one growing in the house, but after Bertie inherited everything, he ordered it destroyed. I suspect he didn't want to know if Father objected to how he ran the household." Millie leaned in closer to stare at the orchid.

Fern gasped at the idea of anyone destroying the flower that allowed spirits to reach beyond the veil, even if their presence came at a terrible price.

"Oh, don't worry. Moyles told me he hid it out among the other orchids in the orangery." Millie winked.

"Moyles is wasted at Warrington Manor." The groundsman had been an ally for Fern when she had worked at the grand estate. How she wished she had the finances to lure him away to help her. Or perhaps she could suggest him as head gardener for Wyndham Hall?

CHAPTER 2

"WHAT HAPPENS if no one determines why a spirit has come back through the veil?" Millie asked as they walked back through the tunnel of arching greenery.

"It will call the souls of others to it." Botanists had written volumes about the physical attributes of the spectral orchid, but only a few paragraphs at most described its ability to draw out a soul from the living.

Millie stared over her shoulder at the cemetery. "So there would be more restless ghosts tapping on headstones at night?"

"No. It summons the souls of the living. The unsettled spirit will slowly drain the life from whoever was closest to them until they pass and join them on the other side. One person for every ten days the soul wanders our realm." From what the Moray sisters told Fern, it had only happened once in the last thirty years. The orchid had flowered, and no one had either the time or inclination to investigate. Or possibly they hadn't truly believed the old tales.

A healthy young man had weakened and wasted away before their eyes. When he was placed in the ground near his mother, they determined she was the cause of the tragedy. Only when the spirit's sister had weakened in the following days had the villagers realised the spectre wouldn't be content with just one reluctant soul for company. With no time to discover the cause of the unrest, the spirit had been banished. After that, Fern's father had vowed to personally investigate whenever the spectral orchid flowered. A task that Fern had taken over when he died.

Millie sucked in a breath. "Oh. I had read about that but thought it was just a story to scare people. I never realised that a restless spirit could turn into...a ghostly killer. Perhaps it is just as well the one at Warrington Manor never flowered, or Bertie and I might have had our souls consumed by it." She halted as though an idea had struck her, and she patted her pocket for the little notebook before she resumed walking.

"I am sure Moyles knows. Most gardeners do, although it is not often talked about. People find it too disturbing to learn that a dead relative might reach through the veil and snatch them away if they don't complete some task." That was also why few people chose to have a spectral orchid in their homes. Larger cemeteries seemed safer, as only one spirit could reach through the delicate plant at a time. Fern imagined souls forming an orderly queue in the afterlife and waiting their turn to be linked to a bloom. "Given the size of your family holding, there will be more people than just your direct relatives who might have died with unfinished business. Think of all the staff who are needed to run an estate. I can imagine Mr Corby making the orchid bloom after how he met his end." Fern was glad neither of them had to return to Millie's former home. She didn't want to be stuck tidying up the grounds to satisfy the head gardener, who was killed by the *Helix mortifera*. Or he might have siphoned her soul from her body, and she'd have to spend an eternity listening to the unpleasant man complain.

Fern and Millie had a leisurely stroll back to the village. Squib darted ahead at times to chatter with a sparrow or the occasional blackbird. The friends parted ways at Scribbles, but Fern promised to stop by for tea the following day. Then Fern turned her body towards Nemython House.

At the back door, she used the scraper to ensure nothing clung to the soles of her boots before entering the kitchen. Mrs Bentley was showing Lucy how to make pastry for the evening's pie. The housekeeper didn't stop in her gentle instructions, but she narrowed her gaze at Fern as though she suspected her of harbouring clumps of dirt on the hem of her skirt.

Walking on the tips of her toes, Fern crept across the kitchen floor and along the hall to the front parlour. Her uncle Ambrose sat in an armchair by the window, enjoying a quiet cup of tea.

"The cemetery spectral orchid is going to flower." Fern flopped onto the nearby sofa, leaving George's favourite armchair vacant. Only then did she lift her skirt to unlace her boots. She placed her footwear to one side and wriggled her stocking-clad toes.

"I shall have a think about who might have left behind unfinished business. Or a hidden book of poems." Ambrose poured tea into an empty cup and handed it to Fern.

13

When the orchid had flowered three years previously, poetry had been the cause of the soul's restlessness. A shepherd had died unexpectedly after a storm. While out looking for missing sheep, he had been struck on the head by a falling branch. It took some time, and repeated visits to his cottage and bereaved wife, before they discovered the worn journal shoved under a floorboard.

"His widow appreciates the earnings from his poems." Fern sipped the sharp brew. Ambrose must be trying a new blend of tea.

No one had realised that the shepherd had penned such achingly poignant poetry. Ambrose had acted as agent for the widow, and the little volume earned her a small, but regular, royalty income. Among those who understood the hidden meaning in the lines and the poet's inspiration, they remained silent that the widow was *not* the subject of the love poems. George and Ambrose suspected that Benjamin, the town's blacksmith, was the muse who inspired the haunting odes of longing and unrequited love.

As she drank the tea, Fern stared at another spectral orchid—the one that sat on a little plinth to one side of the window. Her father had acquired it after his wife and Fern's mother, Delphine, had passed away. Rowan and Fern had kept a vigil over the plant, hoping for a sign that her loving spirit lingered. Then, after her father died, she continued to monitor for any signs of a flower bud. But none ever formed.

"They are at peace, Fern. That is why they don't need to signal their presence," Ambrose spoke in a soft tone as he followed the line of her gaze.

"I know, it's just...I have so many questions that only they can answer." She spoke to the plant with its thick, glossy leaves and absolutely no inclination whatsoever to flower. She had always thought the mysterious manner of her father's death would surely make him sufficiently restless that his soul would reach out through the orchid. Unless her uncles were right and he truly had longed to join his beloved wife.

"While George and I could never replace Delfie and Rowan, we will help you however we can. Together, we will all muddle through this life." Ambrose seemed lost in his own memories of his sister and brother-in-law.

Thinking of the two couples and what they must have been like in their youth raised a question that her uncle could answer. "Why have you never written about your adventures before Mother had me? If only half of what you tell me is true, there would be an avid audience for such tales."

Ambrose laughed and winked at her over the rim of his teacup. "Who says I haven't? When I shuffle off this mortal coil, you might discover a trunk with a truly salacious manuscript awaiting you."

A hand tightened around Fern's heart at the thought of losing her uncle. "I'd rather hear you tell me such stories. It's your voice that brings my parents back to life once more."

George walked into the heavy atmosphere of the room and glanced from his partner to his adopted niece, both with sad expressions on their faces. "Who died?"

"Delfie and Rowan," Ambrose replied.

"I'm sure Fern already knows." George crossed the room to sit in his favourite armchair and ruffled his adopted niece's hair on his way past.

"The spectral orchid at the cemetery is about to flower, and I lament that this one stubbornly refuses to bloom. Apparently, my parents have nothing more to say to me. But you are right, George. There is a rather gloomy mood in here for such a lovely day outside." Giving in to the sadness that radiated from the hole her parents left in her heart was better suited for a grey and overcast day when rain pelted at the window.

"I hope it's not more poetry again." George picked up his newspaper, which had recently arrived with the other delivery from London. Some weeks, if the rider came straight to their corner of the Cotswolds and didn't get diverted, they were only two days behind on the happenings in the capital.

"I think it's sad that none of us knew Mr Emley possessed the soul of a romantic poet." Fern imagined him pouring all his feelings onto a page out in a meadow with only the silent company of his sheep.

"I think it's sad. The poor fellow had been carrying a torch for Ben, and his wife was oblivious to it," Ambrose said.

George folded back one side of the newspaper to regard the man who had held his heart so tenderly for over thirty years. "Not everyone is comfortable being who they truly are."

George's comment reminded Fern of the morning's events at Wyndham Hall, and she squirmed on the sofa. Lord Drakeman's dragon gaze saw who people truly were, even if they tried to hide behind a mask. It stripped everyone bare to the nub of their souls, exposing them to the alchemist's scientific examination. She nearly told her uncles what the mercurial eye saw but thought that was Lord Drakeman's secret to hide or reveal, not hers.

Ambrose waved his hands in the air around his head as he continued to speak. "I thought we had done better in our little corner of England. The poor tortured chap should have felt supported enough to reveal his romantic feelings for his fellow man."

George huffed. "We have built a community that embraces all sorts of folk, but it's still each person's decision what they share. You can't go around ripping other people's masks off just because you are at ease with expressing yourself."

"Oh, I know that. It's just that unrequited love pains me so. He should never have married his wife when his heart lay elsewhere." Ambrose laid one hand over his heart and shook his head.

"Ben didn't even know, let alone have a chance to consider if the feelings might have been reciprocated. Stop trying to match people. Especially after they have died." George snapped the newspaper back up and returned to the article that held his attention.

Ambrose poured more tea into his cup and took a slow sip. His hazel eyes were thoughtful, with a mischievous glint. "Well, it is entirely understandable that Ben inspired such poetry with all that hammering in the forge. Having to remove his shirt because of the heat. Sweat running down those ridiculously massive biceps. He reminds me of a young George, capable of such wondrous things with those big, strong hands."

Fern swallowed a laugh as a low, annoyed growl came

from behind the newspaper. Her uncle had baited the bear enough, nor did she want to choke on her tea if the conversation got any saucier. There were some things she couldn't scrub from her mind's eye.

"Returning to restless spirits, we have only lost a handful of villagers each year since...since Father died." They were a small village and benefited from the able care of Doctor Dodd. As such, the Reaper only managed to claim a half-dozen or so of them each year from sickness, injury, or reaching the end of their allotted time.

Closing her eyes and making a sad tally of those they had lost, there couldn't have been more than thirty souls plucked in the previous five years. A few were taken far too young, but babes rarely had unfinished business as they weren't given enough time to start any. The elderly sometimes used the orchid to reach out to remedy an old wrong. Or a soul needed someone to know they had written beautiful and evocative poetry.

"I'll go see the sisters and ask them to brew the spray. Judging from the size of the bud, I think the orchid will open in another two or three days." The orchid would reveal its ghostly flower, which would sparkle softly at night as though draped in stars. Its petals would turn in the direction of the spirit, and the bloom would remain open until the spectre had done whatever kept them anchored to the realm of the living. Or it was banished.

Uncovering the name of the restless soul and determining their unfinished task would be a welcome distraction for Fern. A part of her mind worried about what Sir Luxton had been brewing at Sibylcrest Abbey. Why would he need dragon's blood and a kelmsgale? It was yet another question she couldn't answer on her own. Then another part of her mind kept thinking about the dimly lit and windowless dungeon at Wyndham Hall. Where, among the sad remains of dragons, she kissed a drake man.

"Starving dragons," she murmured as she considered the collection of bones on the long table.

"Who is starving, dear?" Ambrose asked. "Do you need cake?"

"Not me, Uncle. I was at the Hall this morning. Lord Drakeman is studying the decline in dragon numbers, and he thinks they are starving." She hoped sharing that part of the morning's events wouldn't be a breach of the earl's confidence.

"How can they be starving when we are surrounded by sheep and rabbits? Not to mention all sorts of other things that I imagine dragons find tasty." A wrinkle pulled at Ambrose's pale forehead.

"I don't know." She kept encountering fauna-related problems when trying to resolve flora ones.

Eurydice had been starving when Fern discovered her, but that was understandable. The poor hatchling had been chased down a hole and couldn't turn around without damaging her wings. Fern kept remembering the sight of a skeleton curled up beside a tree stump. Why had that hatchling starved? The journals of the old drake men she had read said young dragons needed fish. But the skeleton she found had been beside a river. Had the creature been too sick to wade into the water to catch fish? Or did it have to be fish from the river that curved through Drake's Bend?

That might explain why so many dragons frequented the spot.

"They ate all their prey. Or its habitat is gone." The comment from George drifted over the top of the newspaper.

Ambrose made a thoughtful sound, and he gazed up at the ceiling. "That is how we lost the dodo forever. People razed the forests where they lived and ate all the dodos. Surprisingly tasty birds, by all accounts."

Fern considered dragons to be wise creatures who wouldn't have eaten the very last dodo, or whatever they needed to survive. That left the destruction of forests to build the factories and mills that advanced industry across England. Had men destroyed the trees where dragons slept or roamed? She recalled they preferred to slumber in caves dug into hills. Her mind raced down valleys to the river that cut through Drake's Bend and the impossibly hard kelmsgale seeds that fell after fertilisation of the flowers. She had all the puzzle pieces, but they weren't fitting together yet.

Which meant she would have to ask Lord Drakeman.

CHAPTER 3

THE NEXT DAY, Fern packed her tools and asked William to hitch up the cart. While Eurydice grew stronger and larger every day, she didn't want to risk tiring the youngster with the walk to Wyndham Hall. The dragon chirped and flapped her wings as she waddled up the plank of wood like a chicken returning to the hen house at dusk. As the horse and cart trotted through the village, the children called out to them, and Eurydice trilled in response.

"We'll be back this afternoon. See you at Scribbles!" Fern waved them away in case they ran too close to the spinning wheels. She pitied the teacher in the little schoolroom who had to try to make them pay attention to their lessons when they knew the dragon would be waiting for them that afternoon.

When they reached the Hall, Fern took the cart around to the stables and left the placid cob in the care of Denis. Then dragon and woman walked through the long grass to the conservatory. Today, the dragon happily nosed through the piles of dead palm fronds, and Fern marvelled at the change a few short weeks had wrought. The sickly, thin creature that slept all the time now showed a curiosity about everything around her, and she could keep up with Fern on their shorter walks.

But she still didn't try to fly.

Fern found the wheelbarrow and placed it close to where she worked. Progress was slow in the enormous and unloved conservatory. She had weeded all around the base of the sleeping platform. Those plants that had clung to a half-life were given compost (from the pile at the rear of the stables) and water. In her greenhouse at Nemython, Fern grew the delicate greenery that would encircle the warmed stone. Supplying them herself meant she could add the plants to her monthly invoice for his lordship.

Eurydice chirruped to herself as she explored and, at one point, she emerged from under a dead tree clutching a dried seed pod in her mouth. She took the offering to Fern, the dragon's eyes whirling as though she had discovered a great treasure.

Once the dragon had released the object, Fern examined the long and narrow thing that had aged to the colour of strong coffee. "It's from a frangipani. Well done, Riddy. That helps me understand what used to be in here, so I can source replacement plants." She scratched the dragon's hard eyebrow ridges while she stared at the seedpod. "Do you know it's also known as the graveyard flower? If our winters were warmer, we could grow it as a companion to the spectral orchid. Some cultures believe its blooms represent the infinite life of our soul. There are countries where the flower is planted in graveyards and the spent blooms become offerings to the dead."

Slipping the seeds into her pocket to germinate in her glasshouse, she returned to her work. The dragon disappeared behind a fallen palm, and only the sway of skeletal fronds marked her presence. An hour later, a shadow passed over Fern moments before a stone scuffed behind her. She turned as she rose from a crouch where she had been digging free a dead root ball, wondering if Eurydice had become tangled in something.

A single dragon eye regarded her alongside its brown companion.

"Lord Drakeman." Her fingers went limp, and the trowel fell to the dry soil.

"Miss Oakby. Could I speak with you for a moment?" His jaw was set in a tight line.

Fern wiped her hands on her trousers, partly to remove dirt and partly to ease a sudden bout of nerves. He didn't look happy. Would he fire her for her presumptuous actions of the previous day?

"I'm sorry—"

"I apologise—"

They spoke in unison, and then they both fell silent. Fern stared at him and, for once, held her tongue while she first formed a sentence in her head and tested how the words sounded once strung together.

He paced a few steps along the path and then spun to pace back again. His hands clenching and unclenching at his sides.

She needed to say something before she lost her job and the place Eurydice needed to grow and thrive.

"Perhaps we could forget the other day ever happened, and continue as usual?" Fern offered a solution to their unease, with the best-sounding option running through her head. Her initial response of *kiss me silly* would most definitely not be making it past her lips.

"Is that what you want to do? Forget all about it?" He tilted his head, and his dragon eye fixed on her.

A snuffling came from a pile of dead branches as Eurydice emerged from the undergrowth. The dragon pushed past a fallen banana palm to sit at Fern's side and rested her head on Fern's thigh, as though offering emotional support.

Fern could lie to him, but he would know. But still...lying would make it easier. If they both agreed to a lie, did that make it a different form of truth?

She reached down and rested a hand on Eurydice's head as she pondered her next words. It surprised her how much work it took to think about what you were going to say and not just blurt out whatever popped into your head. "I enjoy my work here. I want to see this conservatory restored, and I believe it's helpful for Riddy's recovery to be here. Where her ancestors once lived. I don't want to do anything that puts that in jeopardy."

He remained silent, but his gaze dropped to the young dragon nestled at her side.

"It was only a kiss, after all..." Fern's voice trailed off as his attention shot back to her face.

"Only a kiss?" His words shivered down her spine as he took a step closer.

"Yes. And need I remind you that I am a member of your staff?" Fern thought it repugnant that some lords abused their positions and pressed unwanted advances on their employees. Although technically, she had initiated events.

"I'm not in the habit of kissing my staff." He took one more step and then reached out. His hand brushed the side of her face, and Fern closed her eyes to lean into the warm touch that was gone too soon. He plucked something from her hair, and when she opened her eyes, he held up a piece of twig, twirling it between his thumb and forefinger.

Fern ran her hands through her short locks to ensure no other shrubbery was stuck there, while her mind tried to find something to say to puncture the intimacy growing between them. "Perhaps you should give Quint the occasional kiss on his bald head. It might improve his temperament if he felt more appreciated."

Lord Drakeman barked a short laugh. "The only sort of head kiss Quint appreciates is when he uses his forehead to smash someone's nose."

Fern had no difficulty believing that. The brief moment of levity gave her struggling brain time to form a coherent sentence, even if the words tasted bitter in her mouth as she said them. "I enjoy working alongside you, Lord Drakeman, and think it better to keep our relationship on a professional footing."

He dropped the twig to run a hand through his dark hair and stared up at the stone ribs that held aloft the glass panels. "I've never met anyone like you before."

"Well, that isn't true. We were both born in Drake's Bend and grew up here. Our paths crossed many times as children." Ambrose told her that the young noble had often joined the local lads in their games and adventures.

He shook his head. "Even if we had played together as children, those were two different people from who we are now. Our childhood dreams were dashed against the cruel rocks of adulthood."

Fern rolled her eyes. He was being as melodramatic as Millie. Was he really going to try to tell her how terrible his life was? "First, speak for yourself. I have a multitude of childhood dreams alive and simmering away inside me. And second, you really are a gloomy thunder cloud. Have you thought about getting out more and spending some time in the sunshine? Or taking off your boots to touch some grass? I can thoroughly recommend it, and it might improve your outlook on life."

He crossed his arms and huffed. "As I said, I've not met anyone like you before. I'll not forget that our kiss happened. But neither will I press undesired attention upon you."

He just had to use that word—un*desired*. Fern bent down to retrieve the trowel. She needed to have something in her hands to stop herself from tracing a finger along the scales that framed his right ear. She had discovered in their brief contact that they were soft, like silk draped over stone, and she wondered if he could be tickled through them. "I didn't say it was undesired." Her tongue nearly stuck to the roof of her mouth as she said that. "But if you tried against my will, you'd only make such a mistake once."

She wanted to kiss him again but also didn't, and so found herself in a right pickle. The kiss had been marvellous. Her body had drunk it up like parched soil when it rained after a drought. But a flirtation with his lordship contained many hidden barbs and thorny problems. At least her reputation wasn't one of them. She didn't give a fig what anyone beyond her circle of friends and family thought of her behaviour. If society were outraged, then that would only encourage her to behave worse. No, what bothered her was losing her job. Or worse, discovering that under the physical attraction, she actually...liked him.

If she threw caution to the wind and let herself get close to him, physically and emotionally, it would hurt all the more when the inevitable happened. A summer romance would wither with the approach of winter. Chill winds would batter her heart. No, it was far better to reinforce the armour around her heart and stay away from dark and dangerous, and deliciously enticing, paths.

Eurydice stepped between them and shook her body like a hen shaking loose dirt in its feathers after a dust bath. Flapping wings made them step apart to make room for the youngster. Fern hadn't even realised that while chiding herself to keep her distance, she had moved closer to the alchemist.

"Dragons are rather protective of any human they bond with." Lord Drakeman's eerie gaze slid down to Eurydice.

That reminded Fern of something else that had happened the previous day. Other than a toe-curling kiss. "You keep saying she has bonded to me. What exactly does that mean?"

"You have a connection that will remain in place until death," he spoke softly, as though the idea conjured a sense of reverence inside him. "Usually, they bond to a drake man, but there are rare occurrences of dragons pairing with others under extreme circumstances. Like rescuing a hatchling from dying alone in the dark. Queen Elizabeth came upon a young pair while out riding who were being attacked by wolves. It is said she personally shot the arrows from a crossbow that saved them, and the dragons hardly left her side from that day forth."

"Until death?" Fern knelt down to hold Eurydice's head in her hands. "You are not bound to me like some serf just because I pulled you out of that hole. When you are bigger and strong enough, you must fly and seek others of your kind. I could not stand the idea of you being lonely. But know that you will always have a home in my heart and at Nemython."

Eurydice stretched her body up to rub her muzzle gently against Fern's cheek. Closing her eyes, Fern inhaled her friend's unique scent. The dragon had a tang of salt, like the breeze from the ocean, as though she had been born to skim over waves all the way to the horizon. Cheek to cheek, and with her arms around the youngster's neck, Fern let the dragon's heartbeat thrum through her skin.

"They are like humans. They give their bonds and hearts of their own free will, and only betrayal or death can sever such a connection." Lord Drakeman's voice washed over them as Fern let her love for the creature in her arms seep from her body and through her scales.

Wonder spread through Fern's chest, and her breath came a little shorter as she tried to comprehend what the noble told her. A dragon had bonded to *her*. Until death. Because she would never sever their unique relationship by betraying the dragon.

"I will do my best to be worthy of your trust," Fern said. "And I promise that one day, you will fly above the meadows or out to sea, if you wish."

The conversation had neatly sidestepped the topic of the kiss she had shared with the drake man. Could she risk asking a few questions without reminding him of what had happened in the dim room where he kept the skeletons? She would dare it. Because she needed answers. "You said you found signs of starvation on the dragon bones. How could they be starving when there is an abundance of game and stock in the district? Could it be the lack of fish? That was what your ancestor's journal recommended for Riddy to improve her health."

"I have yet to determine the *why*, or even if it is indeed starvation causing numbers to decline. I have correspondents around the country who send me their observations of dragons in their districts, and they notify me if they find a skeleton." A frown wrinkled his forehead as he mentally reviewed whatever notes he kept on the subject.

"Why didn't you want Riddy here when you are studying dragons? When I asked, you acted as though I wanted to let a rabid dog loose in the Hall." As hard as she tried, Fern couldn't understand his behaviour, and it made her head spin.

"I can study them without being near a living one." Under a half-lidded gaze, he tracked Eurydice's movement. Perhaps satisfied he posed no immediate danger, the dragon snuffled at the leaves piled up to one side of the path.

Fern thought the two of them were like introducing a kitten to an old cat. Eurydice was curious about the earl and wanted to get closer, but he snarled and moved away. Would he eventually soften or lash out?

"Your stance of keeping yourself removed from live dragons would be like me studying trees and plants by only looking at books and pressed cuttings. I have learned a great deal from digging my hands in the soil. You need to take the dry words in your ancestors' journals and make them...real." She couldn't help herself. As she tried to awaken his interest in living dragons, she crossed the few inches that separated them.

Fern stood close enough that she could study the flecks of deep green and vivid blue that were scattered around the vertical pupil.

Bother.

She really wanted to kiss him again.

CHAPTER 4

As FERN STARED at two very different eyes, she pondered how they combined to make a unique form of gaze. Curious and warm and yet coolly piercing. One that saw the truths inscribed in her soul, like words carved in a headstone.

Lord Drakeman leaned closer until his breath feathered by her ear, and he murmured, "Still want to forget that kiss ever happened?"

All she had to do was turn her face a fraction, and their lips would meet. Part of her (that bit that thought it had been far too long since she had last luxuriated in the feel of another person's naked skin pressed to hers) thought that was a most excellent idea. The stubborn part of her refused to comply since he goaded her about it. Instead, she tightened her grip on the trowel. If the insufferable man dared to smirk, she would drive the gardening tool into his stomach and weed out his spleen.

Then an idea flitted through her mind that would allow her to regain the upper hand in a conversation that now seemed more like a chess match. Moving just a smidge so that her cheek grazed his, Fern murmured, "Don't think that because my name is Fern, I am unassuming and innocuous. My middle name is Nerim, for the *Nerium oleander*. All parts of me can be highly poisonous, and I might cause heart failure...even in small doses."

He huffed in amusement, but at least it wasn't an outright laugh. "Ah, your father gave you a warning label. In the future, should you wish to repeat events of the other day, I shall be prepared with my protective gloves and apron. And I will require you to ask me, so it is painfully clear that you are willing and give your consent."

Fern stepped away from him and crafted her features into a bland and slightly puzzled expression, as though she thought him a somewhat confused, elderly person. "This discussion obviously refers to a theoretical alchemic experiment that will never happen. Because I don't have any idea what you are talking about. The other day, you showed me your research into the decline of dragons, and *nothing* else happened."

Now he smirked and tapped the right side of his face.

Yes, well, they both knew she was lying, but if he possessed any gentlemanly blood whatsoever in his dry veins, he was supposed to go along with her version of events. What they needed was a change of topic.

"Is there anything else, Lord Drakeman? As you can see, there is a substantial amount of work to do here. All on my own. Lord Warrington has a most able groundsman called Moyles who would be a valuable addition to your rather... limited...number of staff." At most, there were three people responsible for the massive estate, and she wouldn't be convinced that the cook existed until she laid eyes on the man. She assumed fairies did the housework, since she had yet to encounter a maid during her brief wanderings of the hallways.

He frowned and tilted his head as though he hadn't quite heard her. "You want to poach a man from Warrington?"

"Yes." She liked Moyles. He had an open and honest manner and knew hemlock from Queen Anne's Lace. A mistake that could be fatal for a novice gardener. "From my time working alongside Moyles, I believe you would find him...tolerable."

Now that she understood what he saw with a dragon-eye lens, she appreciated why he was selective about what sort of person he saw every day. Fern had two human eyes and so relied on instinct to weed out those who were decent people from those who should be tossed on the compost heap. How much easier it must be to glance at someone and see if any rot nibbled at their core.

Lord Drakeman arched one dark eyebrow, but he appeared to be considering her request. "I'll have Quint assess him."

She hoped an *assessment* didn't involve knocking the groundsman unconscious, putting a sack over his head, and interrogating him for long hours. Thinking of Quint reminded her of how he had grabbed her in the dark and scared a few years off her life. She needed to devise her revenge, and she knew just the people to ask for help. The Moray sisters.

The alchemist interrupted her scheming of a cunning

prank to play on his butler. "I shall leave you to your work. When you wish to stop for lunch, a tray will be available for you in the library, along with a few more of my ancestors' diaries. You might find something I have missed that will give us a direction about a possible cause of starvation in youngsters." He inclined his head in the smallest of bows. After one last glance at Eurydice, he turned on his heel to stalk back between the corpses of banana palms that leaned on each other across the path.

Fern worked for a few more hours until her muscles protested. Taking off her boots at the library door, she crept across the carpet to find that there was indeed a tray laid out on the table beside the sofa. Someone had draped a sturdy piece of canvas over the furniture for her to sit on in her work clothes. Not wanting to leave Eurydice on her own, Fern grabbed the plate and headed back through the conservatory to sit outside in the cool breeze under a tree.

The plate held a chunky bit of cooked meat that she offered to the dragon. She took it with the gentlest of bites and then held it between her front paws to happily chew on her meal like a dog gnawing on a bone. Fern ate a sandwich with a layer of ham and cheese and read a journal she had snagged off the pile on the desk.

After half an hour, when her lunch was finished, her mind swam with old English, and Eurydice snoozed in the sun, Fern took the empty plate and journal back to the library. Then she tackled a few more hours of work tugging out dead growth. The detritus was added to the growing burn pile, now high enough to torch at least three witch-finders (who oddly mostly went unpunished for their crimes of killing innocent women).

Deciding she had had enough, Fern arched her back, tugged off the gloves, and surveyed her work. She had completed the edge of the sleeping platform and now tackled the space to the left that stretched from it to the grimy glass.

"Tomorrow," she told herself. There was plenty to do tomorrow. And next week. And next month, before the conservatory would return to life and become a thriving jungle of greenery and exotic blooms that would be the ideal place for a young dragon to spend time in winter.

On their way back through the village, Fern guided the reliable cob off the road and onto the grass in front of Scribbles. Eurydice jumped down and waddled to the window, pressing her face to the glass and trilling as she searched for her little friend.

Fern opened the door and yelled, "Squib! Riddy is here to see you."

She didn't see the pixie dragon but heard the excited trumpet as he launched himself from somewhere above, skimmed the top of her head like an arrow, and shot outside.

Millie wasn't at her desk, although the scattered trail of papers indicated she couldn't be far away.

"Millie?" Fern called and picked up a discarded page.

"Here," came a muffled reply, giving the search a direction.

Rounding a stack, Fern found her friend up the rolling ladder, reaching for a book, but the ladder kept sliding in the opposite direction, taking her further away from her goal.

Fern jammed her boot under the brass castor before Millie glided along the length of the bookcase.

"Oh, thank you. The ladder seems to have a mind of its own. Could you roll me a bit that way, please?" Millie gestured to the left.

Fern pushed her friend along until Millie gave a cry of success and then held the ladder still as it tried to sneak back again. "This should have a brake or a stopper on it. I'll have George look at it."

"Only if it won't be a bother. But I do feel as though the ladder is an uncontrollable horse at times." Millie climbed down, clutching a book to her chest with one arm.

"We can't have you being involuntarily dismounted from your charge and dropped to the floor from such a height. Nor will it be any bother to George. Remember, you are family now. What treasure did you spot up there?" Fern peered over the other woman's shoulder at the volume with its deep-red cover and silver lettering.

"*Myths and Legends of Scotland.*" Millie turned the book over and traced a fingertip along the swooping letters. "I have an idea that I want to incorporate into my book, but I need to research the exact details."

Fern had fond memories of her time in Scotland, and her heart ached with the remembrance. "My father and I made several forays to Scotland to find rare plants. They say motes are plentiful in the Highlands and dance like fireflies. It always made me sad I couldn't see them."

"How I long to travel there. It is such a magical place, and I have read there is a rare species of pixie dragon to be found hiding among the heather." Millie clutched the book to her chest, and a faraway look softened her features.

Fern laid her hands over Millie's. "We could go there, you know. Not until Riddy is bigger and I've settled our restless spirit, though. But we can plan a trip for whenever you are ready. I can write to my father's associates in Scotland so we have somewhere nice and remote to stay."

A breathy sigh escaped from Millie's lips. "Remote sounds awfully wonderful. Especially if accompanied by the crash of waves against a rocky shore. Yes. I would love that. Thank you." Then worry lines pulled at her forehead. "Perhaps next spring? I would need to find someone to look after Scribbles."

"Ambrose would love the chance, so don't throw any obstacles in our path. Next spring, you and I, and Riddy and Squib, shall have a Highland adventure." Now that the idea had taken root in Fern's mind, she liked it. It had been years since her last trip to Scotland with her father. Perhaps the misty vales and hills would soothe the restless spirit inside her.

The concerns piling up behind Millie's eyes dissipated like mist under the morning sun. "How about a cup of tea?"

"I'll tell Alice. I should probably scrub my hands before touching anything." Fern turned her hands over. Somehow, dirt wriggled through the leather of her gloves and hid itself under her nails.

Fern popped through to the cosy kitchen and asked Alice for a pot of tea. Then she reached for a short-bristled brush to remove any trace of dirt from her skin, rinsing off in the bucket of water by the back door. Her boots were banged together to remove any lingering clods of mud and left outside. On stocking-clad feet, Fern followed Alice through to the conservatory.

Both women murmured their thanks as the maid set out the tray. Fern tucked her feet up under her on the armchair, making herself as comfortable as if she were in her own home.

"What have you been up to today?" Millie asked as she turned the teapot three times clockwise.

"The endless task of cleaning out the Hall's conservatory. Lord Drakeman appeared, and I apologised for the other day." Fern leaned on the padded arm of the chair. They had both apologised, so obviously events had lingered in his lordship's mind as much as hers.

"Did you tell him that you wanted to forget all about the rather delicious kiss?" Millie poured tea and handed a large mug to Fern.

"Yes. I also threatened him with physical violence if he tried it again, but he seemed to like that idea." Fern wrapped both hands around the drink, appreciating that Alice no longer set out a dainty cup and saucer for her, and sipped the sweetened tea.

"Really? That's an unexpected twist for my story." Millie's hand paused as she was about to pick up her teacup and instead diverted into her apron pocket for her little notebook.

"I don't think it's an actual predilection and was more in the way of light-hearted banter." At least Fern didn't think he was signalling that he'd enjoy her trying to poison him. That seemed more like something that happened to Quint. She could imagine people had tried many ways of doing away with the grumpy man over the years.

"I think it's a shame, though. I rather enjoy hearing about tortured romantic escapades." Millie daintily sipped her tea with her pinkie finger extended.

Past experiences gambolled through Fern's mind. "Tortured certainly describes my romantic endeavours."

The friends chatted as they ate the oven-warm cake Alice had provided. After a while, Millie set down her teacup and plate, and her hand went into the capacious apron pocket, withdrawing a folded sheet of paper. She worried at the edges for a moment before speaking. "I received a letter from Bertie. He asks when I will be returning to Warrington Manor."

Fern snorted. Why would her friend ever want to return to a cold building that didn't offer her the comfort a home should? "I think you should draft a response that is a single word—never."

Millie's fingers crushed the side of the letter, and she bowed her head. "He is my brother."

The small voice of her friend skewered Fern's heart. Unfolding herself from the armchair, she knelt before Millie and placed her hands over the letter. "Yes, he is your brother. And as such, he is supposed to support you and love you. But I saw very little of that when I rescued you from under his roof. Sometimes, family is made up of the people we encounter in life, not those with the same blood in their veins. It's the people who stand beside us through thick and thin. We are forged together by the trials we endure, like metal. Fire binds us stronger than blood."

"A forged family." Millie rolled the idea around in her head. "Like how we are becoming. And George and Ambrose. And Squib and Riddy, because family can include more than humans, can't it?"

"A forged family can most definitely include dragons—big and small. Look how much we have all been through together, and we have only known each other for a few months. Imagine what adventures we will have in the coming years." The idea warmed Fern to her core. How she longed to fly on a dragon over a starlit ocean. Or climb to the top of a snow-covered mountain to find the only specimen of the *Crystallophoenix nivalis,* or Snow Phoenix flower, in the world. A single bloom had been plucked once three hundred years ago, and botanists had searched for it ever since.

Other women might dream of marriage and children, but her dreams were crammed with adventure.

If only she had someone to share them with her.

CHAPTER 5

After a pleasant afternoon tea with Millie, Fern reclaimed her boots and helped Eurydice into the cart for the journey home. With the arrival of summer, there were still a few daylight hours before dinner, so she decided to visit the Moray sisters and tell them about the spectral orchid. And seek their help to exact revenge on Quint.

Eurydice leaned over the back of the seat, her head resting on Fern's shoulder as the horse trotted along the shady road. When they crossed the bridge, the dragon gestured to the water and trilled in a questioning manner.

Fern peered over the side of the cart but couldn't spot any fish darting among the rocks at the edges. "Do you want to try a paddle in the river behind Scribbles? There's a ledge that creates a nice shallow bit there. That's where George taught me to swim."

Perhaps letting the water caress her wings and work her muscles might help the growing dragon learn to fly. When Fern read the old journals at the Hall, she searched for any information about delayed flight in hatchlings but hadn't found any mention of such a problem.

Eurydice chirped and bobbed up and down, which Fern took as a yes. She rubbed the dragon's head.

"Very well, I will finish at the Hall early tomorrow, and we shall have a dip in the river." It was ladies' day at the bathhouse, but she wasn't sure the other residents would appreciate a dragon splashing about in the small pool with them. Nor did she think the dragon would cope with excited children on their day to play in the heated water.

They stopped briefly at Nemython House to hand the cob and cart over to William, then Fern and Eurydice continued on foot to the two whitewashed cottages. Fern followed the sweet tang wafting in the air to find the Moray sisters at the rear of their homes. In their sheltered brewing spot, the old women huddled around a simmering cauldron. She called out a greeting and tucked her arm through Morda's crooked elbow.

Eurydice chirped and made a beeline for the edge of the forest, poking her nose under arching ferns and hellebores.

"She is thriving." Decima waved to the long tail swishing from among the greenery.

"Yes. I think she grows more substantial every day." Fern leaned closer to the cauldron hanging from the metal chain and inhaled. The faint, fresh scent of peppermint rose from the bubbling surface, and something darted beneath.

Nona carried over a bottle and used a glass dropper to add a single drop to the brew. "Yet despite her improvement, you worry about her."

"Why won't she fly?" Fern whispered the worry that nibbled at her mind.

"Fear can keep us earthbound." Morda squeezed Fern's hand.

"What has she to fear?" Fern couldn't imagine a dragon being afraid of anything. Apart from the hounds that had chased her and driven her into the narrow tunnel that turned into a trap. If she flew, she could easily avoid the canines until she was large enough to fight back.

Morda elbowed Fern's side, although given her small stature, it was more like a poke in the hip. "You know, for it is your fear, too. Give it voice."

Events tumbled through Fern's mind as though she fell down a well and drawings were plastered to the stone she passed. The hatchling chased by the baying hounds. Desperately looking for somewhere to hide. Scurrying into the welcoming dark of a tunnel. Only to be entombed for at least a month. Unable to turn around and go back the way she had gone in. Unable to shuffle backwards without damaging her wings on the unforgiving stone. Cold. Alone. Frightened.

While there didn't appear to be any visible damage to the delicate wing membranes, it was possible that the cramped conditions had damaged the tendons necessary for flight. What sort of life would a dragon have if it could never fly? Would it break her spirit to only ever watch birds take flight and play among the clouds, knowing she could never join them?

Fern swallowed and glanced at her companion to make sure she couldn't hear. The young dragon was engrossed in a conversation with a ladybird sitting on a leaf. "What if she tries and cannot?"

"She won't know until she tries. Very few people are guaranteed success without any effort." Nona peered at the brew while Decima stirred. A rose-coloured pattern radiated outwards from where the droplets had disappeared, and the darting shape elongated.

A fracture rippled over the surface of Fern's heart. How did she encourage the dragon to try, knowing she would most likely fail in the first few attempts? Was this what a mother felt like, watching a child stand on wobbly legs and take that first tentative step? She swallowed a lump in her throat. "She needs a safe place to test her wings."

Like a dragon conservatory with a perfectly sized balcony and a bed of soft dirt and leaves below.

Morda cackled, obviously reading her thoughts. "Lucky that you know of such a place."

Fern closed her eyes and muttered under her breath about all-seeing seers and interfering magic casters. "I will try to get her up onto the balcony. That will be a start." If it turned out the dragon didn't fly because she was scared of heights, that would be a whole different problem to tackle.

With one concern relieved a little, Fern moved on to the next one on her list and the main reason for her visit. "The spectral orchid will soon flower. Could you please make up the potion to help reveal the troubled spirit?"

"Of course, dear. It will be ready in two days." Nona nodded to herself, apparently satisfied with whatever concoction they made.

"That will be perfect timing. From the size of the bud, I

think it is two days away from opening." She would enlist the help of George and Doctor Dodd to make a list of those who had passed in the last five years. When she used the mist, it would identify the restless spirit who pushed through the veil separating the living from the dead. Then everyone would need to consider how to soothe the person back to their eternal rest. They only had ten days from when moonlight first kissed the orchid's petals to settle the restless spirit before a villager's energy would be drained.

"You should brew the banishment potion, too. Just in case." Fern didn't want to admit defeat before the orchid even unveiled its spider-like bloom, but they should be prepared.

The women chatted for a bit as they worked, discussing who among the departed villagers might have unfinished business that kept them from their eternal slumber.

"We lost Jessica Tompkins in childbirth two years back. She might want to see if her child survived." Decima took over stirring the soup-like brew.

"Gorgeous wee mite she is, too. Spitting image of her mother." Nona fetched a jar from the bench and pressed it into Morda's hands.

Fern moved Mrs Tompkins' name to the top of the list in her head. Childbirth was a fraught endeavour, and many lives of both mothers and babes were lost in the process. She wondered why so many women took the risk, but then what choice did many have in the matter? Not for the first time, she pondered how different their world would be if it were men who carried and birthed babies. She didn't doubt that the finest minds in the world would have advanced medicine and magic centuries ago to ensure the health of the father.

Not to mention, men would have demanded a foolproof way to ensure that conception only happened when it was wanted.

From a spot on the grass and out of the way, Fern watched the sisters each pluck an invisible mote from their jar and close it in a fist. Morda relied on touch, having told Fern once that the motes tickled like fireflies. Then they each cradled the seed of magic between their curled hands. They crooned a chant that rippled over her skin and raised goose bumps before throwing the golden specks of magic into the cauldron.

Faint green steam swirled off the surface and became three long fish that twirled around each other as they rose into the air. Fern tipped her head back to watch them dart among the leaves and disappear from view. Even fish could fly with magic, but not Riddy.

Nona clapped her hands and brought Fern's attention back to the cast-iron pot. The brew within had solidified, and when Decima stirred it with the ladle, she now kneaded a green dough.

"What is that?" Fern asked. Curiosity drew her near, and she returned to Morda's side.

"Summer dreams for the festival," Nona answered as she fetched a wooden bowl that was large enough to bathe a baby.

On the village green, the last standing kelmsgale was dotted with swelling flower buds. When they opened in just over two weeks' time, they would have their annual festival to celebrate the event. From twilight until the wee small hours, there would be music and dancing. Soon, the brightly painted wagons that were home to travelling entertainers would set up camp in a nearby field.

"What does it do? Is it a bread or a pastry?" Fern was fascinated by the process.

Decima scooped up the stretchy dough, and it pooled in the bowl. Swirls of green and pale raspberry reminded Fern of crisp apples and tangy berries she had eaten as a child.

"This isn't to eat, but it is a dough. The magic will mould into something from your childhood and tug out a memory you might have forgotten." Nona shook the container, and the mass wobbled and levelled out.

"When you have the time, I have an issue with Lord Drakeman's butler, Quint." She considered her words, trying to articulate the way the dour man made her want to needle him as though he were a much older sibling. She harboured no malice towards him. Only a large amount of mischief and a need to settle the score in the game that had sprung up between them. "I'd like to play a trick on him, but nothing nasty or that will hurt him. Just...shake him up a bit." If the three witches could brew something to give him a heart-stopping scare similar to the one he gave her in the forest, Fern wouldn't mind.

Morda huffed a laugh and reached out to find the wooden bowl. Her fingers, with their swollen joints, tugged free a ball of the summer dream dough. "That one was born on the estate. Adventure called him to London," she crooned as she rolled the dough between her palms until it formed a perfect ball.

Fern digested that news. Neither Quint nor Lord Drakeman had mentioned that he was a villager. She assumed the earl had pulled him out of a drain in London. Perhaps they had more in common than she realised. The lights, noise, and activity of London had lured her to turn her back on Drake's Bend. But then it had been her refuge when events did not go as planned. Had Quint likewise returned to the place he was born to lick old wounds?

Morda extended her arm and opened her palm. The green-and-red-swirled ball rested in the centre.

"You think throwing a ball of dough at him will be a worthy joke to play?" Fern plucked the toy and found it surprisingly firm, as though the witch had somehow baked it in the warmth of her hands.

"Place it somewhere it won't be easily discovered. The magic will do the rest, slowly, over a period of time." Nona rested the bowl on her hip and slapped down a tendril of dough that reached out like a seeking hand.

"But what will it do?" Where was the fun in pulling a prank if she didn't know what it was or if it had worked? Nor did she want to wait weeks or possibly months.

Decima flung a towel over the bowl and tucked it under the bottom to keep the contents warm, just like proving bread dough. "It will remind him of something from his youth and, perhaps, find a piece of him he has forgotten."

"Like his hair?" Now that Fern thought about it, she should have asked for a hair formula. She could have smeared it on the door handles so the butler ended up with furry hands.

The witches laughed, and Nona waggled a finger at Fern. "You will have to trust us and be patient."

"It doesn't sound very funny after the way he grabbed me

in the dark." Fern screwed up her face and fought the urge to pout. She shoved the ball into her pocket, fully intending to ignore it.

Decima reached into her apron and extracted something small that she pushed into Fern's hand and muttered under her breath, "If you want a more fitting sort of revenge and cannot wait for the memory dough to work its charms, then rub this on something only he will touch."

That sounded like a more promising concoction. Fern closed her hand around a squat glass pot and nodded her thanks. Hopefully, the middle sister understood that a prank needed to be avenged promptly, and with something funny. A gentle reminder of childhood just didn't sound like sufficient reprisal for grabbing someone in a darkened forest.

Without looking, she slid the container into her pocket before kissing each wrinkled cheek. 'Thank you, ladies. I'll be back in two days for the spirit mist."

As she farewelled Morda, the seer's hand snapped out and grabbed her forearm. Arthritic fingers curled into the fabric of her sleeve, and a milky gaze pierced her as effectively as a silver dragon one. Her voice had a faraway quality as she intoned, "Beware the embrace of shadows. Do not fall unless you can fly."

A chill swept down Fern's spine. The witch's words came from whatever premonition flashed through her mind. Somehow, she doubted Morda meant to be careful of venturing into her garden after dusk. But the problem with cryptic warnings was that one never knew what specific set of circumstances it applied to, so you ended up ignoring it. Not that Fern would ever tell the old woman that. "I shall be careful of my footing when my path is not clear."

Oh, that was good and sounded as vague as anything the seer would say.

She tucked the seer's words away, but as she hurried home with Eurydice in the fading light, the warning faded like a long-forgotten memory.

AFTER DINNER, Fern strolled in the descending dark to Doctor Dodd's cottage, only to find her gone.

"A young lad fell out of his bedroom window and broke his leg." Fern was informed by the old woman sweeping the floor.

"I don't need her assistance, I just need to write down names from her ledger." Fern stepped around the pile of dust and entered the front room used by the doctor as an office. There, on the bookshelf to one side, she pulled down a thick ledger with a black leather cover.

Within the sombre-looking book, Doctor Dodd noted all the births and deaths that occurred within the village. Placing the heavy book on the desk, Fern opened it towards the back. A black ribbon marked those lives that had been lost. A pale-cream ribbon marked the births recorded at the front of the book. Taking a clean sheet of paper from her pocket, Fern unfolded it and used the doctor's quill to copy down names going back five years.

The last name she inked on the list of thirty-two people was an achingly familiar one—Rowan Oakby.

CHAPTER 6

WITH THE LIST IN HAND, Fern returned home and found her uncles in the parlour.

"Thirty-two souls in total." She waved the folded sheet of paper.

The three of them spent a quiet evening reviewing the list of names. Fern added notes next to those she thought were most likely to be their restless spirit. Such as Mrs Tompkins, who never saw her daughter draw breath. Hope still lingered inside her that it was her father reaching through the veil. Both her parents were buried in the cemetery, after all. They could use either the spectral orchid in the graveyard or the one in Nemython House to send a message.

Children and babes, who tragically made up a full half of the list, were crossed out lightly. Young souls rarely lingered, and she would only consider them if none of the other residents were their returned spirit. The same logic was applied to anyone who had passed more than five years ago. Most of the departed should have made their peace in that time, or had decided to stay on in the realm of the living as ghosts tied to a specific location.

"There are twelve who might return." George passed the page to Fern after his last review.

"But only five who might have a reason to leave their eternal rest." Ambrose had added what he had learned from local gossip.

George stared at his partner. "You didn't know about Emley the poet."

Ambrose opened his mouth to protest, then shut it again. He huffed. "Some secrets are buried deeper than others."

"I will check the orchid again later tomorrow and take the map. Even the vague direction of the bud will narrow the list down more." Fern made a mental note to collect the large map of the cemetery that George kept. The graveyard was like an extension of the village streets and houses, as who was buried where was meticulously recorded. All she had to do was look up the names on the list and find the number that marked their location on the map.

She would ask Millie and Squib to join her. Fern suspected the writer would be delighted to help unearth the stories hidden among the weathered stones.

THE NEXT MORNING, Fern was up with the very first blush of dawn and ate her breakfast in companionable silence with George. Her uncle by love had only raised one bushy grey eyebrow in question at her early appearance in the kitchen.

She muttered about having much to do at the Hall and then lost herself in the steam curling from her coffee.

After a hearty bowl of porridge, Fern walked out to the stables with the young dragon's meal. Nestled in the straw, she sipped the last of her coffee and watched the dragonet devour a stew that was more meat than broth. The dirty dishes were left at the back door. Then Eurydice scrambled up the plank into the cart and chirped all the way through the village. Fern suspected the creature had recalled the promise of a swim in the river later. In a basket, she had stowed towels and a change of clothes. Something told her that swimming with the dragon would involve everything within a certain distance getting soaked.

At the Hall, she found the house silent, still blanketed in slumber. Only the slow twist of smoke from a chimney stack was evidence of someone being awake. Around the back, Denis sat on a bench, drinking a mug of tea as the sun crept over the cobbles. He wandered over and took the reins as Fern climbed down from the cart.

"Morning, miss. You're early today. I'm just finishing my breakfast." He waved the mug with his free hand.

"I want to finish early today. I promised Riddy a swim." Fern set out the plank, and the dragon waddled to the ground.

"I wish I could watch the little one playing with ducks, but his lordship wants the carriage ready for first thing tomorrow, and I have all the harnesses to polish today, and that's before I wash the horses to make sure they shine as much as the brass." He drained the last of his tea with a large gulp.

"Oh? Is the earl off to anywhere interesting?" Mentally,

she reviewed all the nobles with estates within a comfortable riding distance whom he might pay a call upon. Or did he head to the Warrington estate to steal a gardener? No. Fern could imagine Quint using the hearse-like carriage to snatch the poor man from the grounds.

"I just get the horses ready, miss, I don't drive them. Mr Quint always does that." He chatted away as he undid the buckles to release the cob from the cart's shafts.

"A butler who is also the driver...how unusual." She injected a lightness into the comment when what she wanted to do was bombard the man with questions.

Denis stopped and screwed his face up. "Is it? I've not worked at any other big house. Mr Quint does all sorts of things for his lordship, and I thought all butlers did the same for their employers."

Fern tucked that little titbit away in the mental ledger where she collected all she could learn about Quint. "I shall let you get on with preparing his lordship's carriage and horses. I have much to do before Riddy can have her swim."

As woman and dragon walked to the conservatory, the stench from the pool drew them both to a halt. The muck in the bottom heated as the day warmed under the summer sun. Algae on the sides baked and peeled off, falling into the bog below, adding more ingredients to the noxious soup.

Fern clicked her tongue. "It will not do, Riddy."

The smell was awful, and she worried she might overlook the edge concealed by the long grass one day and fall in. An idea spun in her head. There would be youths in the village who would be keen to undertake the work in exchange for fair pay and the first chance to use the heated swimming pool. She would suggest it to the earl.

"Wouldn't it be lovely in winter to soak in the steaming water and watch the snow fall?" They had the bathhouse, but that was covered and sheltered bathers from the weather. Besides, anyone could use those as they were public. The idea of bathing under the snowflakes at twilight made Fern curl her toes.

She scratched the dragon's head. Possibly, Eurydice hadn't been hatched last winter and didn't know what awaited in the coming months. The thought of her emerging into the world in the middle of winter, alone, made Fern's heart ache. "Where is your mother, I wonder? Did you hatch when she was away from the nest and the dogs chased you, or did you become separated?"

There was another option: that the dragon had abandoned her eggs. Fern had never seen a drawing with an adult dragon being followed by a handful of stumbling dragonets like a duck with her ducklings. Were dragons not maternal, or had a line of young trailing their mother not been recorded by any artist?

"There is so much to learn about you. Do you think Quint would let me visit in the evenings to study the old journals?" Fern asked as she pushed the doors open to admit her friend.

Eurydice promptly disappeared under a collapsed palm to explore. Fern headed straight for the library. Part of her had been tempted to toss the lump of dough. It seemed silly to hide a token to make Quint remember something from his childhood. That wasn't a prank at all. But she would plant the seed, anyway. The substance had solidified in her pocket and formed an ugly blob. She scanned the titles of books and found a section that, in her opinion, wouldn't draw the curious eye of the butler—the volumes about etiquette, fashion, and dances. They were probably leftover relics from the last Lady Drakeman who had spent time in London.

With that item hidden away, her hand dived into her pocket, where her fingertips caressed the squat glass container given to her by Decima. Her careful inspection of it the previous night had revealed a waxy substance inside that reminded her of polish. An idea had formed, and she would execute her plan if Quint brought her a luncheon tray. She only hoped the results would be amusing...for her.

Returning to the conservatory, Fern tugged on her leather gloves and set about tackling the corner by the sleeping platform. As she pulled out dead growth, she found an odd, remarkable survivor. Near the glass, she discovered a gem. A clump of arching, glossy leaves of a deep green.

"Oh, you look like a *Strelitzia*. How have you managed to cling to life?" The bird of paradise plant was so called for its distinctive flowers that resembled a flamboyant bird's head. The one before her had substantial leaves, far bigger than her palm, and a trickle of excitement ran through her. "*Strelitzia nicolai*," she murmured and cleared away a tangle of dead jasmine that blocked the sunlight.

The rare giant bird of paradise could grow to some fifteen feet in height. Too big for Fern's greenhouse, although she did have a much smaller specimen. How marvellous to watch one soar at Wyndham Hall. Or it would once she saw to its sun-loving needs.

Fern knelt back on her heels and gazed up. The glass above had escaped the worst of the coating of grime. Perhaps the southern exposure had stopped the lichen from growing, and winter storms had lashed some dirt away. If she could clear a circle above the bird of paradise, it had a chance of growing larger before it went dormant for winter. Her thoughts about how to let shafts of sunlight caress the *Strelizia* were interrupted by a heavy tread.

"The boss said I had to bring you a tray. It's by the door so you're not traipsing mud across the carpets." Quint stood a few feet away, arms crossed over his chest as he scowled at the inconvenience her presence created.

Fern smiled. "You know, when you stand just there, the sunlight glinting on your bald head makes you look like a little sun. Or more like a moon, really, as you're not as bright as the sun."

His gaze narrowed, and he uncrossed his arms but didn't seem to know what to do with them. Lord Drakeman had probably told him not to throttle her. With a muttered curse, he spun and strode away.

"I meant brilliance!" she shouted after him. Although that didn't sound any better. Neither would yelling out that she meant he was duller. "Shiny!" Fern called out another descriptor, but only Eurydice heard. The butler had stormed away. "I meant his head wasn't as shiny as the sun, but more glowy like the moon."

Contemplating how sunlight reflected from various surfaces reminded her that the morning had almost passed as warm rays filtered from directly overhead. Her tummy gurgled as it had been some time since the early breakfast, and she hadn't stopped since.

"Lunch is called for, then an early finish and a swim." Fern caressed the dragon's side before she headed for the carved library doors.

Today, the tray held a bowl with chunky cuts of fish in a clear broth. Beside it were arrayed slices of roast beef, cheese, a bowl of pickles, and fresh bread. The cook had obviously heard the same advice about fish being good to help a dragon thrive. Although Fern shared slivers of beef with Eurydice since the dragon watched intently as she placed a slice onto a piece of bread.

After a pleasant meal in the gentle breeze, Fern returned the empty plate and bowl to the tray. She stared at the wooden handles for a long moment as she remembered the fright Quint gave her when he grabbed her in the dark forest. Whatever the small pottle contained, she doubted it would make his heart stop in a similar fashion. But it would do something, given Decima's mischievous wink when she passed it over. Unscrewing the lid, Fern used a dried frond like a paintbrush to smear the waxy substance over the dowel. She decided that extreme caution was called for, as she didn't know what the stuff would do.

It worried her that the paste would be obvious and Quint wouldn't touch the tray. But as she painted it on, it absorbed into the wood. By the time she had done both sides and replaced the lid on the container, only a faint sheen showed that there was anything amiss at all with the handles. Holding the impromptu brush away from her body, she took it outside and tucked it deep into the burn pile so that no one accidentally touched it.

After another hour of work and their lunch had settled, she decided the sun was high enough in the sky that it was time for their swim. Somewhat disappointingly, she hadn't heard Quint return for the tray and could only hope he didn't send a phantom maid to collect it. After watching the dragon scramble up the plank into the cart, Fern climbed in and took the reins from Denis.

Eurydice trilled and bobbed up and down.

"She's keen to get going." Denis laughed as the dragon arched her neck and sang a happy, high-pitched song.

"She knows we're on our way for a swim." Fern rubbed her knuckles over the dragon's head and then waved to Denis as she turned the horse towards the driveway.

When they reached the village, Fern guided the horse over the bridge and left him at the forge. Benjamin gave the equine a good scratch before glancing at his hooves. "I'll give him a trim while he is here."

"Thank you." Fern collected the canvas bag with her spare clothes and glanced at the tall and muscular blacksmith from under her lashes. Ambrose was right. It really was no surprise that his form had inspired poetry. She wouldn't be at all surprised if someone in the village possessed a painting or sketch of him stashed in an attic.

At the bookstore, Fern walked around the side of the cottage to approach the open kitchen door, the dragon waddling behind like an oversized goose. The bag of clothing was dropped onto the slate floor.

"I'll tell Mrs Carlisle you are here." Alice offered and

wiped her hands on her apron before hurrying through to the main part of the cottage.

By the stove, Fern stripped off her boots and stockings and then her trousers and shirt, folding each item and placing it on a chair. Her chemise hung to mid-thigh.

Millie entered the kitchen and stopped with wide eyes. "Goodness, Fern! You are practically naked. How can you go outside like that?"

Fern grinned. "Watch."

Then she ran out the kitchen door. As she jumped, she tucked her knees up, landing with a splash out in the river.

When she surfaced, Eurydice flapped her wings and trilled loudly from the bank. The dragon bobbed up and down with excitement.

Swimming back to the shallows, Fern knelt on the stone that formed a low platform where she used to play as a child.

"You'll be safe here. It's not very deep, and the current is quieter at the edges." She held out her arms to encourage Eurydice to wade out to her.

Millie and Squib sat on the grass, but not too close to the riverbank. The pixie dragon didn't want to get wet, perhaps still remembering his origins as a paper construction.

"Can dragons swim?" Millie yelled out as Eurydice dug her claws into the riverbank and leaned forward.

"Yes," Fern replied as the dragon hopped and splashed into the water before her.

And promptly sank from view.

CHAPTER 7

FERN HADN'T EXPECTED THAT.

Millie shrieked and jumped to her feet. Squib shot up into the air, wings flapping as he emitted sharp cries of concern.

Fern peered into the slow-moving river as panic clawed up her gullet. As she swished her hands through the water to find the submerged creature, the dragon popped up like a cork and floated on the surface.

Relief poured through her as though from a waterfall. "See! Told you dragons could swim!" Although Fern wasn't quite as confident about that now.

Eurydice wobbled from side to side like a boat on a rough ocean and stuck out her wings for balance. One dipped deeper into the water, causing her to spin in a circle.

Fern placed her hands under the dragon's tummy and steadied her until she found her equilibrium. The creature chirped and tucked her wings in by her sides, resembling an odd duck as she paddled back and forth in the shallows.

Millie crept closer and sat with her knees almost at the river's edge. "Riddy is rather good at it already. Do you think dragons are born knowing how to swim, like ducklings? I once watched newly hatched ones leaping into the lake behind their mother, and every one could paddle along behind her with no instructions at all."

"It would seem so." Fern floated near the dragon. If Eurydice was born knowing how to swim, shouldn't she also know how to fly? A new priority formed in Fern's head: clearing a way to the platform in the conservatory so the dragon could leap into the air, as opposed to plunging into the water.

Fern swam a few strokes out into deeper water and turned a somersault before swimming back to the ledge. The dragon watched, her silver eyes flashing with streaks of watery green. Unfurling her wings, she gave small flaps as she paddled towards Fern.

The dragon peered down at her and chirped as Fern floated on her back.

"I am quite all right and don't require rescuing." She reached up to pat the concerned creature. "When you are larger and stronger, we could go to the seaside and play in the waves." Worried about the dragon following her out deeper in the river, Fern nudged Eurydice back to the safety of the ledge and then anchored herself with one hand on a nearby rock.

"Why don't you join us?" Fern asked Millie.

"Oh. No." Millie's eyes widened. Perhaps she imagined how horrified her brother would be to hear his sister bathed in the river like a peasant. Then she wiped a hand over her face and the worry disappeared. "I can't swim."

"We shall remedy that one day." Fern could only supervise one creature at a time in the river, but the bathhouse would be a safe place to teach her friend to float. That pool was shallow enough that Millie would be able to stand and touch the bottom if she needed. "How about a little paddle? The water is lovely, and you would be perfectly safe sitting on the edge and dangling your feet in."

The writer glanced around. Children were crowded on the bridge, watching the dragon, and some curious villagers paused in their daily chores.

Millie shook her head. "Another time."

After a bit longer playing in the water and the dragon getting her feet tickled by a fish, Fern helped her out. The process of getting the creature out of the water was much harder than getting her in. Millie and Squib offered encouragement as Eurydice scrambled up the bank, and Fern shoved from behind. Once she flopped onto the grass, Fern climbed out.

No towel was needed for the dragon, who shook her body and then extended her wings to dry in the sun.

Fern dried off in the kitchen and changed into fresh clothes before joining Millie in the conservatory. She curled up in an armchair, clutching a mug of tea. "If you're not busy, I am going to the cemetery with a list of deceased villagers. Would you like to join me?"

"Is it time to find the spirit?" Millie's eyes brightened at the idea of a supernatural visitor.

"Yes. We have a map of who is buried where. If the bud is indicating a direction, we will be able to narrow down who it might be." Their tea was accompanied by warm scones, with butter sliding over the edge.

A faraway look crossed Millie's features. "An exploration of souls. Of course I will do what I can to assist."

After they finished their afternoon tea, they walked over to the forge and reclaimed the horse and cart for the short trip. As Fern turned the horse off the road, the tunnel of greenery offered cooling shade. She left the horse under the spreading boughs of a tree and, with her friends, approached the waist-high conservatory.

When she opened the glass door, the spectral orchid's bud had elongated and was now two inches long. A faint line of silver ran down one side as it cracked, ready to release the luminous bloom.

"When will it flower?" Millie asked.

"Tomorrow." Fern stroked a finger along the thick bud, encouraging it to unfurl. "Then our time to find the reason begins to count down."

She lowered her head and considered the direction the emerging flower pointed in. Sadly, it wasn't towards where her parents were buried but at the trees on the other side of the cemetery. There was a slim possibility that the flower could unfurl and alter its course, like a ship finding its way home.

Closing the door of the little conservatory, she angled the movable glass plates that formed the roof. With the warmer temperature outside to the liking of the delicate plant, she opened the panels to allow more air to flow around the orchid. That would also help the bloom to break free of the thick bud.

From her satchel, Fern retrieved the map and unfolded it. Then she handed Millie the notebook with the details of who was buried in each grave. For herself, she kept hold of the list of most likely candidates for their restless spirit. She gestured to an area of the cemetery back towards the road and closest to the village. "It looks like the orchid bud is pointing in this direction. So we need to see who on our list is buried over there."

Lying on the grass in the sun, the women found the name George had written next to each number, indicating their plot. Then they found the number on the map. Some names were crossed out for being in the wrong direction, such as Fern's father. After some time and squinting at the map, they had six names in the general quadrant the orchid bud indicated.

Fern tapped one name in particular. "Mrs Tompkins. She died in childbirth two years ago and has a gorgeous wee daughter."

"Oh." Millie exhaled the syllable. "It must be her, wanting to see her child thriving."

"We don't know for certain yet. Let's find each grave so we have a better idea where the mist might lead us tomorrow night." Fern climbed to her feet and held out a hand to Millie.

With the map to guide them, they wandered past a fragrant, deep-pink sweet pea that brightened a tall grave-stone. "Richard Plummer; he died of natural causes and lived a quiet life." Fern pointed to a grave closer to the trees as they walked.

Millie peered over her shoulder as they stopped to orien-tate the map. After a few more strides, they stopped to stare at a grave with fresh daisies tied with ribbon and laid on the grass.

"Simon Dempsey; he was only eighteen. Surely too young to have unfinished business?" Millie asked.

"I remember being eighteen and feeling as though I stood on the verge of a grand adventure. Everything and anything seemed possible. All I had to do was decide what path I wanted to take." Fern closed her eyes as she recalled events from the past. Some she would never regret. Others she possibly could have dealt with differently.

Millie rested her hands on the stone that appeared to be regularly scrubbed clear of moss. "Do you think he might be reaching out for us to have an adventure for him?"

"Anything is possible. Once the orchid flowers, the spectral mist the Moray sisters are brewing will tell us which grave has released the soul. When we have a name, we will determine what has roused them from their eternal slumber." Fern folded the map and tucked it away in her satchel.

"Until tomorrow night." Millie patted the headstone.

THE NEXT DAY at Wyndham Hall was more silent than usual. Both the master of the house and his butler had left by the time Fern halted her little horse outside the stables. Denis advised that they had left at the break of dawn. Curiosity ate at Fern as she worked in the conservatory. Where could they have gone? When she questioned Denis, he didn't know if they would be back the same day or not. Had they gone further afield?

Fern shoved the trowel into a stubborn patch of roots. "I suppose they don't owe me any explanations."

No one delivered a luncheon tray, which increased her suspicions that no one tended to the rest of the Hall in the absence of Quint. Fortunately, she had packed a meal for both herself and Eurydice, and as had become their habit, they sat under an ancient oak tree in the shade to eat.

After an uneventful day, but having cleared a path to the winding ramp in the corner, Fern and Eurydice returned to Nemython House. With little to do until dark fell on the village, Fern roamed the house, stared out the windows, and then glared at the spectral orchid in the parlour. Was that a bump forming on the stem or simply wishful thinking?

Ambrose set up the backgammon set for his evening game with George, who was at his desk in the corner sorting the mail he had received that afternoon. "One for you." He held out several sheets of paper and waved them at Fern.

"Me?" Curiosity stopped her silent inspection of the plant.

"From my Romanian friend." George shuffled everything else into a pile and placed it neatly to one side before joining Ambrose.

"At last," Fern murmured as she tried to read the messy handwriting. George's friend had translated the pages she found in the old journal. "Oh, this is interesting. The first specimen of *Helix mortifera* ate three nobles in Romania before the plant was chopped up and burned by the villagers."

"Three? Goodness." Ambrose's eyes widened. "Did it also sprout after a storm?"

Fern squinted as she tried to follow the script that appeared to have been dashed onto the paper while the writer was being tossed around on a ship. Or that was what she imagined was responsible for the rolling up and down of the lines. "Apparently so. The journal notes that it was discovered the morning after a terrifying and thunderous storm that struck the castle on the hill. I shall add this information to the paper I am writing. Lord Warrington will have to live with the disappointment of not being the first to discover the plant."

Ambrose slid the leather dice holder to George to have the first throw. "Let us hope it is also the last such plant we encounter."

Fern heaved a sigh of regret. What a shame she never had the chance to try to grow a miniature version, like the Japanese bonsai trees. "Millie used up the last of the Storm-borne Serum, so there won't be any more here."

Pouring over the letter and comparing the text to the drawings in the notebook kept her occupied until dusk crept over the old house. "I'm off to identify our restless spirit." Fern tucked the papers away and kissed each uncle on the cheek.

"Take a lantern." George narrowed his gaze at the board and considered how to move his pieces.

Ambrose appeared to be winning, with his black pieces blocking most places that George could slide his tokens to.

Out in the stables, Fern added a lantern and a blanket to the back of the cart before helping Eurydice up. It lightened

Fern's heart to see the dragon thriving. She also now refused to be left behind when Fern went out.

"Ready?" Fern asked her companion.

The dragon's silver-green eyes whirled with excitement and made two eerie reflective points in the dark. Clucking her tongue at the horse, Fern guided them along the drive and over the bridge to the Moray sisters.

Decima answered her knock on the door. "We have it ready for you. Morda insisted we make two batches, and so we humoured her."

"Hello, Fern!" Nona called from by the fireplace, where she stared at a pot hanging over the low-burning flames. Flickering light caressed the underside of the thick oak beams that supported the ceiling.

Morda turned her face to the door and grinned, her bony shoulders shaking in silent laughter at some joke evident to her only.

"Good evening, ladies." Fern rubbed her hands together, keen to discover what spirit had emerged from their grave. As much as she loved spending time with the sisters, tonight she bounced with as much excitement as Eurydice to return to the cemetery.

Decima turned back inside the snug cottage. From a dresser that occupied nearly an entire wall, she plucked two stoneware bottles, a thick cork wedged into each.

Fern took both bottles and hugged them to her chest. A faint warmth tingled under her fingertips, as though the contents were mulled wine to fend off a chill night. "I will be back tomorrow to tell you who they reveal."

"Happy hunting," the sisters called in eerie unison.

Returning to the horse and dragon, Fern tucked the bottles safely in a basket with wisps of protective straw. Continuing on her way, she next called at Scribbles, where soft yellow light came from the lower windows of the cottage.

Millie emerged, wrapped in a velvet cloak with a deep hood. Squib chirruped from his spot nestled within its warmth. "I thought a cloak was fitting for a graveyard at night." She swept in a circle, letting the heavy fabric swirl around her form.

"Very mysterious." Fern held out a hand to help her friend. "I always think a gown with a full skirt is needed for mystical excursions." She gestured to the dress she wore under her coat.

"One must be attired for the part one plays." Millie's eyes twinkled in the dark. The writer was also keen for their midnight adventure.

Squib emerged from under the hood to hop onto the back of the seat, where he could face Eurydice. The two dragons chirped and trilled at one another as they conducted their own conversation.

"Will we really see a ghost?" Millie pulled her cloak tighter around her body to ward off the slight evening chill.

"No. It's more like the shadow of a ghost. We can discover the grave of the spirit by looking for traces of the path it walked to touch the orchid." The basket in the back of the cart contained a metal sprayer that Fern would use to mist the air.

Millie made a *huh* sound as she thought about what they might find. "So it's like looking for footprints? But in the dark and using the mist to make them glow?"

"In a way. Generally, it takes the shape of a head and torso with...sort of legs." Fern became lost in her own thoughts, wondering if ghosts had feet. She couldn't recollect any of the shadows they had unveiled in the past touching the ground. Which meant the spirits didn't walk but floated.

Or did they fly?

CHAPTER 8

As THEY LEFT the village behind, the sounds of night enveloped the little group. The hoot of owls and call of foxes searching for a meal wove with the clop of hooves to make an eerie tune. The tunnel through the trees became a black maw in the dark, but the steady little horse followed the worn path without any signs of concern. On the other side, Fern looped the reins around the brake and hopped down from the cart. Eurydice waddled along her plank, and Squib flew to his human friend to burrow under the folds of Millie's hood.

Fern lit the lantern and held it aloft to guide their way. "We'll have to douse this to see the mist. I hope the dark will not worry you?" Only now did she consider whether Millie might be scared of the velvety night.

"No, I am not scared. We have two dragons to protect us." She raised her hand to scratch Squib's chin, and the pixie dragon sat a little taller.

Approaching the miniature glasshouse, a soft white light came from the thick glass. Fern opened the door to reveal the spectral orchid in full bloom. Its narrow petals were a tangle of spider legs that glowed like a shredded moon.

"*Orchis phantasma*," Fern murmured as she took a moment to marvel at the unusual orchid.

The petals, lateral sepals, and dorsal sepal were indistinguishable from one another. Only their position hinted at which was which. The dorsal sepal was a twisted ribbon at roughly twelve if it were a clock face. The throat column ended in a tiny open mouth in the middle of the flower.

"I don't think it has changed direction and still seems to be pointing to that side of the cemetery." Millie gestured to the quarter where they had roamed among the graves to find the names on Fern's list.

"Yes, it does seem to be pointing to that corner." Fern curled her fingers around the spray bottle that she had filled by the cart. Leaning down, she angled her head to mimic the angle of the flower. "Time to douse the lantern, please."

Millie dampened the wick, and full night wrapped them in her blanket. Four luminous eyes kept watch over them, and Squib trilled from his perch on Millie's shoulder. Eurydice butted her head against Fern's knees, in case she thought she was alone in the dark.

"Thank you, Riddy." Fern blinked, and her eyes adjusted to the dimness.

Millie clutched the lantern and watched as Fern misted the air in front of the orchid. Tiny silver specks spun in the dark. Most fluttered to the grass, but a dozen appeared more solid in one particular spot. They hung for a heartbeat longer than the rest, before breaking apart and vanishing among the grass. Eurydice sniffed at the specks and must have breathed some up as she snorted them back out of her nostrils. Three specks shot up into the air and then spiralled back down.

"Oh, it is like we are doing magic." Millie's voice was touched with awe as she held out her hand to catch a dancing mote.

Fern studied the pattern of silver dust and turned her body to where the spots had seemed more substantial for a heartbeat. "This way," she called over her shoulder.

She took two careful steps in the signalled direction, stopped, and misted the air again. It was a slow process. Each time, Fern and Millie held their breath as they watched the dancing specks and waited for some to cling to one another, showing them the way. Squib became bored and took to hopping between headstones. Eurydice never left Fern's side. The dragon keenly focused on the silver mist. She crooned, low and rhythmic, each time the mist spun in the air and stopped when it disbursed.

At times, Fern took a step too far and all the silver dots winked out like stars hidden behind clouds. When that happened, she retraced her step and tried again, paying attention to how the young dragon reacted. It seemed to her, if it were at all possible, that Eurydice acted like a compass needle. The dragon's head swung in the right direction as she emitted the eerie sound, her tail held straight, making her into an arrow.

They reached the grave of Mrs Tompkins and stopped. Fern touched the cool headstone. "I think it must be her."

But Eurydice swung her head towards the trees and ignored the site that held the most likely cause of the restless spirit.

"Riddy might be distracted by a hedgehog in the forest," Millie said, peering to catch what had caught the dragon's attention.

Squib hopped to the headstone and chirped, but Fern couldn't tell if he agreed or disagreed with them.

Fern watched the dragon, who seemed fixated on something closer to the surrounding trees. "Regardless of whatever Riddy can sense, if our spirit is Mrs Tompkins, the mist will take a more solid form over her mortal remains." Once more, she sprayed the air, this time aiming directly over the woman whose life ended as she brought a new one into the world.

As though a breeze blew through them, the droplets spun away from the grave and hovered over the long grass to the side. This time, they took a little longer to disappear, a few trailing off towards the trees before falling to the ground.

"I don't think it's her," Millie whispered. "Unless she was inadvertently buried somewhere else?"

The idea sent a chill down Fern's spine. How sad for the daughter if one day she poured out her heart to her mother, like Fern did, only to discover someone else lay under the ground. Impossible, though. Such a mistake would never be made in Drake's Bend. Particularly since George always double-checked sites before a grave was dug, and he noted the name and plot number on his map. "She is definitely here. It's just that I am wrong in thinking Mrs Tompkins is the soul reaching out. Perhaps you were right, Millie, and it is young Simon Dempsey."

Changing her grip on the cool metal of the sprayer, Fern waved it back and forth as she released the fine mist. A veil of silver hung before them as though she splashed paint on a dark wall. Then the dots clung together in one spot that appeared to surround Eurydice. The dragon trilled, and they danced in the air with her exhales.

"It seems we need to follow Riddy." Fern thought it had to be a coincidence that the spirit spray coalesced exactly where the dragon sat and stared at the rustling trees.

They continued onwards to the outer corner of the cemetery. Night grew more solid as the trees stood shoulder to shoulder to protect the eternal slumber of the residents. An owl hooted and took flight, its body casting a shadow across the moon as it hunted for its dinner. Scented stock perfumed the air as Fern brushed past another gravestone. One more time, she misted the air, more than a little worried they would run out of potion in the sprayer and have to fetch the second bottle the sisters brewed.

This time, more of the silver flecks clung to one another in a particular spot where Eurydice sat, watching the spiralling flecks. As they hovered, suspended in the air by the dragon, they formed a slender column.

"Is it that one?" Millie whispered, as though afraid to wake more of the deceased.

"I believe so. Yes." Watching where she placed her feet, Fern approached the grave. Grass had regrown, so it wasn't a recently deceased villager. Eurydice sat near the foot end. Her eyes were two small moons as she stared at the silver veil.

One by one, the tiny specks winked out until a lone one drifted to the grass by the headstone.

"Let's see who we have." Fern relit the lantern while Millie held onto it. Yellow flared for a moment, and she turned her head to blink away the patches of red that danced before her vision. Then she trimmed the wick and closed the glass hatch.

Millie held the lantern high before her with one hand, her other clutching the sides of her cloak. "Richard Plummer. 1770 to 1819. Beloved husband, father, and provider," Millie read the inscribed words, now gently illuminated. "Well, Mr Plummer, there is not much to your tale for nearly half a century spent walking this earth. Do you think his unfinished business is that he'd like another line or two carved on his gravestone?"

Fern tried to recall what she knew of the man. Each name on the list had been briefly discussed with George and Ambrose as they decided who was most likely to have been unprepared at their end. "I don't think spirits come back because they want *lover of kittens* added to their headstone."

Millie waved the lantern up and down, perhaps looking for a smaller, secret inscription. "Of course not. Everybody loves kittens, so that is assumed about a person. His restlessness might be caused by an unrecognised passion. Perhaps he wrote operas for squirrels, or he might have been a painter with a future masterpiece hidden in the attic."

The image of squirrels wearing fine gowns and singing arias in high-pitched voices drifted through Fern's head—along with a scantily clad portrait of Ben the blacksmith stashed under a roof. "It wouldn't be the first time someone died without revealing a hidden talent."

Millie made an excited, "Oh."

The light swung in Fern's direction, and she screwed her eyes up as the world went bright yellow.

"Sorry." Millie lowered the light. "But you need to elaborate on when it happened before, and please tell me it involved squirrels."

"We had a shepherd who wrote the most beautiful poems. But not about squirrels. No one ever knew about his gift. The journals were hidden under a floorboard. With his widow's permission, Ambrose had them published." Fern's attention fixed on the unremarkable slab of oolitic limestone, which came from a local quarry. The stone was a warm honey colour when first cut, and over the years weathered to a mossy-grey patina.

From what she could recall of the Plummers, the family lived on the north-western side of the village. Ambrose had recalled that Mr Plummer's funeral had been a quiet affair, and the couple had three children who were now adults. "Mr Plummer was some sort of labourer and did work on farms around here."

Millie hummed quietly as she thought. Then the noise stopped abruptly. "The most obvious thing would be an unfinished job, but I prefer to think he had a more creative flair. What if he had a love of sewing and he laboured by candlelight at night on a magnificent, embroidered waistcoat fit for a duke? Only Death snatched him before he finished the last panel."

"If he did, don't go looking at me to finish it. I am a rudimentary sewer at best and never had the patience or skill to master anything beyond darning socks." Fortunately, there were women in the village who could weave magic with a needle and thread. Although if Mr Plummer had possessed a secret passion for needlework, his wife might have spotted the workbasket. Embroidery would be harder to do while sitting out in a field, unlike penning poetry.

"When I'm not writing, I like to embroider pansies. They have such cheerful round faces," Millie said. "Although often, I spoil my work because I have ink stains on my fingertips I haven't noticed, and sometimes my pansies look like they are crying."

"While your idea would add a colourful touch to what we know about Mr Plummer, I doubt his spirit has returned because of an embroidered waistcoat, or even so much as a handkerchief. We'll visit his wife during the daylight hours and see if she has any idea." Sand began running through a spectral hourglass as soon as the unique flower bloomed. They had ten days to discover what made Mr Plummer rise from his grave before his chilled hands would collect his widow's soul to keep him company.

Fern walked around the grave to rest a hand on the stone. Having identified the restless spirit, and with nothing to learn from the scant information on his tombstone, the women lingered a little longer in the cemetery. The moon played hide-and-seek with the clouds, and shafts of gentle light flickered over the stones as though more souls darted between the monuments.

"How goes your work at the Hall? You haven't told me what happened after your kiss in the dragon dungeon," Millie said as they walked in front of the handful of mausoleums with their backs to the forest.

Fern paused at the largest and most ostentatious mausoleum. The one for the Drakeman family. If it were a cottage, it could have housed an entire family with a dozen children. The stone had weathered to a soft grey, and moss clung to the north side. Dragons sat on the corners in the place of gargoyles and guarded the eternal slumber of the occupants. "There is nothing to tell. We...well, *I* have agreed to forget it ever happened."

"That would be more believable if you didn't touch your lip when you said it." Millie's voice ended with a soft giggle.

Fern stared at her hand and hadn't realised it had acted of its own volition. Again.

Turning her back to the Drakeman tomb, she leaned against the stone and stared at her friend. There were questions and emotions crammed inside her that she needed to discuss with another woman. As wonderful as her uncles were, there were some things she didn't want to share with them. And while Fern unburdened herself at her parents' graveside, her mother never answered.

"Did you ever kiss someone who made you tingle?" Fern wondered if Millie had found love with her husband in what had been an arranged match.

"Yes." That one word carried longing and a tinge of sadness. Millie put the lantern on the ground and held out her hand for Squib, who flew to her from Eurydice's back. The pixie dragon walked up her arm to nestle on her shoulder.

"Did you love him greatly?" What would it be like to have a love that endured like the stones surrounding them?

"Him?" Millie found a comfortable spot of grass and sat before the mausoleum, tucking her feet under her skirts and velvet cloak. Eurydice plonked herself down next to the writer and rested her head on Millie's knee.

"Peter, your husband." Fern decided to join them. Dragons and women sat in the peaceful cemetery while nocturnal creatures and restless spirits went about their business unseen around them.

"Oh. It wasn't him." Millie fell silent and fussed with Squib, preening the pixie dragon's papery hide.

"I'm sorry. That was presumptuous of me. I have a habit of speaking before my brain has considered if I should have said anything at all." Perhaps they were more alike than she realised, if Millie had also given her heart unwisely. "Let's forget I said anything."

"It was so long ago. Positively years and years. I don't mind telling you, and it would be nice to remember such kisses again. We met when I returned from London, and Father said I didn't have to go back for another season if I didn't want to." Millie spoke of her father with a fondness missing from her reminiscing about her brother.

Fern considered what to say next, curious but also not wanting to offend her friend. "What were they like?"

"Kind. They...she...was very kind. I always found being around her was like we stepped away from this world and hid in our own little place for the few hours we could snatch." Millie closed her eyes, and her shoulders heaved with a long sigh.

"An escape sounds wonderful. How did you meet her?" Fern asked.

"She was a modiste, and it was easy to spend much time together. After Father died, there were the mourning clothes to be made, and Bertie had no idea how long such appointments could take. Then one day, Annabelle arrived to collect me and...well, she told Bertie what she had seen. Not long after that, he announced I was to marry Peter Carlisle." Millie wiped a single tear from the corner of her eye.

Fern clasped her friend's hand, and her dislike for Lord Warrington deepened. "I'm sorry he couldn't let you be happy. Have you thought of writing to her now that you are free?" Such relationships were not unusual among women. Spinsters often lived together to *reduce their expenditure* and make a small allowance stretch a little further.

"No. She found another. And anyway, I am not the same person I was back then." Millie's smile didn't erase the sadness in her eyes.

Fern vowed to find someone who would make Millie touch her lip as she spoke of a shared kiss. And no one, not even the horrid Lord Warrington, would stop her friend from being happy and loved again.

CHAPTER 9

AFTER ESCORTING Millie and Squib back to their cottage and tucking Eurydice into her blanket in the stables, Fern found Ambrose and George reading in the parlour.

"It's Mr Plummer," she said as she dropped onto the sofa.

"Really?" Ambrose took off his reading glasses. "I am surprised. I was sure it would be Mrs Tompkins."

"So did I. At first, the mist seemed to be directing us to her grave, but then it continued on towards the trees, and the mist is never wrong." Or had the mist been pulled off course by Eurydice? The silver specks had seemed attracted to the dragon, or had she somehow sensed where they needed to go?

"We'd best figure out what he wants. They have three children, and we don't want to bury either them or their mother." George barely looked up from his book, which held his attention as he turned another page.

"No," Fern said in a quiet voice. That was the horrible price to be paid for a loved one returning. The longer they lingered, the higher the chance they would gather more souls to them. "I'll go visit Mrs Plummer tomorrow. I am sure we will easily discover his task."

She would prefer to run chores around the village than labour alone at Wyndham Hall. Neither Lord Drakeman nor Quint had returned from whatever matter called them away. While she would never admit it out loud, the enormous old house was far emptier without either of them in it.

Determined to enjoy the summer warmth, Fern decided to walk to Scribbles and to visit Mrs Plummer on the other side of the village. She even donned one of her favourite walking gowns in a soft green print covered in swirling leaves and flowers and grabbed a straw bonnet that would keep the sun from her eyes.

"Why, you make a delightful picture this morning." Ambrose beamed on seeing her appear in the kitchen doorway.

Fern held her skirts out to one side and dropped a brief curtsey. "Why, thank you, kind sir. Today felt like a floral dress kind of day." She took her seat and placed the bonnet on the end of the table.

"We all have days like that, dear," Ambrose murmured into his teacup.

After selecting two golden-brown crumpets from the plate in the middle of the table, she added a blob of butter in the middle of each. Next, Fern poured a fresh cup of coffee and added a splash of milk.

"Millie is going to join me when I talk to Mrs Plummer. I am hopeful that whatever awoke his spirit, it won't be too hard to discover so he can go back to...whatever it is spirits do in the other realm." She gestured with a crumpet as she spoke, waving it from side to side to roll the melted butter all over the hole-riddled surface.

"George and I have little to contribute that will aid your quest, unfortunately. Mr Plummer lived a quiet life. I still can't believe he is the one the orchid means. Do you think it could be a mistake?" Doubt lingered in his hazel gaze.

Fern shared his concern. But just because someone led an uneventful life, it doesn't mean they died without any regrets or unfinished business. "Quiet waters can conceal deep currents," she spoke softly, her thoughts elsewhere.

"You sound like George. Some days, I wonder if you are related to him, not me." The warm smile returned to Ambrose's handsome face.

"I think after a lifelong association, he has rubbed off on me. I just meant we don't know what secrets Mr Plummer might have harboured when he passed." Fern finished her crumpet and then reached for a napkin to wipe butter from her fingertips. "I am going to take Riddy with me. It will be a slow walk, and we can have lots of stops if she gets tired." It would be the furthest the youngster had ever walked, but she seemed capable. Fern hoped that having to walk everywhere might give her an incentive to stretch her wings. Even ducks and geese occasionally took to the skies and didn't waddle everywhere.

"We shall reconvene over dinner, and you can tell us what you learned." Ambrose poured himself more tea and seemed content to stay at the kitchen table for the morning, with the sun at his back and Mrs Bentley for company.

Outside, Fern tied the bonnet under her chin and fetched Eurydice. The dragon had finished her breakfast and chirped as the stall door swung open to let her out. "Ready for our walk? We will stop whenever you need to."

Side by side, they strolled along the road, following the gentle curve of the river to where it bent like an elbow. Every day, the heat of the sun intensified. Tight buds had appeared among the greenery of the kelmsgale as the tree prepared to flower at the height of summer. An air of excitement grew among the villagers as the annual mid-summer festival approached.

At the quaint bookstore, Fern walked around the side to the open back door. Eurydice flopped onto the grass in a sunny spot.

"Good morning, Alice," Fern called out as she stepped into the kitchen.

The oldest Bentley daughter rolled pastry at the long bench under the window. "Morning, Miss Oakby. Will you and Mrs Carlisle be wanting tea this morning?"

"No, thank you. We have a call to make this morning. Perhaps when we return, though?" While Fern would never tell Mrs Bentley, she thought Alice's rendition of her mother's teacake with currants was absolutely delicious and possibly surpassed the original.

Millie was between the stacks today, shelving an armload of books. Squib perched on the row above, squawking instructions.

"Hello. Ready to start our spectral mission?" Mischief

gleamed in the writer's eyes. No doubt imagining the possible stories that events would inspire.

"The sooner we start, the sooner we will find Mr Plummer's purpose for returning." Fern took a book from the pile and placed it back in the row where the little pixie dragon indicated.

The task was soon done, and they headed out. Squib sitting on Eurydice's shoulder. The women walked over the bridge and then headed north-east, away from the high street with its pretty shops, each with bay windows. Past the fifteenth-century building that housed the Drake's Rest tavern, and the old stone forge where the clang of metal rang out.

They took the packed dirt path that wound by cottages with glorious gardens, or some were growing vegetables instead of flowers, and cucumbers clambered over fences to dangle their fat fruit. Eurydice started to slow as they finally approached the Plummer cottage, with its pretty garden of lavenders, roses, larkspurs, and cornflowers. Flowers in tones of blue and purple were intermingled with white, making a soothing display.

"Why don't you and Squib sit by those trees, Riddy?" Fern pointed to a stand of birch that clustered to one side of the road. "You are getting too big for going inside, and not everyone appreciates dragon visitors." She rubbed the hard ridge above the dragon's eye.

Eurydice sank to the shady grass with an appreciative *oof*, while Squib roosted on a branch above, like a lookout.

Fern knocked on the door, and footsteps came from inside before the door was flung open. A woman in her mid-forties, with the beginning of silver streaking the sides of her hair, greeted them. She wore an apron over her gown, and flour indicated that they had caught her at work in the kitchen.

"Hello, Mrs Plummer. I don't know if you remember me. I'm Fern Oakby. This is my friend, Mrs Carlisle. Could you spare us a little time, please, to talk about Mr Plummer?" Fern didn't want to blurt out that the woman's deceased husband had returned until she was sitting down.

Worry wrinkled the widow's brow, and then she drew a deep breath and nodded. "Of course, come in, ladies. I shall put the kettle on." She stepped back to allow them to enter the modest home.

"You might have heard that the spectral orchid has flowered..." Fern decided to jump right into the reason for their visit.

"It's him, isn't it? My Dick." Her hand went to her chest.

"I believe so. Last night, we used the spectral mist, and the spirit manifested at his gravesite." Fern was a bit out of practice at gently teasing details of the deceased's life from their remaining relatives. As she considered how to ask the widow what unfinished business or secrets might have pulled him back through the veil, Millie jumped in.

"Do you think your husband left behind a secret family?" The writer leaned forward, a keen glint in her eyes.

Mrs Plummer recoiled, the hand at her chest now clutching the fabric of her bodice. "A secret family?" Her wide gaze darted from Fern to Millie and back again.

"Or perhaps he was a highwayman and has a stash of jewellery and coins hidden in a tree trunk that you must find." Millie's hands turned into the branches of a tree as she spoke.

Fern stared at her friend. She had expected Millie to quietly observe as she usually did, but the idea of finding the spirit's unresolved business had unleashed her creative side. Reaching out, Fern took hold of Millie's hands and hoped it likewise stilled her mind. Catching the other woman's gaze, Fern made what she hoped was interpreted as a *don't scare the poor woman* expression. "I am sure Mrs Plummer knows her husband best, Mrs Carlisle. Why don't we let her gather her thoughts and then tell us what she thinks is the most likely cause of his soul's return?"

"Oh. Of course. Why don't I pour the tea?" Millie busied herself setting out the mismatched cups and turning the pot.

Fern suspected she needed something to do with her hands to stop her from reaching for the notebook and pencil hidden in a pocket.

Mrs Plummer was silent, her attention on her hands in her lap, where she plucked at the edge of her apron. She took the offered cup of tea with a silent thanks and sipped for a quiet minute before speaking. "He was a good man. Quiet and steady. Dick never had any fancies like other men. He was always happy to lend a hand with the children if I needed one. In the evenings, in warmer weather, after he had tended the vegetables, he was content to sit on the porch and smoke his pipe. In winter, he sat by the fire with a book."

None of which seemed important enough to Fern to bring his spirit back from wherever he was supposed to be for eternity. Unless Millie had been correct and he wanted to know how his book ended.

"Something has made him reach out across the void that separates living from death. Did you perhaps argue in the days before his passing?" Fern dug deeper, trying to find the problem that roused the spirit.

The widow remained silent.

"We're not here to judge, Mrs Plummer. It might seem trivial to you, but it may have pressed upon your husband's soul, and he wishes to make amends." No one was perfect. Even the mildest person could snap if sufficient cause was heaped upon them.

"We never slept on an argument. Not that we had many. He did his chores, and I did mine. We had little cause for complaint." Her brows drew together, and her gaze turned inward for a few moments.

"But?" Millie prompted.

"It's nothing." A brief smile lit the older woman's face, and then it was chased away by a sombre expression. "Dick worked long hours, but that's our lot in life. He was a labourer, and he always worked as many hours as he could over spring and summer to tide us through the winter months."

Millie let out a breathy, "Oh." Her eyes widened, and she turned to Fern with questions burning in her bright gaze.

Fern cleared her throat. "Do you think he was occupied elsewhere, and not necessarily on a farm?"

Perhaps Millie had been right with her opening question, and Mr Plummer had another family in a nearby village. It wouldn't be the first time a man spread himself thin. Although usually, it was pirates and sailors who kept a lover in every port they visited.

Mrs Plummer's lips set in a thin line, and she set her teacup down with a rattle. "You think he had a woman somewhere and dallied away his time with her? I think you should leave, Miss Oakby."

Things were not turning out as she had hoped. "We mean no offence, Mrs Plummer, but we have limited time. We need to settle Mr Plummer's spirit within ten days, or you will succumb to the spectral sickness. To do that can require asking difficult questions. We all have sides to ourselves we keep private, sometimes even from those closest to us."

The older woman drew a ragged breath and stood. "I will have a good think and talk to the children. There was some squabble with a couple of his friends not long before he died. But with men, such things blow over quickly. I'm sure it was nothing that would rouse him from the grave."

To Fern, an argument between good friends sounded exactly like the sort of thing to make a spirit restless. "Could you find out more, please? Just so we can be sure."

"Our lad might know more than me. He and his father often spent time out in the vegetable patch in the evenings. He won't be back until this evening. He works just as many hours as Dick used to."

"I will return tomorrow to see if your son knows the details of the disagreement. We must find the reason before you are afflicted with the weariness." Fern didn't want to panic the woman. But if the cause was not found, she would weaken every day until she joined her husband.

With no more to learn that day, Fern stood and took Millie's hand, practically pulling the writer to the front door.

"Thank you for your time," Fern said as they stepped back into the sunshine.

Eurydice lifted her head from where she lay by the path. Squib dived from his perch on a branch and landed on Millie's outstretched arm.

After settling the pixie dragon on her shoulder, Millie looped her free arm through Fern's and leaned in close. "I am confident we will have this matter sorted in no time at all. It is most likely another woman. Mrs Plummer suspected but didn't want to say so out loud. She needs a day or two to make her peace with the situation, then she will confess all to us."

"You seem very sure." While Fern had seen the widow's hesitation when the idea was raised, that didn't mean her husband had been unfaithful. For all they knew, he could have been secretly attending dog fights or any number of unsavoury ways men found to while away the hours they were supposed to be working.

"All men bicker among themselves at some point, so I don't put any weight on this disagreement among friends. I imagine there will be some deep, dark secret that has tormented him beyond the grave." Millie let out a sigh, no doubt imagining all sorts of furtive activities the mild-mannered man had engaged in.

"I'm not so sure." Fern stared back at the cottage, and her attention drifted down from the top of the stone chimney stack to the vegetable patch at the side, enjoying the most sun exposure. "The things people hide can often surprise us."

CHAPTER 10

The two women exchanged ideas on what awoke Mr Plummer's spirit as they walked back into the village. Squib moved from Millie to ride on Eurydice's back, looking like a small jockey. The dragons chatted in their own musical tongue. As they stepped off the old stone bridge by the bookstore, Eurydice flapped her wings and trilled. She turned and looked expectantly at Fern.

"What is it, Riddy?" Fern wondered what had got the dragon excited. Possibly, she wanted to spend more time with Squib.

As they stepped on the grass, the young dragon waddled in a direct line to the river.

"I think she wants another swim," Millie said as they followed behind.

Fern glanced down at her walking dress. She hadn't come prepared to jump into the river and might have to dry out in Millie's kitchen before returning home. "Perhaps we could come back later?" she called out to her companion.

Too late. Eurydice ploughed on. Literally. The dragon walked out into the river and, a second later, dropped with a splash and a plonk. This time, she stretched out her wings and didn't go under. After rolling one way and then another as she overcorrected, she soon tucked her wings into her sides and paddled in a circle.

"At least she didn't sink this time." Millie stopped well short of the riverbank. Squib's agitation made it clear he didn't want to get wet.

"Stay on the shallow side!" Fern sat on the grass, unlaced her boots, and rolled off her stockings. Next, her light cotton coat joined the pile of clothing as she removed as much as possible to save it from getting soaked in case a rescue was needed.

The dragon paddled in circles and appeared pleased with her new skill. At one point, she ducked her head under the water and seemed to be peering into the depths of the river. At times, she would drift out a little and let the gentle current spin her around before paddling closer to the bank again.

"It is a marvel how confident she has become for only her second swim." Millie edged closer, while Squib nestled against her neck and used the side of her bonnet as a shield in case Eurydice splashed.

Fern watched the dragon like a nervous mother with a child learning to swim. The youngster grew bigger, stronger, and braver in water. But she was still flightless—like an ostrich. Morda's words wafted through her mind. *Fear can keep us earthbound.*

What more could she do to prod the dragon into trying?

"Clear the ramp to the balcony," Fern muttered.

Thinking of the metal stairs that curved up to the second level in the conservatory.

"What balcony?" Millie glanced around at the cottages that overlooked the river further down.

"I was thinking of all the work still to do in the conservatory. I will be labouring there through winter, and at least my fingers won't get frostbite." Given the thermal spring that heated the pool and sleeping platform, the glassed space should keep a lovely cosy temperature through the colder months.

Millie sat down and tucked her skirts around her legs. "I love winter. There's something about curling up in an armchair by the fire and watching the flames crackle while snow falls outside."

Squib gave a worried squawk. Apparently, flames were something else he wanted to avoid. Even though magic had made him real, he still thought of himself as a paper construction.

Fern thought Millie's love for winter showed she never had to work outside to make ends meet, all the while worrying that her nose would freeze and fall off. Not everyone had the luxury of burrowing in a warm parlour and waiting for spring like a hibernating bear. But she bit her tongue. It wasn't her friend's fault she had been born to the upper classes and had a different experience. Thinking of her tender background made Fern worry about how draughty the bookstore might be in winter. She would seek out one of the knitters in the village and ask them to make fingerless gloves for the writer when the temperature dropped.

They watched Riddy play for a little longer, then Fern

gestured for her to climb out of the river. The dragon gave a rebellious stare and paddled out of reach. Fern crossed her arms. "I have work to do, Riddy, and Millie needs to open the bookstore. You either come back in now, or you will be left here on your own."

The dragon huffed and peered up at a passing blackbird. Only then did she swim back to the bank and clamber out, where she shook droplets from her scales.

"When Lord Drakeman returns, I will ask him about cleaning out the pool. Then you can keep on swimming even when the river gets too cold." Fern tugged her stockings and boots back on, more than a little thankful that she hadn't had to jump in because the dragon had gotten into trouble.

The friends parted company, and Fern and Eurydice continued back to Nemython House in silence.

Fern had a sneaking suspicion the dragon was sulking at having her swim curtailed. "I shall leave a change of clothes at the cottage. That way, when you want a swim again, I can go with you and still have something dry to put on afterwards."

Her idea mollified the creature, and Eurydice stretched out her neck to sniff a flower.

Back in the walled garden, the dragon picked a sunny spot and flopped on her belly. Her iridescent scales soaked up the sunlight and glinted in tones of blue and green. Fern pushed open the kitchen door with a weariness in her bones as though she had spent all day chopping up wood. A trickle down her spine warned that settling Mr Plummer's spirit would not be as easy as she initially hoped.

"What did you discover?" Ambrose looked up from the

papers spread before him on the kitchen table. "Did our wandering soul have a secret hobby he wants his widow to know about?"

Fern pulled out a chair and sat opposite her uncle. She poured a still-warm cup of tea from the pot as she gathered her thoughts. "No. Mrs Plummer had no idea why he has returned. She is going to talk to their son tonight, as there is a possibility Mr Plummer said something to the lad he wouldn't say to his wife. I will go back tomorrow to see if she learned anything. Apart from that, she said he was a quiet husband who worked hard and liked to tend to his vegetable patch."

"Don't lose hope yet, Fern. We might yet reveal a secret life as a highwayman." Ambrose picked up the sheet closest to him and held it up.

"You sound like you have been talking to Millie." The writer had suggested the most outrageous reasons for the dead man to return.

Ambrose chuckled. "I have been editing her story for the *Midnight Chronicle*. It is about a highwayman who is actually a woman. She only ever robs wealthy men and kisses the women senseless. Our readers are clamouring for more. This is instalment three that will go out this week."

"How have I missed reading that?" Fern turned her head to try to read the story upside down.

Her uncle covered up the papers. "Oh, no, you don't. The first two parts are on the table by my armchair in the parlour."

While the idea of taking her tea and curling up in the sun to read was certainly enticing, Fern couldn't relax until Mr Plummer was back in his grave. "I shall save them for after dinner. I need to spread the word about Mr Plummer and see if anyone in the village knows anything remotely helpful."

In a small village, everybody usually knew everybody else's business. To a certain extent. It was still possible to keep secrets. Those who dwelt in Drake's Bend were a bit more circumspect than in other villages and towns.

"George and I are doing our bit. For his bulky size, George is rather adept at creeping up on secrets." Ambrose winked over the rim of his teacup.

"I'll start with Mr Plummer's family and friends and circle out from there."

Ambrose filled Fern in on the details she was missing. The Plummers had three children. Two boys and a girl. "The younger two married before they reached twenty," he said with a wink.

Some people were in a hurry to find a match, get married, and settle down. Others had different goals to achieve first. The oldest lad remained a bachelor and lived with his mother. Fern would visit the younger siblings and sow the seed of their father's return. Hopefully, it would germinate in the next few days.

After a cup of tea, Fern found Eurydice snoozing in the sun. The dragon's muzzle wrinkled, sniffing the air as she approached.

"Do you feel like a bit more of a walk?" Fern asked as one slitted eye half-opened.

The dragon let out a snort, and the eye closed again.

"I'll take that as a no. I won't be too long. I need to visit the two younger Plummers, and then I plan to work in my greenhouse this afternoon." There were orders to fulfil for alchemists and apothecaries in London and Europe. As well as cuttings to tend that would one day be planted out in the conservatory at Wyndham or sent to the far corners of England.

Setting off once more, Fern didn't have too far to go as Sophie, the youngest Plummer, lived in the village. She found the little cottage, with a modest and rather neglected garden, and rapped on the door.

Miss Plummer, now Mrs Cooper, flung the door open to Fern with a flustered look. "Is this important?"

From within came a screeching yowl that drove through Fern's ear canal like a spike. Before Fern could answer, the other woman hurried to a side room to scoop up a fractious baby. She jiggled the babe on her hip, which only made the noise worse.

Whether a woman longed for motherhood or had it thrust upon them, they all seemed to roll up their sleeves and get on with the job of child-raising. Fern didn't think she was cut from the same cloth. Watching the tiny red face balled up as she screamed only reinforced her conviction that life never intended her to be a mother.

"It's the colic. Nothing is settling her poor wee tum," Sophie said.

"I'm sure either Doctor Dodd or the Moray sisters will have a cure." Fern wriggled her fingers but failed to distract the child from the ache in her stomach.

"They both said beer. But I can't get my child drunk." Sophie wiped a strand of hair from her forehead with the back of her arm and switched her daughter to the other hip.

Fern had heard of beer being a remedy for horses and

didn't know it also worked for infants. Or not, since the crying had continued. Perhaps the beer was meant for the mother? "Did they have any other suggestions?"

"Gripe water, but I don't like the look of it. Beer might be safer." She pointed to a glass bottle on the mantle with greenery suspended in a yellowish liquid.

Fern peered closer at the brew, trying to identify the plants. If she were stuck with the infernal screaming for hours on end, desperation would make her try anything to soothe both babe and her ears. "Camomile, lemon balm, a pinch of dill. These are all edible herbs, and there is nothing that will harm her."

Sophie's arms tightened around her child. "Are you sure?"

"Yes. It is my opinion as a botanist that you may safely give a little to your baby." If both the doctor and the three witches had told her to try the remedy, she would have tried it immediately. But perhaps the new mother needed extra reassurance.

Fern grabbed the bottle and nearby found a spoon. They dribbled a little of the fragrant water over the baby's lips. The crying soon lowered to a grizzle.

Fern spoke quietly as they tended to the child. "I don't know if you have heard from your mother, but it is your father who has reached out through the spectral orchid. I need you to think if there was any reason for his soul to be restless."

Sophie paled. "It's Pa? Did you see his ghost?"

Even the baby fell silent, as though she too wanted to

hear the answer. Or it could be that crying had exhausted the poor mite.

"It was more like the shadow of a ghost, but he led us to his grave. Your mother is going to talk to your oldest brother to see if they can think of any reason for your father's return. It could be something simple like an unfinished project, something he said he always wanted to do, or...an argument?" Fern added the last on impulse. She remembered the hint of scandal around the young woman marrying at the tender age of eighteen. And the child that followed not many months after.

The young mother turned away and bowed her head. She half murmured a lullaby under her breath, and the child fell asleep in her arms as the gripe water soothed the upset tummy.

"He didn't approve of Jim. Didn't understand how much I love him. I wish..." she spoke in a quiet tone so as not to disturb the baby. When she turned to face Fern, a single tear rolled down her cheek.

"You argued about it. And you never got the chance to smooth things over." It wasn't too hard to guess what pained the young woman. Young lovers whom her family had tried to separate. Heated objections making their devotion more urgent and most likely tinged with a bit of the forbidden. Fern only hoped the young woman didn't regret any hasty decisions made.

"He never got to see his granddaughter." Sophie tilted her head to wipe her cheek on her shoulder.

Fern's feelings about babies softened as her gaze dropped to the small bundle. The girl's features had relaxed in slumber, and, with her little button nose, she appeared delightful. Not enough to tempt Fern into wanting one of her own, but she could appreciate a content baby and marvel at the stamina of those who cared for them.

"It's not too late to make your peace." Spirits were mollified by simple but heartfelt ceremonies.

"But he's dead." A frown marred her perfect young forehead.

"So are my parents, but I still talk to them. I think you should take your daughter to his graveside. Introduce her. Tell your father that you are sorry you argued, but that you love your new family and only wish that he could have seen that you are happy." As she said the words, Fern examined Sophie's face, looking for any hint that she wasn't happy in her new role.

Mrs Cooper looked down at her daughter, and an expression of pure love washed over her features. "Yes, I will do that. Jim really is a good man. A bit of a hothead, which is why he argued with Pa, but he's settled now and takes good care of us."

"Tell your father that. I am sure it was worry for you that made him reach through the veil." Fern dared a gentle touch on the baby's dark hair. They were quite sweet when fast asleep.

She left on quiet feet, congratulating herself for discovering the cause of the spirit's unrest in just two days.

CHAPTER 11

FERN WALKED BACK to Nemython House in a good mood. Ambrose had gone from the kitchen, but she found him and George out in the workshop. The men were discussing plans for a piece of furniture George was making. Or rather, Ambrose was waving his arms around, and George was sketching ideas on a plank of wood.

She stuck her head into the fragrant building, the aroma coming from the cut pieces of wood on a long bench. "Mr Plummer argued with his daughter over her relationship. She is going to take her baby out to his grave and have a good chat to settle things."

Ambrose's hands stilled, and recognition lit his face. "Oh, yes. Young Jim. Bit of a bother, that one. Used to throw rocks through the windows of people he didn't like."

"He stopped when I caught him," George growled. He put the length of lumber down and tucked the pencil behind his ear.

Fern could imagine a swift bit of justice had happened.

Most likely, George's boot connected with a posterior, and Jim was made to repair the damage. "Well, Sophie says that marriage and fatherhood have settled him down."

Ambrose hummed as he accessed his local knowledge. "I have heard that. The young malcontent has grown up with a bit of responsibility."

"I will let Mrs Plummer know. If the family makes it a ceremony of forgiveness and celebrates the new addition, I am sure Mr Plummer will return to his grave, content with his daughter's situation." All Fern had to do was watch the spectral orchid. Once a spirit had been soothed, the petals would fall from the bloom.

Satisfied with herself, she walked to the rear of the barn and checked on the kelmsgale seedlings that grew in the compost. The new shoots were now some six inches tall and had sprouted at least four leaves each. "Gosh, you lot are doing well. I shall leave you to carry on growing until autumn. Then I shall pot you up to winter in the greenhouse."

The afternoon was spent working in the greenhouse, filling orders and taking notes on what seeds she needed to gather in autumn. After dinner, Fern settled in the parlour with the *Midnight Chronicle* and dived into Millie's tale of robbery and daring on the shadowy and forested roads.

THE NEXT DAY, straight after breakfast, Fern watched Eurydice waddle up the plank into the cart, and they set off to the northern end of the village. She left horse and dragon outside the cottage, with its thatched roof and rapped on the door. It swung open within seconds.

"Good morning, Mrs Plummer. I think we found the reason your husband's spirit is restless." Fern launched into the good news to brighten the widow's day. No one wanted to contemplate having their soul slowly pulled from their physical form by a deceased loved one.

Mrs Plummer gestured for Fern to enter her cosy home, and they walked through to the sunny parlour. "I saw my Sophie yesterday afternoon. She told me about the fight with her Da. Silly girl. He loved her dearly. That's why he was upset about Jim. Always thought she deserved better. But they make a fine wee family."

"I suggested she take the little one to your husband's grave and perhaps have a ceremony to introduce her to him and tell him that his fears were unfounded. I am sure once he is reassured that Jim has grown into the role of husband and father, he will return to his eternal slumber." With the more pressing concern settled, Fern could turn her mind back to discovering whatever Sir Luxton Davies had been up to at Sibylcrest Abbey. A man who thought nothing of slaughtering a dragon and destroying rare trees needed to be stopped before he did something else equally horrid. The noble's total disregard for the impact on the forest around the abbey or the health of the villagers was a slow-burning rage inside Fern. Like a coal seam that had ignited and burned for hundreds of years deep underground.

"Yes. We all plan to gather there tomorrow, when my lads are done with work for the day. Will you join us, Miss

Oakby?" Mrs Plummer's smile deepened the lines around her eyes.

"If you do not mind, and I will stay under the trees so I don't intrude. Afterwards, I will check on the spectral orchid." As an afterthought, she added, "Did your oldest have any other ideas of why his father might have roused? Although I am sure the argument with Sophie is the reason." It didn't hurt to delve a little deeper, just in case.

Mrs Plummer shook her head. "No. He said Dick had been quiet those last few weeks. We wonder if he had been feeling unwell for some time but kept it quiet."

"I have heard some men don't like to worry their families about such things." Thankfully, that wasn't an issue in Fern's family. A wide range of health issues, including sometimes far too much personal detail about the exact location of aches and pains, were discussed at every meal.

Fern said her goodbyes as they walked back to the front door. Unable to help herself, she cast a gardener's eye over the front yard and the vegetable patch that basked in the sun. The potatoes had yellowed and fallen over, but the tubers were still tucked in the earth below. Beans clambered over a woven willow fence, and birds were feasting on the last of the tomatoes. The garden was functional, but could have been more productive with a bit of loving attention.

"Perhaps Mr Plummer has returned because of the state of his potatoes," she wondered to herself.

Eurydice trilled as Fern strode back down the path and climbed into the cart. "We have a full day at the Hall ahead of us, Riddy. I'd like to clear the ramp to the upper level so you can stretch your wings."

Taking up the reins, she urged the horse along the road towards the village and over the old stone bridge. Once on the other side of the river, they carried on northwards to Wyndham Hall. Where Fern immediately struck off through the narrow track she had managed to carve to the base of the ramp. A slow, sweeping path rose from the ground, hugged the side of the conservatory, and gave access to the upper level. A balcony jutted out from the middle and overlooked the lush garden below.

Wielding a hoe like a machete, Fern hacked dead branches out of her way to venture to the base of the cast-iron walkway. A closer inspection revealed that dragons with wings outstretched formed the balustrades. A rail ran along the tops of their heads and joined them together. The incline wasn't too steep as it curved up towards the mezzanine floor, and very different from the tight spiral staircases often found in conservatories. The design made sense since young dragons learning to fly would waddle up to leap from the balcony, testing their wings in the warmed currents of the conservatory.

"For Riddy." Fern touched a metal dragon, then grabbed hold of a long-dead palm blocking the bottom of the ramp.

She had spent a couple of hours clearing a mostly dead vine clinging to the balustrades and fallen palms beside it, when a low vibrating hum from Eurydice alerted Fern to them not being alone. She turned as Quint ventured a few steps into the conservatory.

"You're back," she called out, wiping sweat from her face with her forearm. His smiling face had been missing for four days. Not that she was keeping count of how much time the earl and his butler spent away from his ancestral home.

"Obviously." He stopped and scowled, tugging at the end of his sleeves. "Boss wants to see you."

Fern peeled off her gloves and tucked them into her leather apron before untying it and draping it over the wheelbarrow. "You know you are supposed to call him his lordship, not boss." If she needed any proof whatsoever that the man wasn't any butler, it was the way he addressed his employer.

"He's the boss, isn't he?" He scratched at his wrist, and the movement caught Fern's attention.

Unusually for Quint, he wore dark grey gloves with a whimsical splash of pink trim at the wrist. Then the pink disappeared as he scratched. Not a trim...but some sort of lining?

"Technically, he's your boss, yes. But that's not how you address an earl." She curled her nails into her palms to stop herself from asking why he wore fluffy, pink-lined gloves.

He huffed and crossed his arms. "Since when did you care what we're meant to do?"

Good point. "Where might I find him?"

"Laboratory." The butler walked off before she could ask anything else.

Fern glanced at Eurydice. "I am off across the meadow in search of *the boss*. Do you want to come for a walk or are you happy here?"

The dragon closed her eyes and hummed for a moment, and Fern marvelled at how she seemed to understand everything said to her. Then she opened her eyes and rose to all four feet and stretched out her neck. A gesture that Fern was learning meant she was ready to go.

A thought occurred to Fern as she imagined the long tail and wings knocking experiments off tables. "You won't be allowed in the laboratory, though. But the meadow is a lovely place to sit in the sun."

They took their time walking around the side of the brooding house and across the field. Grasses swayed in the light breeze, and Eurydice disappeared at times in the longer patches, possibly chasing rabbits invisible to Fern as they scurried through the undergrowth. At the stout little building, Fern rapped sharply on the door and waited. Today, there was no shout of *go away*; instead, the bolt rattled in the solid piece of timber, and then the door swung open.

"Good. Quint found you." Lord Drakeman's gaze dropped to the creature at Fern's side, and he ground his jaw. "She stays out."

"We've already had that conversation." Fern patted the dragon's head.

Eurydice lay down and rested her head on her crossed front paws. After a pointed look at Lord Drakeman, which seemed to convey that she didn't want to go inside his smelly old laboratory anyway, she closed her eyes and made what sounded suspiciously like fake snoring noises.

Fern followed him into the cool building. "Where did you go?" she blurted out. Then belatedly, she added, "Not that it is any of my business." She bent down to stare at a terrarium that held a miniature ocean and beach instead of plants. An unseen moon pulled at the water, which lapped against the golden sand. There didn't appear to be any sort of clockwork mechanism, so how did he make it work?

"Two pieces of business drew me in a similar direction. Like you, I want to know what Luxton was doing at Sibylcrest." He leaned on the square tabletop, his long fingers spread wide as though he held the solid piece of wood down.

Fern gasped, and hope of solving one mystery surged through her. "Have you discovered what he brewed?"

Not knowing why the baron made such a horrid concoction tore strips loose in her mind, but she had no way to figure it out on her own.

"I did not have much of the substance to examine." Here he paused to stare at Fern, but she refused to look away or be made to feel guilty over her actions. She stopped the smoke that was poisoning the land and was unrepentant about it. "Despite the small sample size, I was able to determine that the trace of blood that was combined with the wood was from the dragon you found by the stump."

"Oh. Tree and dragon were slain at the same time." She mourned the death of the creature and hoped it had a quick and painless end. Possibly one better than starving while predators circled it.

"So it would seem. And I know what for." He pushed off the surface and paced to a shelf where the pulpy mixture sat in a glass beaker. A faint blueish shimmer came from the substance as he swirled it around. "My family has kept many old books recording what alchemists and magic casters have created with the assistance of dragons. Scales are the most common ingredient, like in the potion I brewed to cure the villagers. They are given willingly by the creatures. Sometimes there is also a shed claw or a clipping taken. Then there are those who seek to conjure darker things with blood and bone."

Fern stared at him with equal parts fascination and horror. Her mind imagined ancient recipe books containing instructions on how to use an entire dragon without wastage. Somewhere out there, some rich noble probably had luggage made from dragon hide. Or riding boots. She wet her lips before speaking in a hushed tone. "What did you find?"

He turned his back to the shelves of vials and crossed his arms. "*Sericum draconis*. Dragon silk. I thought it was as mythical as the Stormborne Serum. It is mentioned in a grimoire from the twelfth century, and supposedly, our family holds the only copy. But somehow, Luxton found another. The grimoire reveals that when the wood pulp from the *Sorbus celmsgeul beatha* is blended with dragon blood, a unique alchemical reaction is triggered."

"You mean *Sorbus celmsgeul*. The kelmsgale rowan." Somehow, the men had known the unusual tree had been a kelmsgale when her father had overlooked it. What had they noticed, or had it been a simple coincidence?

"*Sorbus celmsgeul beatha*." Slowly and clearly, he pronounced each syllable. "It is mentioned more than once in the text."

Fern's head spun. An unknown variety of kelmsgale. How was that possible? "Can you show me? Please?"

He paused long enough that she thought he would refuse. Then he strode into the dim earthen tunnel at the rear of the laboratory. Without a light, not that he needed one with night vision in one eye, the shadows swallowed him.

Only a faint shuffle marked his movement. The clang of heavy metal was followed by a scrape. A few moments later, he reappeared cradling a tome in his arms.

Gently, as though it were a baby, he laid it on the table. The book was almost square, with a distinctive scalloped pattern to the iridescent leather.

"Is that...?" Her hand hovered over the surface, her fingers longing to stroke the familiar-looking hide.

"It's bound in dragon skin. A foul practice and not one ever sanctioned by any king or drake man." His hand curled into a fist before he used it to push through his messy hair.

A knot formed in Fern's stomach as she imagined Eurydice being used to bind novels on the shelves of Scribbles. Not that Millie would ever condone such a practice, either. She would be equally horrified when Fern told her later.

A black silk ribbon dangled from both ends of the book, and Lord Drakeman opened the book at whatever it marked. "This is the formula for *Sericum draconis.*"

Fern moved closer until the heat from his body prickled over her skin. She didn't mean to, but she inhaled and drew in the odd combination of scents that he emitted. Something earthy that reminded her of warmed soil after the rain. An undertone of freshness, like pine. A spice she couldn't identify, perhaps book dust and inhaled residue of dragon. Most likely, she was sniffing whatever he used to clean his beakers and vials. So why did it make her want to lean closer and take a lick to see what he tasted like?

CHAPTER 12

Spread before Fern was an illuminated version of some alchemic process. A piece of equipment that looked like a spindle was painted gold. There was something else with cogs and metal bits all covered in runes and symbols. Vibrant colours were used to illustrate the ingredients, but her brain had to glance over the dark-red stain seeping down the side of the page from the slain dragon at the top. The image on the right-hand side drew her eye.

Rooted at the bottom of the page, the tree bore some vague resemblance to the kelmsgale in the shape of its leaf and the boughs that spread across the paper. But the leaves were a dark burgundy, like those of a copper beech. "You were hidden in plain sight. Disguised as your more common relative. Only the flowers and seedpods would have revealed your true identity." She spoke to the tree, which laced its branches through the words of the formula.

"The last of its kind..." Sadness washed over Fern, and

then she gasped as it was swept away by a fresh breeze in her mind. "The seeds!"

"You have seeds?" Lord Drakeman glanced up from the book.

Past events collided in Fern's mind and, with a flash, they clarified and made sense. "That's how I knew it was some species of kelmsgale. I found a seedpod in the dirt beside the stump. That then got squashed in my pocket during the... umm...upheaval at Warrington Manor." Fern paused and swallowed a giggle at the remembered sight of Lord Warrington being chased by the monstrous *Helix mortifera*. "The pod made a bit of a mess of the lining. As I was sitting with Riddy, picking sticky seeds and lint from my fingers...she licked them off."

"The dragon ate the seeds? But they are inedible." A frown drew a line across his forehead.

"That's what we always thought. But this tree"—Fern tapped the drawing—"has seedlings growing in my compost heap. I believe the seeds had to pass through a dragon's digestive system in order to germinate."

Fern closed her eyes and pressed her hands to her face. There was so much racing around inside her head. The dominant thought was how much she wished she could tell her father about the rare subspecies of kelmsgale. She plucked at a question the alchemist could answer for her. "I still don't understand how combining a tree and dragon blood makes silk?"

He tapped the ornately written formula, as though it were obvious. "The dragon blood activates the latent magical energies in the kelmsgale pulp, breaking down the remaining lignin and releasing a pure, reactive cellulose. That substance becomes a thread that is then perfectly primed for weaving into luxurious fabric, known as dragon silk."

"Fabric made from wood." Was there anything science couldn't do? Fern couldn't imagine wearing a gown made of wood. But then Squib had started as an origami creature, and magic had made him real. Perhaps there was another sort of magic that transformed paper into silk instead of hide.

But to what end? He had said dragon's blood was used to make *darker* potions. A chill washed over her and raised goose bumps under her sleeves. "Why did that take you away from Drake's Bend?"

"Once I discovered this dark alchemic process, it narrowed down my search. I have had a man in London sifting through Luxton's interests, and one caught my attention. He owns a small cotton mill, but we could not find any evidence it ever produced cloth." He slid the book to one side and unfolded a map to place next to it. "We went here, Banbury, in Oxfordshire. Luxton has a mill close to the River Cherwell. When we paid a call, it appeared not long abandoned."

"I still don't understand how he makes fabric from two incredibly rare and special specimens. Or why?" She flung out her hands to scramble for the seat of the stool and slid it under her bottom as she slumped. Cotton and wool were spun from fibres. Silk was gently teased from the silkworm's cocoon. But how did slushy, boiled wood become a shirt?

Lord Drakeman huffed, reluctant to become a teacher. But he tried. "It's complex and requires both knowledge of alchemy and someone who can mould motes. Quint and I paid a nighttime visit to the mill and discovered that Luxton had certain unusual modifications to the spinning equipment. The old spinneret has alchemical runes etched along its surface, which match this formula. From what I've learned from the book, that is crucial for channelling the reaction's energy into a continuous filament. Then it passes into a room known as the curing chamber. There, the extruded fibre passes through a steam-powered machine inscribed with more protective glyphs. Here, the enchanted cellulose solidifies and emerges as a lustrous, silk-like fibre—*Sericum draconis*, or dragon silk. Rather like the thread that a silkworm spins, it is then ready to be woven into cloth."

Fern stared at him and wholeheartedly wished it to be a horrible joke. "You said it had not been long disused? Perhaps he failed, and the dragon died and the tree was cut down for nothing."

He rolled his sleeves up his arms, drawing Fern's eyes to the movement of muscles in his forearms and the silvered scar. "We asked in the nearby taverns. It was being used until a few weeks ago, although no one local worked there. Whatever Luxton was doing, he has moved on. Most likely, he transformed all the pulp he had from Sibylcrest and could not source any more."

"What does one do with dragon silk?" She didn't want to know but had to at the same time. How did one use silk to advance a nefarious scheme?

"For centuries, men have searched for a holy chalice or fountain of youth to prolong their lives. But what if I told you it could be found in a bolt of fabric?" He held her gaze, and a quest for such knowledge gleamed in his human eye.

She tried to understand how fabric could increase a life-span. A beautiful gown could have a transformative effect on the wearer. Or did he mean more literally? A dress of fine silk hung in her wardrobe, and she recalled the sensation of slipping it over her body. "Silk can feel like water when being worn."

"It's not about a fancy gown. *Sericum draconis* is said to reverse the ageing process. Wear a shift made from it every night, and you will turn back the hands of time and regain a youthful form and face." He crossed his arms, and his dragon eye narrowed as though that part of him found the idea repugnant.

She wondered that he didn't go cross-eyed, trying to reconcile the two different ways he saw the world. Fern washed her hands over her face as the implications slammed into her brain. "You are telling me that centuries ago, someone discovered you could kill a dragon and fell an incredibly rare tree just to...to...look younger?"

He curled one hand into a fist as he rested it on the table-top. "The production is a slow process that cannot be rushed, and Luxton hasn't started selling the garments yet. We may still have time to find where he took the thread to be woven into fabric."

"What was the second thing?" Fern whispered. Her over-whelmed mind was still processing what he had told her, but she figured she may as well tip every last thing into the brew swirling in her head.

"Second?" One dark eyebrow quirked.

"Back at the beginning, you said two things called you

away in the same direction." She needed a change of topic and hoped his other business had been lighter in tone.

"A dead dragon."

Nope. That wasn't any better. "Another drained by Luxton's men?" Chills swept over her body as she considered that the appetite of the wealthy to look young was behind the decline in dragon numbers. They would slaughter every creature in their pursuit of vanity.

Lord Drakeman turned the map and, after studying it for a moment, tapped an area by a river. "No. An associate had written to me about an adolescent some weeks ago. It was found in poor condition on a riverbank. I wrote to advise him to give it fish broth since that had a remarkable effect on your companion."

With difficulty, Fern swallowed the lump that had formed in her dry throat. "I'm assuming the fish didn't work, since you said it died."

He closed both eyes for a moment and pinched the bridge of his nose. It appeared she was not the only one struggling to find reason in everything laid out before them. "I cannot fathom why your dragon recovered but this one did not. Both were fed broth made with fish caught in the local river. It is possible there were other factors that caused the adolescent to expire, such as disease or injury, that weren't obvious."

Fern had the tiniest kernel of an idea, but she wasn't sure if it was worth voicing yet. "There are types of birds that require stones in their gizzard for digestion. I wonder if the kelmsgale seeds served such a purpose for Eurydice. Perhaps the whole fish might contain pebbles from eating off the river bed. Could dragons be starving without them?"

He folded up the map and slid it to one side. "Possibly. It certainly appears that this creature starved. Although we didn't have time to conduct an internal examination. My associate will do that and report any findings. He'll also send a bone sample so I can analyse the mineral density."

The words sounded cold from his lips, yet he spoke about a fantastical creature that had the life drained from it. Rather like when a person has a restless soul and doesn't have their unfinished business resolved. That sparked a new fear in her head. What if some spectral being reached through the veil that separated living from dead and gathered young dragons to it?

"There is so much we don't know." Fern stored their conversation away. Later, in the quiet of her room, as she stared at the ceiling, she would pull it back out to examine. She struggled to imagine what their world would lose, just so shrivelled up nobles could wrap themselves in dragon silk and restore the fullness of lost youth to their features.

At least they could stop Luxton from profiting from such a heinous thing. "When your London man finds where Sir Luxton has moved the *Sericum draconis* thread, I want to be involved in depriving him of it."

She met his odd gaze and held it until he nodded. The tension in the room eased a little, as though they had reached some silent agreement.

Lord Drakeman closed the rare grimoire and rested one hand on the dragon hide cover. "I have a question for you— would you happen to know anything about Quint's *condition?*"

Mentally, Fern compiled a list of different things that

could be afflicting Quint. "You cannot blame his surly demeanour on me. I am sure he was born like that."

His lips quirked in a brief smile. "No. I was referring to the unusual pink fur that has grown on his palms in the last few days. Although he does seem to be shedding it now."

Ah. Now she understood the flash of colour she saw when he told her that the earl wanted to see her. It wasn't a whimsical trim on his gloves, but something that sprouted from his skin. "Quint has pink fur?" She repeated the question mainly because she enjoyed the way it bubbled up her throat.

"Yes." He crossed his arms.

His simple gesture affected Fern's mind in an odd way as her eyes lingered on the shape of muscles under linen. Struggling to pull her attention back to the matter at hand. Or *furry* matter at hand. "On his palms?"

"Yes." While he didn't smile, humour glinted in his eyes. "It also sprouted on his nose and in a stripe over his scalp. Almost as though it took root wherever he touched himself."

Well played, Decima. It took all Fern's self-control not to burst out laughing. Quint deserved fur and more for scaring her in the dark. *He grew fur wherever he touched himself.* Did he have a pink furry...No! She slammed a door in her brain before she conjured the image of where else, exactly, Quint might have touched. "Need I remind you, Lord Drakeman, that you have both been away these last few days? How could I possibly have caused such a thing? Isn't it more likely that Quint has been exposed to something in here?" Fern gestured to the array of bubbling experiments. Some even emitted faint wafts of steam.

His dragon eye bored right through her. Oh, he knew she had been responsible, but she refused to own up.

He arched one dark eyebrow. "Quint does not come in here. Nor have I ever brewed a potion that would cause pink fur."

Was she the only person he admitted to his laboratory? Questions sprouted in her mind like dandelions, and she struggled to ignore them. "Assuming you do not have a valet, is it possible Quint touched your clothing? You may have had traces of something on your sleeves or the edge of a waistcoat or jacket and not realised. I have little knowledge of alchemic experiments, but if Quint had traces of something else on his hands, such as silver polish, might it not react with one of your experiments and create an unexpected result?" She congratulated herself on an entirely feasible-sounding explanation.

He grunted, and it was surprising how much disbelief he infused into the sound.

"Well, it shall remain a mystery. It is time I left you to your work, Lord Drakeman. I have a restless spirit to settle before his wife joins him in the graveyard." After their morbid discussion of dead dragons and dark artefacts, she needed to walk in the sunshine.

He reached out and caught her arm as she passed. Gently, his fingers encircled her wrist, and his thumb rubbed along her pulse point. "I will keep you informed, Miss Oakby, of what my man discovers. Luxton harmed this community, and we shall ensure he pays for that. Together. I have slumbered too long, but you have awoken me, and I will tend to my responsibilities."

Together. Fern couldn't draw her attention away from where he held her. Or the slow caress. Words fled her, and if she tried to speak, there was a good chance she'd forget how to breathe anyway and choke on her tongue. "Um..."

He unfurled his hand, and she was free. But now didn't know if she wanted to be. Perhaps he could have stroked a little higher up her arm? He did mention tending to his responsibilities. Was she on that list? No. Best not to ask that. What had they been discussing again?

"Thank you, Lord Drakeman," she murmured as she hurried back out into the warmth of the day.

It was probably her imagination, but she thought for the briefest moment she heard a low chuckle before the door of the squat building slammed shut behind her.

CHAPTER 13

OUTSIDE, with the warm breeze tugging at her short hair, Fern bent down and wrapped her arms around Eurydice's neck. After discussing so much death, she had to reassure herself that the dragon would continue to thrive. "Let's go, girl. I think it's too nice a day to labour in the conservatory, and we have a ceremony to witness later this afternoon."

They would return to Nemython House for lunch and sit out in the garden beside the pond. The gentle ripple of water over rocks might soothe her thoughts and restore some sort of focus. But Fern would have to watch the dragon, who showed a keen interest in the darting fish. They had already had one conversation that the koi in the pond were to be left alone. If the creature wanted fish for dinner, she would have to learn to catch them in the river.

Fern unlaced her boots by the back door while Eurydice wandered along the path to the pond.

"I know how many fish are in there!" Fern called out to

the dragon, who disappeared behind a dark green *Hebe speciosa* covered in soft lavender, brush-like flowers.

Darting across the kitchen floor, Fern made for the parlour. She wanted to grab the latest *Midnight Chronicle* to read in the sun.

"Where did I leave you?" she spoke to the periodical as she surveyed the room.

Fern glanced to her left and froze for two heartbeats. Then she practically jumped to where the spectral orchid sat on its plinth in the corner where it received morning sunlight.

"You're going to flower." A bud of at least an inch in length had grown from the odd bump she had noticed on the arching stem just a few days before. Fern's vision misted as tears formed. Five long years of waiting, and her father was finally reaching out. While her heart desperately wanted a little more time with her mother, they had sufficient warning of her impending end to ensure she had nothing unfinished when Death gathered her up. Or nothing as unfinished as Delphine could make it. No amount of preparation could make up for the decades of living that were snatched from her.

"Uncle Ambrose! Father is here!" Fern yelled, hoping to summon her uncles without having to move. Her gaze fixated on the swelling bud. What if she turned away, and it retreated back into the stem or fell off?

Pain swirled with hope and formed a tight knot inside Fern. Her father's unfinished business simply had to be who had slipped poison into his tea. That would erase all doubt from George's mind, as the big man believed otherwise. Then worry niggled at her. What if it was something else? Her father might want to see the lunanavis bloom, or had plans to acquire a particularly rare plant and forgotten to tell her.

Ambrose rushed into the parlour, patting his thinning hair that had been disturbed on the way into place. His face was pinched in a quizzical expression. "What do you mean, Rowan is here?"

Only now did Fern risk glancing over her shoulder to wave him closer. "It has a bud," she whispered.

"Oh, Fern." Ambrose's words choked up in his throat.

George was drawn to the parlour from upstairs by her yells. He leaned close to the orchid and examined the stem with the obvious swell of an expectant mother nearing her due date. "Might not be Rowan. This is an old house. Dozens of people would have died here, unlike Rowan."

"That's a cheery thought." Ambrose cuffed his partner on the shoulder.

"The previous owner died over there. Might be him." George gestured to Ambrose's favourite spot with one hand.

"You are jesting. Only Delfie slipped away in here. Old people die in bed." Ambrose's voice became higher in pitch as he stared in horror at his armchair warmed by the sun and with its view of the front garden.

"That spot. He didn't have any family, and it took a few days before anyone found him." George turned the orchid around to check for buds on the other side before putting the plant, with its graceful stem, back on its plinth.

"My chair?" Ambrose repeated. His mouth hung open, and his face drained a little paler.

"Rowan had it recovered to remove the corpse smell."

Not a flicker of emotion crossed George's rugged and lined face.

A strangled gasp came from Ambrose, and he buckled at the knees to sit down, realised he was aiming for the piece of furniture in question, and staggered left to land on the sofa instead.

"Father might not have died at Nemython, but he has a strong emotional tie to this house." *And to me*, Fern added in her mind. *Surely he has a message for me?* "That bond is what allows him to use the orchid to show he is here."

"Fern is quite right. People don't usually die in cemeteries, but their restless souls can use the orchids kept in them to reach their families." Ambrose pointed out as he fanned himself with the periodical Fern had been about to retrieve.

George huffed. It appeared he rather liked his theory of the previous owner wanting his armchair back. His features softened as he stared at Fern. "It could be Delfie. She might want to see the fine woman you have grown into."

Fern drew a ragged breath, and her eyes stung. Before emotion overwhelmed her, she flung her arms around George's barrel middle. "I miss them both so much," she whispered against the rough cloth of his shirt.

George patted her back. "Love never goes away. They are both always with us, and we don't need an orchid to feel that."

He was right. Of course. Fern's heart and mind were full of love for her parents and their love for her. She still missed their physical presence, though. Her conversations with their memories were rather one-sided.

Fern swallowed the lump in her throat and wiped away

the moisture in her eyes. "When the bloom opens, we will know for sure."

Bother. Then she would have two restless spirits to placate.

But Mr Plummer would be content once he was presented with his granddaughter and saw how happy his daughter was as a married woman. Another worry wormed its way into Fern's brain. If her father was returning because of the manner of his death, she only had a matter of days to solve a mystery that had defeated her for five years.

The Moray sisters often warned that you should be careful what you wished for. Fern had always thought it nonsense. Not understanding how anything that was much desired could have unintended consequences. Now, she stared at the orchid with a creeping sense of dread.

"Oh, no," she whispered. What had she done?

LATE THAT DAY, as the sun lazily descended behind the horizon and twilight bathed the cemetery in golden light, Fern stood under the trees as the Plummer family gathered. Sophie was accompanied by her husband, the former ruffian who had found his purpose with a wife and daughter to provide for and protect. Mr Cooper tugged at his collar and eyed the grave nervously. Perhaps expecting his father-in-law to rise up and challenge him to a duel. The oldest son of the deceased Mr Plummer escorted his mother to the graveside.

The other brother, whose wife was not in attendance, stood on the other side of the widow.

Eurydice lay at Fern's feet, the dragon watching the grave as though ready to pounce if an arm punched up through the soil. The two sons, their mother between them, stood on the opposite side of the grave to their sister and her little family. Sophie had dressed her daughter in a cotton gown with pink smocking, and a tiny bonnet shielded the baby's face from the last of the sunlight. Fern let out a sigh of relief that the bout of colic had passed and there was no screaming, only the babble of a contented child.

Mrs Plummer held a wreath made of lavender, forget-me-nots, and jasmine. The fragrant tribute was placed against the grave marker, and she rested a hand on the cold stone for a moment. Then she glanced over her shoulder at Fern. Straightening up, Mrs Plummer clasped her hands before her stomach and stared down at where her husband rested before she began.

"Richard," Mrs Plummer began in a strong and clear voice, "we know you worried about our Sophie, but Jim has grown into a good man. You'd be proud of how he looks after our girl." Here she stopped and smiled at the young man, who blushed and stared at the toes of his boots.

Sophie reached out and took his hand, and the love between the two was evident.

"They have a wee daughter, Sarah." Mrs Plummer gestured to Sophie, who held the baby over the grave.

"She's a gorgeous thing, Pa. You would have loved her, and she has your dimples when she laughs." As if on cue, little Sarah let out a giggle and waved her arms in the air.

Eurydice lifted her head and stared at something. A chill washed down Fern's spine. Had Mr Plummer's ghost waved to his granddaughter, an action seen only by dragon and baby?

"Jim has a good job at Putnam Farm. Just like you did. And he's providing for us. You don't have to worry no more, Pa. I love you, but you can rest." Sophie returned her child to her hip and glanced at her husband.

"Until we meet again," Mrs Plummer said in a softer voice.

Having said their piece, the family turned to stare at Fern.

"Will that have worked?" Mr John Plummer, the oldest son, asked.

"I am sure that it will. It was lovely. Tomorrow, I will look at the spectral orchid. When a spirit's task is complete, the petals turn black and fall to the ground." They would shrivel upon themselves and resemble glistening obsidian tears among the bark at the base of the orchid.

Having reassured the family that no one would be imminently joining Mr Plummer in his grave, Fern helped Eurydice into the cart, and they returned home. They would have dinner late, and she decided to enjoy the cool of twilight while strolling her garden. She was deadheading a rose, carefully snipping off spent blooms and avoiding vicious thorns, when Daniel came running along the path.

"Miss Oakby!" he shouted on finding her. "Alice says come quick. Lord Warrington is at the cottage."

The words dripped cold fear through Fern. "No," she

whispered. Had Millie's horrid brother come to drag her away to an institution?

Shaking her brain free of shock at the announcement, Fern kicked her body into action. She dropped her secateurs into her apron and tugged the item from around her waist as she ran for the stables. Inside, she clicked a lead rope onto the chocolate-brown mare and urged her from the comfortable stall. Using a wooden box to jump onto the horse's back, Fern kicked her straight into a canter, and they burst from the barn.

They took the western side of the village, cantering along the riverbank and across the village green, digging up divots of turf in their wake. Fern hopped off her horse at the forge (the equine immediately dropping her head to snatch at lush grass) and yelled out to Ben, "Can you take her, please?"

Without looking back, Fern raced across the bridge and burst through the back door of Scribbles. She combed her hands through her short hair as she strode through the stacks of books and then brushed the knees of her trousers. About to enter the conservatory, she heard a voice that took her a moment to recognise.

"Mrs Carlisle will not be abandoning her business. Don't be ridiculous, Lord Warrington," the woman said in a stern tone.

Mrs Garrick. Whatever was she doing here? Fern slowed her pace and stopped at the archway to peer within.

Lord Warrington stood on the other side of the small table, which held a tea tray and a stack of books. Millie sat on her favourite sofa, her head bowed. A protective Squib flapped his wings and puffed from her lap. Mrs Garrick sat on the other sofa, calmly drinking a cup of tea.

"You have had your fun playing shop, Millicent. It is time to return with me. I have found a lovely cottage for you by a beach up the coast. You know how you love the seaside," his voice dropped to a croon, as though he tried to lure a scared kitten from under a set of drawers.

Fern swallowed a snort. A lovely cottage by the seaside was most likely a private sanatorium where Millie would be confined to a small cell for the rest of her life. Unable to stay silent any longer, Fern crossed the room to sit beside Millie.

"Hello, Mrs Carlisle. Mrs Garrick." Her voice became cool as she regarded the arrogant noble, now the only person standing in the cosy space. "Lord Warrington."

"You! You!" Colour rose in his face, and he jabbed a finger in her direction. He would have lunged at her, but Squib squawked and flew up in the air, batting him away like a fierce magpie protecting its nest. "You planted one of those horrible seeds under my study window! How dare you! I should have you arrested for attempted murder." He paced back and forth with a jerky motion, like a wind-up toy running out of tension.

"Seed?" Fern frowned and stared up at the corner of the room. "Did Moyles only recover one? I was sure I planted two there." She tapped one finger against her chin and hummed in a contemplative manner.

"Two?" Lord Warrington roared and spun around. One hand went to his chest as he started coughing or possibly having a fit of apoplexy.

"You really must calm down, Lord Warrington. It is impossible to have a rational discussion with you when you're being so overly emotional," Mrs Garrick murmured over the rim of her teacup.

Fern had forgotten how much she liked Mrs Garrick.

Rather than calming down, Millie's brother seemed to lose the power of speech, his mouth opening and closing as he gasped for air, and he went as bright red as a freshly boiled lobster.

Millie roused from a stupor that was no doubt induced by the yelling from her brother and poured a cup of tea for Fern. She flashed an appreciative smile as she passed it over.

"Thank you, Mrs Carlisle. The bookshop has been such a valuable addition to Drake's Bend. No one here wants to see it closed, and we have all become rather protective of our resident writer." Fern caught the gaze of Lord Warrington as she stressed how the village would defend Millie, if necessary.

He glowered at her but seemed at a loss as to how to respond when not one but *two* troublesome women refused to be intimidated by him and refused to let him bundle Millie into a carriage and transport her to who knows where.

"This is ridiculous, Millicent. You cannot run a business, and you will make me the laughing stock of London." Lord Warrington huffed and crossed his arms.

"Mrs Carlisle asked me for advice, and having reviewed her accounts, she is managing perfectly fine. Most women are capable of managing any enterprise, if given the opportunity." Mrs Garrick finished her tea and placed her cup back on the table with deliberate care. "You will leave Mrs Carlisle alone,

Lord Warrington, or your lovely wife may find her name missing from a number of guest lists."

"Are you...threatening me?" Bertie's eyes widened.

CHAPTER 14

Mrs Garrick rolled her eyes and took a breath to gather her patience. "I do apologise, Lord Warrington. I forget that men are creatures with much smaller intellects than women. Yes, I am threatening you. Or rather—your wife. Who will be cut from all good society if you ever try to remove your sister from this charming little cottage again."

Fern was enjoying watching the other woman cut Lord Warrington down to size. But she knew it wasn't easy for Millie to argue with her only sibling. Reaching out, she took Millie's hand and squeezed it in support. Squib had returned to perch on his mistress's knee. With a narrowed gaze, he made short, sharp spitting sounds in his lordship's direction.

Lord Warrington's expression turned thunderous as he rounded on Mrs Garrick. "You wouldn't dare. You have no sway in society and are as ruined as that creature there." He pointed a finger at Fern's head, but his attention stayed on the woman calmly sipping tea.

Far from being insulted, Fern thought she kept the best of company.

"You are correct, Lord Warrington. Well done." Mrs Garrick's patronising tone turned praise into an insult. "I might have no sway, but my brother, Lord Blair, is the darling of parliament and tipped to be our next prime minister. He is also deeply concerned about the welfare of women and children. His wife will be a valuable addition to his political career as she shares his beliefs. Have you met Lady Blair? She is the only daughter of the Duke of Geraldine, who is himself a close friend of the Prince Regent."

Silence fell, but Fern could practically smell smoke as Bertie thought through all the ramifications. His desire to spirit away his sister faltered at the idea of telling his wife that she would no longer be admitted into the best parlours in London. She clutched her teacup. No London stage show could be as entertaining as she waited on the brink of anticipation to see what he would do.

Throw another tantrum, as it transpired. Millie's brother hurled his top hat to the ground and stomped up and down on it in frustration, all the while growling like an old dog in its death throes. Having vented some of his anger, he combed a hand through his thinning hair and glared at his sister. "This is a den of inequity. If this is where you wish to moulder, Millicent, then so be it. But you will be cut off. I will no longer be responsible for you, nor can you ever return to Warrington Manor. Think on that. I shall await your apology letter when you realise there are consequences to consorting with..." His hand pointed from Mrs Garrick to Fern.

Fern grinned and toasted him with her cup.

Lord Warrington spun on his heel and stalked from the conservatory, leaving behind the ruined hat. On his way out, he slammed the door so hard the bell tinkled for nearly a full five minutes. With his presence removed, the chill edge to the atmosphere dissipated.

Millie sobbed and twisted her hands in her lap. Squib climbed up her arm and rubbed his face against her cheek, all the while making low crooning noises. Bit by bit, the spell of hopelessness her brother cast over her was broken by the kindness of her friends. She took Squib in her hands and kissed his head. "Thank you. All of you. You must think me terribly weak for not saying a word."

"Not at all. I think you are a woman who has suffered much at the hands of a dominant sibling, and you have not yet found your voice to enable you to stand against him." Mrs Garrick helped herself to another slice of currant cake.

"Most people don't like confrontation, Millie." Fern set down her tea to give her friend a quick hug without disturbing Squib. "Mrs Garrick and I have a bit more experience in standing up to people such as your brother. You can always rely on your friends to do so on your behalf when required."

Mrs Garrick nibbled on a corner of cake and, with a remarkably impassive expression, said, "Your brother should learn to rein in his temper before he meets a terrible accident on a staircase."

Fern swallowed a laugh at what must have been a reference to how the horrid Mr Garrick met his ultimate demise. "I once used Lord Warrington as bait for a carnivorous vine." Some days Fern wondered if she did the right thing disposing of the *Helix mortifera* before it had taken a bite from his lordship.

"It's not your fault the thing didn't snap up the bait," Mrs Garrick said with a wink in Fern's direction. "I believe somewhere amongst his overly emotional outburst he made reference to seeds from that plant. Perhaps you should consider growing another?"

Fern snorted. Mrs Garrick was becoming exactly the sort of friend Fern liked. Direct and not above giving members of the patriarchy a shove out the door. Or a push down a steep stairwell.

"It is an odd coincidence that you were here when Lord Warrington chose to try to seize his sister, and I am thankful that you were able to stand between Millie and her brother. But what brought you back to Drake's Bend at precisely this moment?" Fern regarded the other woman, curious as to why, after so many years of estrangement, the Fates brought her back into her life twice in as many months.

She put down her cake and dabbed at her lips with a napkin. "Two matters. One is that I have visited Miss Hambling, who used to be in our circle when you came to London. Or rather, attempted to visit the poor thing. Her father watches her closer than a hawk that has spotted a three-legged mouse struggling through the undergrowth. The woman is being drained of all life, and we must take action."

"Do they have a spectral orchid in the house? There might be a restless spirit siphoning off her essence?" A keen, inquisitive glint entered Millie's gaze.

"If you mean her father, then yes," Mrs Garrick spoke in a dry tone. "Although he still walks among the living. I need assistance to craft her escape, and you are rather good at that, Miss Oakby."

"Always happy to oblige. Particularly to save a friend from family members who don't appreciate them." It would be harder to get Miss Hambling out from under her father's thumb. Not impossible, but they would need to concoct a plan between the three of them. If more subtle ways failed, they could always bundle her out a window and down a ladder. "What is the other thing that brought you here?"

A slow grin softened the other woman's usually stern features. "I am inspecting Sibylcrest Abbey. My brother has heard that it will shortly be for sale. Something to do with fire damage and blocked chimneys. Would you happen to know anything about how that happened?"

Fern sucked her lips together and, unusually for her, kept her silence on the matter. There were only a handful of people who knew what transpired that night, and she doubted that either Lord Drakeman or Quint had said anything. Most likely, the men guarding the abbey had told their employer about the man with the liquid silver eye and his bald accomplice.

Millie laughed and tapped Fern on the arm. "That is brilliant news, is it not? That means Sir Luxton won't be trying to brew any more of whatever it was that poisoned the locals and trees."

That reminded Fern that she needed to tell Millie everything that transpired when she visited Lord Drakeman and what the baron had been brewing. More immediately, the haste with which Sir Luxton abandoned his property gnawed at her. "He is leaving the site rather easily."

Mrs Garrick huffed. "Sir Luxton is known for dissolving like sugar in rain at the first hint of trouble. The man is all puffery and no substance."

Fern rose to stare out the window at the river beyond. The water rippled, and the last vestiges of daylight caught the edges to sprinkle it with diamonds. Her gaze rose to the kelmsgale, its boughs heavy with the solid buds that would soon open into magical blooms.

"He's moved on because he has done all he can here," she spoke to the tree standing guard over the village green.

"Oh! Do you know what he is making?" Millie asked.

Fern turned and regarded her friends. She chose her words carefully. "Yes. Something very rare and dangerous called *Sericum draconis*. Or dragon silk."

Millie's eyes rounded. "That sounds so pretty for something with such terrible ingredients."

"You will have to catch me up with this man's activities. What is so terrible about dragon silk?" Mrs Garrick glanced from Millie to Fern.

"It is made of dragon's blood and wood from an incredibly rare tree. Both must be destroyed to make a fabric that can turn back the hands of time." Fern crossed her arms, and her fingers dug into her sleeves. If she ever had the man before her, she would punch him in the nose. "Not to mention that smoke from the process was poisoning the people of Drake's Bend."

Mrs Garrick let out an astonished sigh. "Silk that makes the wearer younger? Good grief. Nobles will slaughter every last dragon in England and fell all the trees for such a thing."

"Not all nobles, surely?" Millie spoke up in defence of

their kind. "We would not, and there must be others of a similar mind to us. Once they know that two rare things would be destroyed forever, I am sure they will agree that the production of the silk is repugnant."

Mrs Garrick and Fern exchange glances. They had a more sceptical view of their fellow nobles.

"We don't have to worry about a dragon cull if society never learns about the *Sericum draconis*." Fern rolled around in her head what Lord Drakeman had told her. The barrels of pulp had most likely been taken to his mill in Oxfordshire to be turned into thread. That then had to be spun into cloth before it could be turned into nightcaps, chemises, or whatever else they needed for the magic to take effect.

"Ah. So we may yet nip his plans in the bud?" Mrs Garrick leaned forward. Her dark eyes shone with sharp intellect.

"Yes, he has completed the first two stages. The blood and pulp have been turned into thread through an alchemic process. Now the thread must be spun into cloth. Are you able to find out anything about Sir Luxton, please? It is possible we are only weeks behind his endeavours, but we need to know where the fabric is being manufactured. Lord Drakeman has his man trying to find the factory, but two heads are better than one."

"Lord Drakeman?" Mrs Garrick's eyebrows shot up, and she leaned back in her chair. "My, you do have a range of acquaintances. I shall do a little digging of my own about Sir Luxton Davies and keep my ears open for any rumours of such fantastical garments."

"Thank you." As a plan took shape, Fern was able to settle and stop pacing. She returned to her seat beside Millie.

Now that the writer's distress had eased, Squib had flown to the windowsill to watch as the gloaming surrendered to night.

Fern had only to settle the spirit that reached out to the orchid at Nemython House. Then she could turn her full attention to stopping the wealthy and entitled noble who thought little of destroying flora and fauna in the pursuit of shallow things.

THE NEXT MORNING, the very first thing Fern did was rush to the parlour and inspect her spectral orchid.

"Oh, you are so very close to opening. Tonight, I think," she murmured as she traced a fingertip along the swollen bud that had the faintest crack. Then a thought occurred to her, and she stared at the ceiling. "Morda." The name huffed from her chest. A few days ago, when she visited the Moray sisters for the spirit mist, they had brewed two bottles for her. She hadn't thought anything of it at the time. A spare bottle never goes amiss if she had trouble finding where a soul lingered. But a niggle in the back of her brain whispered that the seer knew Fern would need an additional bottle for when the other orchid flowered.

"Well, at least I don't have to wait for them to brew more mist. As soon as you unfurl your bloom today or tomorrow, we shall see who you lead me to," she said to the plant.

After a quick breakfast, Fern helped Eurydice into the cart, and they headed straight for the cemetery. The warmth of the rising sun caused an eerie mist to rise from the moist earth, and it almost appeared as though all the residents were climbing out of their graves to greet the day.

Leaving the dragon to snuffle around a gravestone, Fern walked straight up the path towards the waist-high glass house. Bending down, she opened the door.

"No!" Fern couldn't believe what she saw. Or didn't see.

Blackened, tear-shaped petals should have been scattered on the bark at the base of the plant. But the spectral orchid's spidery bloom remained as unblemished as always. No matter how hard she looked, Fern couldn't see a hint of discolouration.

"But we resolved Mr Plummer's concerns about his daughter." She tapped the glass above the flower, not wanting to accidentally knock the petals away, as that wouldn't help at all and could make the spirit even more aggravated.

She pressed the heel of her palm to her forehead and muttered, "It's something else. But what?"

A different argument. She recalled her first visit to Mrs Plummer and her words about a possible disagreement between her husband and some of his friends. Fern glanced at the sun. The oldest Plummer son would have already left for work. Most labourers were out of bed with the first blush of dawn and tilling the fields or tending stock as others were only just contemplating their first pot of tea while still wearing a robe.

"Come on, Riddy. We need to go back to see Mrs Plummer." After helping the dragon walk the plank into the cart,

Fern climbed onto the seat and guided the horse north. There was another crossing over the river not far away, and once over, they would be closer to the Plummer cottage than going south back into the village to cross by the bookshop.

This time, the dragon chose to stay in the cart and turned her face to the sun to watch birds flitting in the trees. Fern rapped on the door, but there was no reply. As she waited, she made a list of jobs needed for the garden. Perennials that needed a tidy up, annuals with spent blooms that could be dug back into the earth, and a rose with thrips that needed a spray.

When there was still no response, she knocked a bit louder, like she did to rouse Quint. Just as she wondered if Mrs Plummer might have spent the night with her daughter, the bolt rattled and sunlight lit the hall inside.

"I am sorry, Miss Oakby. It was ever such a struggle to get out of bed this morning." Tired lines pulled at Mrs Plummer's eyes, and her hair was only loosely contained in a bun. Strands flopped over her ears as though a determined wind had tugged them free.

She appeared exhausted. Like a mother who stayed up all night tending to a sick child.

Or like a widow having her essence drained away by a restless spirit.

CHAPTER 15

"Why don't we go inside, and I'll put the kettle on for you?" Fern let herself in and closed the door. Gently, she guided the older woman down the hall to the kitchen at the rear of the cosy home.

Mrs Plummer sat, and Fern filled the kettle from a barrel by the back door and then set it to boil on the range. She busied herself finding the tea things while she considered how to break the bad news to Mrs Plummer. *I am sorry, but it seems your husband's spirit is siphoning off your soul because we haven't found his unresolved business yet* seemed to the point, but possibly a bit blunt for so early in the morning.

"Yesterday has been a weight off Sophie's shoulders. I never realised how the poor thing had tied herself in knots about the angry words with her Da," Mrs Plummer said as Fern poured boiling water over the tea leaves and popped the lid on to let it steep.

"I'm glad we have brought her some peace," Fern murmured as she dragged two mugs closer together. She spun them around as words swirled through her head. "I went to the graveyard this morning and then came straight here."

"Did you bring the tears?" Mrs Plummer asked.

Some people kept the solidified petals that fell from the flower as a reminder that a spirit had returned to their family. Over time, they hardened until they almost seemed to be carved from obsidian and could be worn on a chain as a remembrance of their loved one.

Fern turned the teapot three times clockwise and then poured the strong brew. She pushed one towards the widow. "That is why I came to see you. There won't be any tears just yet."

Mrs Plummer wrapped her hands around the mug and inhaled the fragrance. "Have they not quite fallen off yet?"

"No." *Not at all*, she thought. "There is no sign of any blackening, and I am afraid that your husband's business wasn't smoothing over the argument with your daughter. We must keep looking."

The mug jolted back to the table with a thud. "He's...he hasn't returned to his grave?" She clutched at the collar of her gown. "That's why I feel so tired, isn't it? He's pulling me to him."

"I am afraid so." There was never a good way to deliver bad news.

"How long?" the other woman rasped.

Fern did a quick calculation in her head. "Six or seven days. But we will find the reason before then. I give you my word, Mrs Plummer."

"I'll never see little Sarah grow up." Tears shimmered in

Mrs Plummer's eyes, and she dug into her apron pocket for a handkerchief to dab them away.

"We are not defeated yet. The first day I spoke to you, you thought your husband might have exchanged harsh words with a friend. Did your son know anything further?" Fern tried to distract the woman away from thoughts of her impending demise.

Slowly, Mrs Plummer raised her mug to her lips and took several short sips of tea. "Yes. He quarrelled with two of his friends. John thought there were some insults thrown against him and his brother from what his Da said. Dick muttered about it while they were tending the vegetable patch."

"See? We were on the right path; we just had the wrong disagreement. What are their names, and we shall think of a way to smooth over whatever it was?" Fern tried to keep a light tone; the poor woman didn't need to see her start to doubt herself.

Mrs Plummer sipped her tea and seemed lost in the steam that escaped over the rim. Just when Fern thought she had nodded off while sitting upright, she lifted her head. "I think it was Edward and...Thaddeus? John wasn't sure, either."

"I will ask around. Try not to worry and get some rest." Fern left the woman slumped at the table.

Eurydice trilled as she returned to the cart. Fern scratched the dragon's head as she told her about the visit. "She looks so drained, Riddy, as her husband's spirit feasts on her soul." Everything was happening faster than she expected. Like the spectral orchid at Nemython House, which seemed about to bloom already, when a few days ago there was only the barest hint of a bud.

There was a terrible price to be paid for the comfort of knowing a loved one could use the delicate orchid as a conduit. Some families refused to bury their deceased members in a cemetery with a spectral orchid, not willing to risk the person rising from their grave. Fern thought it would be horrible to spend eternity with some incomplete task gnawing at you, or harsh words that were never forgiven. Or knowing you were murdered when others did not.

But the risks...

Fail to settle the spirit within ten days, and death awaited you. Then it would collect other family members until it was sufficiently sated. A spirit could be forcibly returned to the other realm, but that was no easy task, either. Larger cemeteries with hundreds or even thousands of interred people often didn't have a spectral orchid. By the time anyone figured out who a returned soul was, it was too late for the family. Far better to never give the deceased the chance at all.

"No time to waste." Fern climbed back into the cart and headed directly for the best source of information about what the village menfolk got up to when women weren't looking— the Drake's Rest. Mr Douglas Tindale, owner of the tavern, didn't miss a thing. Or rather, his wife didn't.

She left the cart and patient horse at the forge. Eurydice was instructed to stay in the back, in case she startled any of the horses in the barn who weren't used to dragons. Her eyes whirred as she watched Benjamin hammering a shoe, the metal bright red from where he had heated it. Satisfied with the shape, he plunged it into a bucket of cold water. The sudden rush of steam made the dragon sit back on her hind, and she nearly toppled over. Only a frantic wing flap kept her balance.

Fern laughed and rested a hand on the creature. "Lucky you don't have hooves, Riddy, or Ben would place the hot shoe on your foot to ensure a good fit."

The dragon narrowed her gaze and snorted. Apparently, she didn't want to wear shoes.

"I'll not be long!" she called out, then made for the tavern next door.

The pub's foundation was rooted in the sturdy stone of an old hunting lodge, originally built as a retreat for the king's drake men when they accompanied the dragons to their favourite fishing spot. The men could keep an eye on their charges from within the solid walls, while the dragons fished in the river. Then they bathed in the heated waters on the grounds of Wyndham Hall long before there was a grand house on the land.

The thick lower walls of the tavern were cool even in the height of summer. In winter, they kept the warmth from the fires within. Narrow, deep-set windows peered out like watchful eyes. In Tudor times, the original single-level building was expanded and a second storey built. Now parts of it had dark, weathered beams and sparkling whitewashed plaster. The top storey jutted slightly over the first. Its overhanging eaves cast a shadow over the entrance below and also provided shelter when the weather turned.

Fern pushed on the grand oak door, its surface worn smooth by centuries of travellers' hands. Standing just inside as her eyes adjusted to the lower light, she drew in a deep breath. Whatever the time of day or season outside, the Drake's Rest was always scented with spiced cider, roasting meat, and wood smoke. It was a place of rest, stories, and secrets. Today, she would try to ferret a secret from the darkened woodwork.

Despite the early hour, the pub was busy, open and serving breakfast to those who had stayed overnight in the rooms upstairs, or delivering a hot meal for those who didn't have one at home. A handful of travellers sat at a table, staring at their meals and exchanging subdued conversation. Fern walked to the bar where the owner polished glasses and kept an eye on the patrons.

"Morning, Fern. We don't usually see you this early." He had a cheerful disposition and a lean, wiry build.

"Good morning, Doug. I need your help." She rested her hands on the polished wood and peered at the array of glasses and tankards stacked neatly on the shelves.

Drake's Bend had its own peculiarities. There were people whom Fern always addressed as Mrs or Mr, just as she was always Miss Oakby. Then with other residents, like Doug, she was on a first-name basis. It had nothing to do with age or rank and was more based on how entwined a person was in Fern's life. The closer someone stood to her and her family, the more formalities were stripped away.

"Do you need me to spit-roast a cow for that dragon of yours?" Doug grinned, and deep wrinkles formed around his eyes. His hands never stopped polishing the glass as he talked. Round and round the white cloth went, and Fern had to blink and look away from the mesmerising effect.

"Riddy is still content with Mrs Bentley's cooking. But I

am sure it won't be too long before she needs something bigger to chew on." And fresher. Fern presumed dragons ate their food raw. Or did they use their ability to breathe flames to cook it first? "It's Mr Plummer who has brought me here."

Doug let out a sigh and placed the glass back on the shelf. "I've been thinking about Dick since I heard he's the one who touched the orchid. Quiet man, kept to himself mostly but always did his share if help was needed."

Fern laced her fingers together on the bar to stop herself from fidgeting. The *quiet man* obviously had a secret big enough to rouse the dead. She just had to find where he hid it.

The publican flung the towel over one shoulder and put the glass away as he turned his mind to the deceased patron. "If it were possible, Dick was even quieter those last few days. Or it might have been because of the squabble."

"Mrs Plummer thought he had words with Edward and Thaddeus?" The widow had also said her husband was more subdued in the days leading up to his death. The doctor speculated it was the early symptoms of his troubled heart about to give out.

"Ted and Tad. That's them. The three of them usually sat in that corner." He waved the towel like a morris dancer to indicate the far corner by the fire. "They would talk, and hardly a raised voice was heard between them. Until the row."

"Do you know what it was over?" She mentally crossed her fingers that whatever disrupted the usual quiet between the three friends was the root cause of the disturbance.

"I've mulled it over with the wife, and we think it was

about their lads. Tad claimed his boy was more dependable and not a delicate thing that needed coddling like Ted's son." He stared up at the ceiling as he recalled the conversation from over a year ago.

"That seems rude for friends to throw comments about their children." It didn't make sense to Fern. There had to be some underlying cause. Perhaps the argument was between the young men and their fathers had taken sides?

He wiped his hands on the cloth before tossing it over his shoulder once more. "It was right odd for them to argue, and this was before the whisperwoods were setting everyone at each other."

Mention of the ancient stand of trees made a shiver run down Fern's spine.

"It might have been the very early stages of the poisonous smoke." She ran through the calendar in her head. Mr Plummer must have died about a month or so after Sir Luxton bought the abbey. Had they been brewing the rare ingredients then? There was a chance, no matter how slim, that smoke might have washed over the three men when they were out together near the hill.

Doug kept talking as more of the argument tumbled into the publican's memory. "I recall Dick called Tad's lad all showy nonsense and a disappointment. Said his boy was sturdy, and he never sulked when it rained. Ted got right upset and said they were both wasting their time when his boy was resilient and more handsome."

Fern let Doug talk, hoping that the real cause of the dispute might be buried in the insults.

"Tad said he much preferred his boy to be dull and

steady, rather than flashy and soft like the other two." Doug rapped his knuckles on the wood as he remembered the last bit.

"Oh, dear. It sounds like there was a nasty rupture in the friendship. Thank you, Doug. I shall go talk to Ted and Tad." Fern waved to the tavern owner and walked back into the morning sunshine to reclaim Riddy.

She found the dragon still in the rear of the cart, her head stretched along one side as she watched the blacksmith at work. Her tail twitched as Fern approached. She slowed her steps, trying to sneak up on the creature, when Eurydice swung her head around with a gleam in her silvery eyes, as though she said *I knew you were there.*

"Fancy a stroll along the high street?" she asked her dragon companion.

The dragon chirped and sat up, waiting for the back of the cart to be lowered and her plank set out.

They set off towards the main street lined with its pretty two-storeyed cottages. Hanging baskets and pots adorned the front of the shops and added splashes of red, orange, and pink. People strolled the street, some carrying baskets for their shopping. Clusters of two or three formed when friends spotted one another. There were nods of greeting to Fern and Eurydice, who waddled along with her tail held off the ground to make sure no one trod on it.

Fern headed for two particular shops that were close together. Ted Cornhill was the baker, and she followed her nose to his door. Tad Beswick was the cobbler, and he repaired shoes and boots two cottages along from Ted. The cottages were on the forest side, their front windows pointing towards the river. Most of the shop owners lived in the rear and upstairs of their cottages. Which was particularly useful for Ted and his family. Their day started long before dawn as they set yeasty starters to rise and form the day's bread.

There were three customers in the bakery when she stuck her head through the door, so Fern decided to grab Tad first. The cobbler sat alone at his bench, a worn boot on a specially shaped piece of wood before him.

"Hello, Miss Oakby. Time for a new pair of boots or apron?" he asked as she entered his domain.

Apart from shoes, he worked on a variety of leather goods.

"Not today, Mr Beswick. I need you to come with me, and we're going to the bakery." She pointed in the direction of the other shop. "And before you tell me that you are busy, it's about Mr Plummer. We need to get to the bottom of why he has returned before his widow joins him in a few days' time." She stressed the urgency of her mission.

His lips tightened for a moment, then he nodded and put down the little hammer he used for the tiny nails holding a sole to a boot. "He is sorely missed. His family has suffered enough without losing his wife. I'll do what I can to send Dick back to his eternal rest."

CHAPTER 16

THE COBBLER FOLLOWED Fern to the door of his cottage, but he stopped in the doorway and gripped the frame with one hand. Wide-eyed, he stared at Eurydice.

"Come along. Riddy doesn't bite," Fern said. Not an entirely correct statement, as the dragon possessed lethal teeth within her jaws. She just didn't bite humans. Yet.

Mr Beswick's gaze slid sideways to Fern, then he edged around the curious dragon as though she were some dangerous dog. Two cottages down, they reached the baker's shop. Fern asked her companion to stay outside.

Eurydice cast a longing look at the delicious-smelling interior. The dragon's nose twitching.

"I will buy you something sweet. Promise."

The dragon huffed, then plonked herself on the ground beside a tall pot with a standard lavender.

Inside, Mr Cornhill, the baker, greeted them as he wrapped a warm loaf in a square of cotton for a customer. "Tad, Miss Oakby. You both look serious this fine morning."

"It's about Dick, Ted," Mr Beswick said, moving out of the way of the customer who gripped her purchase, nodded, and hurried out the door.

"I am told that just before his death, there was some dispute between the three of you and insults were hurled." Fern glanced from one man to the other. They should have known better at their age, but friendships could fracture at any point in time.

Mr Cornhill huffed and scratched up the old disagreement. "My Lumper can't be beaten. It's hardy and a good doer."

Mr Beswick rolled his eyes and visibly bristled. "You and your Lumper. Come winter, you'll be knocking on my door asking about my Pink Eye. Or you'll be offering Mrs Plummer your currant bread for a few of Dick's Shaws."

Fern let out a groan and stared at the ceiling. Lumpers. Pink Eyes. Shaws. The root source of the dispute became obvious to her. They were all varieties of potatoes.

"You three argued over potatoes?" Naturally, she could understand being passionate about a tuber. But she struggled to imagine a resentment about a tuber festering so deep it roused a dead man.

"He needs to stop growing those Lumpers. Things fall over at the first sign of blight, and they taste horrible." Mr Beswick levelled an accusing finger at his friend's head.

Fern agreed with him. "He has a point, Mr Cornhill. Pink Eyes are much better for lasting through winter. Although I think Mr Plummer had the right idea growing Early Shaws. They are delicious roasted. But have either of you tried the Rough Purple Chilli?

The purple skin is quite unique, but it's a good all-rounder."

Both men turned to stare at her.

"Purple Chilli?" Mr Beswick repeated, as though the words were entirely new to him.

"It came to us from South America about thirty years ago. It's very popular in some areas." An idea struck her, and enthusiasm lit through her. "It would make an excellent cross with a Pink Eye, or perhaps the Early Shaw." She shot an apologetic look at the baker. "I'm not sure the Lumper would be a good match, though."

The baker crossed his arms and slid a basket of sweet rolls away from Fern and closer to his side of the counter. Perhaps she shouldn't have insulted his favourite potato until after she had bought a treat for her and Eurydice. She pulled her gaze away from the rolls, with their shiny glaze, and back to a more mundane edible.

"How deep did this argument go?" She struggled to imagine that it was a potato debate that roused Mr Plummer from the grave rather than worry over his daughter and harsh words thrown between them.

"It was a friendly rivalry. We used to see whose crop was ready first, whose had the best yield by weight, which ones lasted through winter best," Mr Beswick answered while Mr Cornhill protected his baked goods.

"Did any of you ever do...anything...to ensure your potatoes performed the best?" She watched each man's reaction, waiting to see who twitched or squirmed.

"I don't know what—" Mr Cornhill blustered, but his friend interrupted him.

"Hot water. A prong through a growing tuber. Letting a pig loose in the potato patch. That year, things went a bit too far." Mr Beswick appeared embarrassed and couldn't meet Fern's gaze as he listed the sort of garden sabotage the men had enacted against each other like a bunch of young lads.

"The pig was right funny, though." Now the baker relaxed a little, his shoulders heaving in quiet laughter.

The cobbler laughed, then cut himself off. "Dick didn't think so. We let the pig go into his garden. It dug up his crop in mid-spring and ruined half of it. I don't know if he ever truly forgave us before he died."

Both men fell silent, remembering the lost member of their little group. Fern was sceptical that the ghost needed an apology for a rampaging hog, but you never knew what moments in life stuck in someone's soul.

"Right, you two. You are to go to the cemetery at twilight and apologise for the pig prank and what you did to Mr Plummer's Early Shaws." She pointed at each one in turn like they were naughty schoolboys instead of fifty-year-old fathers and grandparents.

"Yes, Miss Oakby," both men intoned as they stared down at the floor.

The shop had filled around them, people drawn by the yeasty aromas. Fern stepped out of the way of a man waving a cotton bag and gesturing to the basket of rolls. It was time for her to leave before she was squashed against a wall by the growing crowd. "Good. I will check the spectral orchid first thing tomorrow morning, so make sure you do, or you will answer to my dragon." That elicited a gasp and a startled look from both of them. Satisfied that the men would do what she asked of them, she fished a coin from her pocket and placed it on the counter. "Two sweet rolls, please, Mr Cornhill."

Outside, Eurydice took the offered bun from Fern's outstretched hand, and the entire thing disappeared in the space of a heartbeat.

"Did you eat that, or inhale it?" Fern peered at her friend, expecting to see a bulge slide down the dragon's long neck.

A polite burp came from the dragon, and she stared at the remaining roll in Fern's hand. Then a long, blue-tinged tongue flicked out and swept around the creature's mouth.

Fern moved her roll to the other hand. "Oh, I don't think so. Next time you might want to chew yours."

Dragon and woman wandered slowly back to the forge, Fern savouring every bite of her treat while trying to ignore the pleading dragon's eyes. To distract herself from the image of a spectral Mr Plummer slowly drawing his wife's soul to him, Fern collected the horse and cart and struck out for Wyndham Hall. Today, she decided, Eurydice would fly.

She left the dragon snuffling in the undergrowth while she tackled the vines clinging to the iron balustrade. Fern hadn't even noticed her progress until her boot hit the level surface of the upper level. Her brain took a few seconds to realise she was no longer on a slant.

"Oh," she breathed out as she peered over the railing. Far below, sunlight splintered through the dirty panes and painted wobbly stripes across the conservatory floor. With a bird's eye view (or should that be dragon's eye view?), the dead palms and dried earth created a muddy scene with no greens from leaves or bursts of pink from flowers to relieve it.

"Next spring," she promised the neglected garden.

Eurydice emerged from under a tent made of fronds and trilled.

"Up here!" Fern called out and waved.

The dragon arched her neck and chirped, then set off in the direction of the ramp.

Fern walked halfway back down and encouraged the youngster to join her. "Come along, you brave girl, and see how marvellous it is to see things from higher up."

With its soaring stone ribs, the silence in the conservatory was like that of a church. Hushed. Waiting.

A tap, scratch, tap came as Eurydice waddled up the curving path. Today her iridescent scales were the colour of storm-washed moss.

"A little further," Fern crooned as they neared the top. She walked backwards, one hand on the balustrade as they made their way to the verandah that ran the length of the shared library wall. Thirty feet below, the conservatory's central aisle ran like a brown nave between dry beds that should have contained orchids and towering fronds. Fern licked a finger and held it out. While there was no wind inside, there was a slight updraught. Enough that, hopefully, the dragon would be able to glide to the ground and learn that she could trust her wings.

Up here, the library was separated by a sheltered verandah with curving arches at regular intervals. Rattan furniture and faded cushions were grouped around glass-topped tables. The perfect place to sit with a pot of tea, a good book, and the warmth of the conservatory.

Eurydice's nostrils flared as she sniffed the wooden planks and followed an unseen trail along the walkway. She stopped at the balcony that jutted out from the verandah. The perfect spot for Juliet to stand and lament her Romeo hidden below. Fern examined the curved balustrade and found hinges on either side of a section, indicating it swung open. It took a moment of fumbling to find that the metal wings of a dragon in the middle acted as a latch. Tugging it up, she pulled the two sides inwards.

Do not fall unless you can fly. Morda's warning drifted through Fern's mind. Perhaps this was what the old seer had meant. She curled one hand around the railing. Since she didn't possess wings, she had no intention of tumbling off the side.

Eurydice shuffled forwards, joining Fern on the circular platform. A warm draught wafted upwards, carrying the scent of earth and decay.

The dragon trilled with a questioning, uncertain tone. Her spine twitched, and her claws scraped as she wrapped them around the brass edge and peered below. Her wings unfurled instinctively and cast two delicate triangles of shadow onto the balcony floor. The youngster inhaled, her chest like bellows expanding and contracting. Then she chirruped and scrabbled backwards, her wings snapping tight to her sides.

She burrowed her head in Fern's side, and a tremble shook her body.

Fern sat on the ground and cradled Eurydice's head in her arms. "Oh, Riddy, don't be scared. It is like swimming. You just need a little hop and stretch out your wings." In Fern's mind, flying and swimming seemed to involve a similar process. Although granted, water was more supportive. "You need to be courageous, even though you are afraid. Bravery is grabbing hold of the fear and using it to compel you forward."

A throat cleared within the shadows. "Is there a problem?" Lord Drakeman leaned on an arch, his dragon eye catching the sun and flashing like quicksilver.

"I think she has stage fright." Fern hugged the dragon's neck.

"I have been reading the old journals. My ancestors reported delayed flight in young separated from their mother too young." He didn't move, but his gaze flicked from the dragon to Fern.

"So they are like birds? A mother would know when her offspring were ready to test their wings." A pang shot through Fern's heart. Both of them needed the guidance of a mother. But without one, they would muddle through together. "I believe in you, Riddy."

"My predecessors used another dragonet to demonstrate for a reluctant youngster," Lord Drakeman said.

Fern heaved a sigh. Bother. She didn't have another dragonet. Then something small and huffy batted at her mind. "Oh! Squib. Of course. The little fellow is a confident flyer. I shall ask Millie if he might accompany me to show Riddy how it's done."

Eurydice tilted her head and trilled at the mention of her friend's name.

"Or you could show her." Lord Drakeman pushed off the archway and walked towards the balcony, spreading his arms as though testing a horizon only he could see.

"If you are going to jump, shall I fetch Quint to catch you?" While Fern had never seen the earl without a shirt—

and that thought heated her skin—she was fairly certain he wasn't hiding wings to match his dragon eye and scales.

He held out one hand, and mischief glinted in his human eye. "I'll show you."

She stared at his outstretched palm. "This had better not be a ploy to push me off the balcony."

With his other hand, he drew a cross over his chest.

Not entirely convinced, she rested her hand on his. He curled his fingers and steadied her as she stood. Then he drew her closer, his hand sliding along her arm and around her waist. She stood a little too close to the edge for her liking. The solid chest of the alchemist was at her back. He took each of her hands in his and stretched out their arms.

Fern's heart tripped. Her gaze darted to the floor. The drop churning in her stomach. Yet beneath it, a bright thread of exhilaration hummed.

Eurydice watched, eyes whirring and her head tilting from side to side.

"There's a draft rising from the thermal vents," Lord Drakeman said quietly, his lips grazing her ear. "Feel the lift? Wings are like a cape that catches the wind."

Fern exhaled and let her eyes flutter closed. For one dizzy instant, she imagined herself winged, covered with orchid petals instead of dragon scales. The air embraced her, ready to toss her into the air to soar across the conservatory. Fern leaned forward, ready to fly...

Eurydice emitted a startled shriek. An arm wrapped around her middle, and she was plucked from the air and shoved up against a stone wall.

Opening her eyes, her hands were splayed on Lord Drakeman's chest, and he held her tight.

Mismatched eyes conveyed alarm. "Don't jump, Miss Oakby. Quint would not appreciate having to clean up the mess."

"I...I wasn't going to..." But she had. For the briefest moment, her soul had wanted to soar. He had caught her before she fell. Her entire body thrummed, and she found herself tilting her head and staring at his slightly parted lips.

Eurydice chirped and butted her head against Fern's thigh. The hatchling wormed her way between them, and Lord Drakeman released his grip to step back to the verandah.

"I'm sorry, Riddy, I didn't mean to alarm you." Fern bent down to reassure the dragon. "But you have wings, and the warmed air will lift you up. I promise."

The dragon narrowed her eyes and had the distinct sceptical look of Squib.

"Perhaps she does not yet have sufficient motivation. Or she requires a push." Lord Drakeman stood at the railing.

"No one is pushing Riddy off the balcony. It has to be her decision." Fern drew the gates of the balcony closed and dropped the winged latch into place, just in case Lord Drakeman decided to give the creature a nudge. "We'll try again another day."

"Yes. We shall," Lord Drakeman murmured before retreating back into the shadows.

As she gazed at the spot where he had been, Fern wondered which leap into the unknown would come first— Eurydice's, or her own?

CHAPTER 17

FERN'S PREDICTION of that morning had proven correct. By the time she returned to Nemython House, the spectral orchid was unfurling its bloom like a woman shaking out a sheet. After dinner, the family gathered in the parlour as dusk fell. Without the soft glow of the lanterns, the room was soon bathed in grey and shadows. Eurydice had been banished to the stables, even though she had wanted to help. Fern was curious to see if the dragon picked the direction of the spirit or if the mist would cling to the creature. But there wasn't room inside for her growing form and sweeping tail. Nor did they want to risk the porcelain urn on a plinth being accidentally knocked over.

"Temper your expectations." George patted Fern's shoulder as she stood before the orchid.

"I know, but..." The hand on her shoulder squeezed a little firmer. Fern held in a sigh. It had to be her father. Apart from her mother, in recent years, no one else had died who was connected to their household. While it could be a ghost from decades ago, it was unlikely.

"An open mind walks through closed doors." Having said his part, George moved to pick up a lantern sitting by the door. He would follow with the light once Fern had found where the orchid's spectre led them.

Ambrose kept quiet, which was odd for him. Nor did he hover nearby. Instead, he took up a position by the fireplace and seemed lost in his own thoughts.

Caressed by the rising moon, the orchid's elongated petals had the soft shimmer of a polished pearl. Standing beside the plant, Fern misted the air in front of the spider-like bloom. The room held its collective breath as the silver motes spun in the air and then coalesced to one side before breaking apart and disappearing.

Taking a step in the indicated direction, Fern misted the air again. This time, the shining pillar appeared closer to the door before dissolving on a moonbeam.

"It seems we are heading out into the hall," Ambrose murmured, and he followed at a distance like a mourner behind a funerary carriage.

With its dark-panelled walls, the night sat heavier in the hall. Shafts of light stretched down the stairs, creating a pattern of silvery squares as they filtered through the mullioned window above.

Fern clutched the metal sprayer, creeping forward as though she followed a tiger through dense jungle. One cautious step at a time, she advanced. Straining her gaze in the dim to spot her prey. There. To the left.

Having grown up in the house, she knew every floorboard

and door. Even with her eyes tightly closed, she could navigate the old building. But tonight she followed the shimmering glimpses of the spirit. Inch by inch, they were drawn towards the study tucked by the stairs.

An open mind walks through closed doors. Mentally, she repeated the caution from George even as hope flared inside her. The spectre could still lead them up the steps to the bedrooms above. Once more, she misted the air. The silver specks turned like tiny globes, spinning with purpose as they clustered together to create a shimmering pillar...right before the slightly ajar study door.

"It's him, George. Isn't it?" Fern whispered. Her heart ached to finally have a sign from the orchid that her father's soul reached out to her.

The older man didn't answer, but a large hand pushed through the gloom and tapped the wood to open the door wider.

"Do it again, Fern, and see if he leads you in." Ambrose stood close behind her now, as keen as she was to see where the trail would end.

She closed her eyes for a moment and offered a silent prayer to whatever entity oversaw the eternal rest of souls. Then, standing a little taller, she sprayed the air just inside the study. This time, the specks moved faster, quickly spinning towards each other and holding firm for a few moments longer. The silver column took on the rectangular form of a tall person for long enough for Ambrose to let out a sad gasp. Then the dots disbursed and fell to the old rug like drizzly rain.

Fern shook the sprayer. She had used nearly all the mist; only a few squirts remained.

Show me it's you, Father, please. If it had been her mother, her soul wouldn't have led her to the study but would have remained in the parlour, which had always been her favourite room. Not to mention, she had passed there, lying on the chaise in the sun and surrounded by family.

The metal container only held a splash of the magical brew. Holding it at arm's length, Fern released the last of the mist into the air by the bookshelf. The specks clung together before the botanical books. A few detached from the main column and drifted towards a particular section, like a hand reaching out, before dropping. The tiny glints of light were gone before they hit the ground.

Fern concentrated on the spot and rested her hand on the closest book.

Yellow flared as George lit the lantern first, then the candles in the sconce attached to the wall by the door.

"What is it, Fern?" Ambrose asked. He stood on the threshold, the small room crowded with Fern and George within.

Her fingertips curled around the small, battered book and tugged it free. She swallowed the lump that formed in her throat, and tears clouded her vision. "It's Father's journal."

"Good. We can settle the argument of what happened that day once and for all," George muttered. Then he stalked back out of the room.

His absence left a vacuum, which Ambrose filled. He hurried over and hugged Fern. "We will finally have the truth."

She placed one hand on the leather cover. "Yes. At last."

"Time for tea, I think." Ambrose kissed her cheek and left her in the silence.

Fern clutched the journal to her chest as an unsettling thought took root in her mind. The orchid revealed that her father returned with unfinished business. But how to resolve it before his restless spirit drained Fern until she was as empty and spent as the container of mist?

In five years, she had not made any progress in proving that another hand took her father's life that day. How would she find the person responsible in just ten days?

"Bother." Her fingers curled into the book. "I'm not sure how well thought-through this plan is, Father. You had better send me a clue or two to follow, or I shall be asking you what happened in person before very long."

That night, Fern slept with her father's journal tucked under her pillow, hoping that the absent pages might wander through her dreams. She awoke no more rested than when she had pulled the quilt over her head. Sliding her feet to the ground, she stared at the hand-knotted rug that stopped the winter chill creeping up her legs.

"It shouldn't happen this fast." She washed her hands over her face. "I am simply worried about Mrs Plummer."

After dressing in a simple gown that suited her mood, she headed for the kitchen and a hot drink to revive her senses.

"You look terrible," George said. Wrinkles pulled at the corners of his eyes as he stared at her over the rim of his enormous coffee mug.

"My sleep was troubled with thoughts of Mr Plummer. His friends promised to visit his grave yesterday at twilight and apologise for their great potato feud. And for letting a pig loose in his vegetable patch." Fern smiled her thanks to Mrs Bentley as the housekeeper pushed a warmed plate with sausage and eggs in her direction.

George poured coffee and placed it at her elbow but kept his silence. He didn't need to say a word. They had argued, at times heatedly, over the circumstances surrounding Rowan Oakby's death. While her father's lifelong friend wanted to believe another had been involved, there simply wasn't any evidence. An unpalatable truth was still a truth.

She swallowed a sigh, along with a mouthful of strong black coffee.

This is different, she reassured herself. *Father is reaching out and will show me the way.*

Or he had better. While she loved and missed her parents, she had far too much living to do to join them before the kelmsgale festival. She wanted to see Eurydice fly. And she had promised Millie a trip to the Scottish Highlands. Then they had to go to London and scandalise society over something while they rescued Miss Hambling from her horrid situation. And...possibly...if the circumstances were right, she intended to kiss Lord Drakeman again.

Ambrose was late to rise and entered the kitchen as Fern was preparing to leave. Her uncle had dark shadows under his tired eyes. When he glanced at her, a deep worry line creased his pale forehead. It seemed Fern was not the only one whose sleep was interrupted by wandering spirits.

Fern threw her arms around him and hugged him tight. "You are not to worry, Uncle Ambrose. Father will lead us to a clue, and his soul will be back with Mother within a few days. You wait and see."

He stroked her hair but remained silent. When she let go of him and searched his features, he had a tight set to his lips. She suspected that a terse discussion had taken place between the two men during the midnight hours. George might already be writing her eulogy. Deep in Fern's bones, she believed that she would find the missing piece of evidence she had been hunting for five years.

But first, she had to confirm that a loose hog and being overly devoted to a tuber had been responsible for Mr Plummer's spiritual wanderings. After William had hitched the horse to the cart and they guided Eurydice into the back, Fern climbed onto the seat. Her dragon companion gave a low chirp and butted her head against Fern's arm.

"I'll be fine, Riddy. My mind is miles away." About twenty miles to the southeast, in Oxford, to be exact, and a small townhouse where her father had stayed while doing research. The place where his landlady had discovered his body, slumped over the table.

Soon she would have the answers her battered heart needed. Knowing what truly happened the day her father died would make it easier to let him rest and continue on with her life.

They took a slow journey through the village and out the northern side, enjoying the warmth of the sun. Bees buzzed between flowers, becoming drunk off nectar and the choice laid out before them. A honeysuckle was alive with the fuzzy insects.

"That will make the honey even sweeter." Fern told the

dragon how certain flowers that the bees fed on would flavour their honey.

At the cemetery, once more, she left the horse and cart in the shade. Today, Eurydice didn't need any help. With her wings outstretched for balance like a tight-rope walker, she waddled down the plank with confidence and even jumped to the ground before reaching the end. The fledgling signs of confidence warmed Fern's insides. Perhaps the balcony in the conservatory had been too far off the ground for a first jump. They would start smaller, and she would encourage the dragon to leap from the cart without the need for a plank at all.

When she reached the little greenhouse, Fern offered a silent prayer to whoever was listening that Tad and Ted had done as promised. Then she flung open the door. Hands on hips, she stared at the spectral orchid. Its spindly flower was still as ethereal and healthy-looking as ever.

"Well...rotted toadstools!" She had wanted to utter a more foul oath, but you never knew who was listening. And rotted mushrooms were disgusting. "Those dratted, useless men didn't do what they promised to do!" She would tear strips off them for not making their apologies to the dead man. If she had to, Fern would take them by the ear and march them straight to Mr Plummer's graveside.

"Of all the inconsiderate, selfish..." she ranted to herself as she strode back to the cart and waited for the dragon to catch up.

Eurydice warbled and lurched from side to side as she hurried behind.

Fern drew a deep breath and knelt down. The dragon

rushed to her and buried her head in Fern's arms. "Sorry, girl. I'm not angry at you but at those men. Mrs Plummer grows weaker every day, and they couldn't be bothered to soothe their friend back to sleep."

From the cemetery, Fern drove the cart back into town and over the bridge by Scribbles. Such was her mood that she barely had time to register Squib peering out the window overlooking the road, and she didn't return his wave. On the other side of the river, they navigated the busy main street and all the foot traffic. Fern left the cart close to the bakery, where Eurydice could peer into the shop and inhale the mouth-watering aromas.

"You need to come with me. Now!" Fern levelled a finger at the baker's head.

He finished his conversation with a customer and glanced at Fern. "I am busy, Miss Oakby. Can you come back this afternoon?"

Fern crossed her arms and glared at him. She hoped a scathing look would work and she wouldn't have to physically manhandle him, as he had muscular arms from kneading dough for years. "You promised you would talk to Mr Plummer, but you obviously did not. Are you saving your words for his widow's funeral? Which will now be only six days away. In case you forgot, her husband is draining her essence."

The bakery fell silent, and all the eyes in the room fixed on the baker.

Mr Cornhill frowned and slowly wiped flour from his hands onto the apron tied around his waist. "We did exactly as promised yesterday afternoon. We even took Dick a pint and had a quiet drink with him."

"You both went?" That took the heat out of Fern's outrage.

Without taking his gaze off Fern, his hands continued to move, and he plucked a dozen golden rolls to place inside a string bag before handing it to the waiting customer. "Of course. What sort of man wouldn't do as much? No one wants to see his friend's family suffer."

"It wasn't potatoes." Which surprised her. She could imagine her or her father being roused from beyond the grave by a garden-related issue. Her shoulders heaved, and she kicked a solid oak sideboard displaying fancier loaves.

Bollocks. We still haven't found the reason.

"It didn't work?" Mr Cornhill paused before reaching behind him for a square, sourdough loaf.

"No. The petals still haven't fallen." A tendril of desperation wound around her heart. What would they do? In good conscience, she couldn't tackle the reason for her father's return until she had proof Mr Plummer had toddled back to his grave.

"I'll talk to Tad. If Dick was hiding something, we'll find it." He gestured to a young lad to come forward and serve the customers.

People in the store parted as the baker rushed out the door, and Fern trailed, unseeing, in his wake. Instinct guided her to Eurydice. She rested one hand on the dragon and leaned against the sun-warmed stone as she gathered her thoughts.

What to do now?

There was hope that Mr Plummer's two closest friends would uncover whatever secret drove the spirit to touch the orchid. But right now, Fern needed the sort of advice only George and Ambrose could impart.

"Let's head home," she said to the dragon and climbed back into the cart.

As though in a dream, she returned to Nemython and handed the horse to William. Fern drifted through the garden, Eurydice leaving her side to sit by the pond. Into the kitchen she wandered, dropping into a chair, and her head hit the table with a faint thud.

"How can one person be so...boring?" she said in a muffled tone, given she spoke directly to the tabletop.

A hand patted her shoulder. That would be Ambrose, who had been drinking his tea and working at the kitchen table before her dazed entrance and had witnessed her flinging herself to the worn oak.

Mr Plummer's wife couldn't think of any reason for her husband to linger. There was no other dispute in the family, and the obvious one between friends had been resolved. A search of the Plummer cottage had failed to reveal any loose floorboards or journals stashed behind walls or in the attic. Fern was starting to think Millie's idea of him being a secret highwayman with a collection of jewels in a hollow tree might be her best line of enquiry.

"Perhaps you just need to dig a little deeper?" Ambrose suggested.

She lifted her head. "You think he might have buried something in the backyard? Like the body of a rival potato grower?"

CHAPTER 18

ONE OF AMBROSE'S pale eyebrows arched, and a bemused expression settled on his face. "I think our resident writer is rubbing off on you, dear niece."

Fern pushed off the table to prop herself upright and sighed dramatically at her uncle. "We have spoken to his wife, family, and friends. Two arguments were resolved and haven't affected the orchid. Apart from a little gardening, Mr Plummer doesn't seem to have any great secrets or unfinished tasks. Not even an unread book." Why couldn't the solution be as easy as sitting in the summer warmth and reading the last chapter of a gripping novel out loud at his graveside? "There's nothing left." She dropped her forehead back to the cool timber of the table. She couldn't begin to tackle the reason *her* spectral orchid had flowered until she knew Mr Plummer was back where his soul was meant to be and his family were safe.

Tick tock, tick tock went the reliable old grandmother clock (which is shorter than grandfather clocks) in the hall.

"What about his employment?" Ambrose lifted a lock of hair that covered her eye and peered at her.

"Work?" Fern hadn't given any particular thought to how Mr Plummer had earned sufficient coin to keep his family fed and warm. All she knew was that he worked for the Putnams as a farm hand.

"Yes, dear. I am told some people are remarkably conscientious about their jobs." Ambrose tsked under his breath, as though he couldn't imagine such a thing himself.

Fern was dedicated to botany, but that didn't always mean she was conscientious. She was, however, running out of options. "Perhaps he left an untilled field when he died."

She rolled the idea around in her head. Nope. That wouldn't make *her* leave whatever happened beyond the veil to tap at the orchid and gather up family members. No matter how much she enjoyed a baked potato topped with a slice of butter.

"He seemed rather devoted to potatoes. Perhaps his work on the farm involved them, too." Ambrose reached out and patted her hand.

Any idea was worth pursuing. *Six days*, she counted in her head how many remained for Mrs Plummer before she joined her husband. "I shall change clothes first and leave Riddy here, as I doubt the livestock at the Putnam farm will appreciate a dragon sniffing around them."

After tugging off the gown and doing up her trousers and boots, Fern explained to the dragon that she had to stay behind. Eurydice's shoulders slumped, and she narrowed her gaze. If Millie was rubbing off on Fern, Squib was definitely making an impression on Eurydice. She perfectly mimicked the pixie dragon's disdainful glare.

"I'm sorry, girl. We can go swimming this afternoon, if you like?" That made the little creature perk up. With the dragon mollified and the door to George's workshop propped open so he could see her, Fern collected her horse.

As she buckled up the girth, she recalled everything she had learned so far about Mr Plummer, hoping there was a detail she had overlooked.

The mare swung her head around and pinned her ears, making Fern still for a moment.

"Sorry, girl." Suitably warned by the horse to pay more attention, Fern scratched her wither and made soft crooning noises. Just like human women, mares could be more reactive at certain times in their cycle. This mare hated her girth being done up, even though Fern always buckled it gently and never did more than one hole at a time. But when half a tonne of female was cranky, it was much better to apologise and make amends, rather than argue you did nothing wrong and she was being overly sensitive.

Once she was sure the mare was comfortable, Fern led her out to the mounting block before she checked the girth once more. And tightened it one more hole when the horse wasn't looking.

They rode south-east and navigated by Sibylcrest Abbey perched on the hill. Before they reached the base of what had once been a fort, they turned off the road and headed inland again. They rode around the edge of the field where the lads had picked the poisoned apples as she sought out the Putnam family.

They wound up the driveway to the old stone house where the family lived. Outbuildings and barns were dotted around a central yard, and the fields spread out on three sides. Fern dismounted and looped the reins over a rail by the stables. The Putnams had three sons who farmed the surrounding land. She needed to talk to one of them, and they would probably be out in a field, not tucked up in the parlour.

Turning her back on the house, Fern followed a worn path from the stables out to where the crops grew. The wheat and barley had ripened and would need harvesting in the next few weeks. When the time came, most of the village would be enlisted to work in the fields. The men reaping with sickles and scythes, while women and children followed behind to bind the stalks into sheaves.

The Putnams had the largest holding of land around Drake's Bend, apart from the Wyndham estate. Lord Drakeman commanded mostly forest and a few meadows where deer, used to feed the dragons, roamed. Unlike Wyndham Hall, the Putnams employed many locals. While it could be hard labour ploughing, tilling, and planting fields, it was reliable work for many hands, and they earned a fair wage. A good, steady employer ensured the entire village flourished.

She found one of the Putnam men out amongst the wheat. The sons were distinctive, as flaming-red hair ran in their family. Each Putnam shone like a beacon under the sun. Unlike Fern, in whom the Reid family red mingled with the earthy browns of the Oakbys and mostly surrendered to her father's side of things.

"Mr Putnam!" she called out as she approached from behind. She didn't know which son it was, but that didn't matter, since they weren't on a first-name basis.

He turned, a single stalk of wheat in his hands as he ran a thumb along the forming seed head. Clear blue eyes, like the sky above, regarded her. "Miss Oakby. What can I do for you?"

His face wrinkled in a frown at her popping up in his field like an unwelcome mole. Fern had little to do with the family beyond polite greetings when their paths crossed. The Putnams had farmed the land for over two hundred years and relied on knowledge handed down from father to son to ensure the crops thrived.

Since they weren't friends, that also meant she could cut out all the social chitter and get straight to business. "I'll not keep you long, Mr Putnam. I wanted to ask you about Mr Plummer. His spirit has returned, and I have yet to uncover the reason why. I know he did labouring work for you, and I was wondering if anything happened in those last few weeks?"

He shook his head and narrowed his eyes against the bright noon sun.

"Could you think about it, please? It might be something that was unimportant to you but has made Mr Plummer restless. Perhaps a task he failed to complete? A disagreement over something? The matter is urgent." The man argued with his friends over potatoes. Perhaps he disagreed with his employer about chickens.

"He was an honest worker, and we were on good terms. That's why it surprised me when he left to work at the abbey." Mr Putnam tucked the stalk of wheat behind his ear.

"The abbey?" Fern stared at him, sure she had misheard. "That abbey?"

She pointed to the stone fortification perched on the hill that dominated the skyline to the south.

"Aye. Sibylcrest." He pronounced each syllable slowly, as though he suspected her to be a bit slow.

"Sibylcrest?" Fern repeated. Admittedly, it was taking a bit for the words to drip into her brain.

"Sibylcrest Abbey. That one. Right there. On the hill." Mr Putnam pointed to the same landmark that Fern had indicated, on the off chance that there was another such place with the exact same name nearby. "I can't blame a man for wanting to do better for his family. They were offering a higher wage than we could match."

Fern's mouth opened and closed, and she struggled to form a coherent sentence. She swallowed to push down all the sentences and questions crammed in her gullet. Closing her eyes and drawing a calming breath, she picked the most pertinent question and asked it. "When, exactly, did Mr Plummer leave your employ for the abbey?"

Mr Putnam huffed as he sorted through his memory. "I seem to recollect it was only a week or two later that we heard he had died. He might not have been here when it happened, but we still look after Mrs Plummer to honour all the years he gave us. She gets a basket of produce once a week from the farm."

"Because you are good people," Fern murmured as she stared at the old Norman fort. Ideas burst into life inside her and spread like an enthusiastic nasturtium. She didn't know how her skin contained them all, and she thought she would erupt like a pot boiling over.

All roads lead to Sibylcrest. It had to be an odd coincidence. There hadn't been many men employed at the abbey from the brief moments she had seen inside, but some might have been drawn from the surrounding area.

"Did Mr Plummer ever say how he heard that men were needed at the abbey?" she asked.

"My southern field and the abbey share a boundary. From what I recall, Dick was approached while sawing up a tree that had fallen in a storm." He waved his hand in the general direction of the field in question, where the old trees of the forest formed a thick line along one edge.

"Thank you, Mr Putnam. That has been most helpful." Leaving him to continue his inspection of the crops, Fern returned to her horse.

"We need to see if we can rouse anyone at the abbey," she told the horse as she balanced on a fence post to ease herself into the saddle.

This time, the mare only flattened one ear. Fern let out a relieved breath that her attempts to mollify the sensitive equine were working. They cantered along the dirt road, the faster pace blowing some of the loose threads from Fern's mind. She only slowed the mare to a rhythmic trot as the road became steeper and harder as it wound around the hill. She walked the mare over the causeway and dismounted before the portcullis.

Peering through the bars, the kegs that were once in the corner of the courtyard had gone. Silence blanketed the old stone building, and she couldn't discern any movement behind the thick glass of the windows.

"One way to tell if there's anyone about." Selecting a rock, Fern climbed up the rails to bang on the old brass bell.

The clangs bounced off the stone walls and echoed around the enclosed space. After several more attempts and several minutes without any response, she climbed back down. Chancing her luck, she tugged on the smaller gate, but the iron didn't budge.

Closing her eyes, she strained to hear if boots rang out on the stone. Or if she could detect a whiff of smoke from so much as a tobacco pipe. Nothing. The abbey was wrapped in an eerie emptiness as though it were bound in a shroud, ready for burial. Not a single creature drew breath within its walls to lend it life.

"They must have moved on with their horrid concoction." Mrs Garrick had told her the abbey was for sale, and after the mess she had made of the great hall, the men must have vacated the draughty place. Lord Drakeman had discovered they'd taken the magical pulp to be spun into thread at a mill in Banbury. "Where are you now?" she murmured to the shadow of Sir Luxton, who threatened two things she cared deeply about. Kelmsgales and dragons.

Since she was here, curiosity demanded she know for certain that the robber-baron had moved on. And it would be much safer in daylight.

Climbing back on the horse, who gave Fern a filthy look for mounting from the ground, they headed back down the hill. Turning off the road, Fern guided the horse along the edge of the forest, then slid off the saddle to lead the mare through the dense trees. The horse was left to graze in a little clearing before the tumble of stones from the collapsed wall.

Taking her time and testing her handholds since no one knew what she was doing and she couldn't afford an accident, Fern climbed the pile of stones to the breach in the wall. On the parapet, she took a moment to appreciate the view back over the fields and towards the village. The wheat and barley were golden squares in the patchwork laid out by nature.

Some people might like bigger towns and cities, with their constant activity, stone buildings, and streets crammed with all manner of conveyances and people. Fern preferred the countryside, the swathes of greenery and the call of birds in the trees.

"Oh!" she called out in excitement as a dragon swooped through a cloud and plummeted to the earth like an arrow. Its scales were an iridescent bluish green. At the last moment, it unfurled its wings like sails and extended its hind claws. When it rose into the air again, a bleating sheep dangled in its grasp.

"Oh, poor thing." This time, her voice lowered to a sad tone as the dragon and sheep ascended through the cloud cover once more. Turning back to where the dragon had snatched its meal, Fern scanned the area for the nearest cottage. "The Herberts."

The elderly couple had recovered from the effects of the tainted smoke that had permeated the sheep's fleece. The illness had blunted Mrs Herbert's tongue—to everyone's relief. An old law itched at the back of Fern's mind, something George had told her about once. If dragons feasted on local livestock, they were entitled to compensation from the drake man. She would verify the archaic law with George and then ensure Lord Drakeman paid the price of the animal to the Herberts.

Tucking that task aside for later, she struck off along the parapet's narrow walkway to the stairs in the corner. Across the courtyard, Fern kept glancing around for signs of anyone rushing to stop her. She tugged on the door leading inside and was relieved that it remained unlocked. The occupants must have thought the portcullis enough to deter the curious and forgot about the breach in the wall.

Comparing the twists and turns to her two previous visits, Fern soon navigated to the open area with the curving stairwell and the double doors to the grand hall. Pushing them aside, she waited behind one solid oak door in case anyone remained inside and called out. Hearing nothing, she peered around.

"Empty," she whispered. Even alone in the abbey, she couldn't bring herself to speak in a normal tone. The place encouraged murmured words and snatched conversations, the centuries having layered conspiracies into its stones.

Fern crept further into the chamber with its soaring ceiling. An unpleasant odour, not unlike rotten eggs, assaulted her nose. "Ugh!" She held one arm over her face.

The pulpy goo that had exploded from the cauldrons had solidified into a metallic-looking substance that emitted the noxious stench. Timber from the shattered kegs littered the slate floor like autumn leaves, and many shards were embedded in the transformed pulp, jutting upwards.

"No wonder they abandoned the place." It would take

the assistance of the three witches to undo the damage their spell had wrought.

Once satisfied that no one remained to answer her questions, Fern retraced her steps and descended the tumble of stone to her horse.

"It is empty, and I will never know what Mr Plummer did in those last two weeks," she told the mare as she stood on a chunk of wall to climb back into the saddle. "He might have been the first victim of what they brewed in those cauldrons."

Villagers had been poisoned by the tainted smoke, but what might have happened if someone ingested the pulp that was spun into thread in a Rumpelstiltskin-like transformation? There was one person who could tell her if Mr Plummer had truly died of a heart attack or if there had been foul play involved. Doctor Dodd.

CHAPTER 19

WHEN FERN RETURNED to Nemython House, she found Eurydice lounging in the sun by the kitchen porch. The dragon lifted her head, and her long tail gave a slow thump against the ground.

"I haven't forgotten my promise, Riddy. It's just that I have to find why Mr Plummer's soul is restless, and there are only a few more days before his wife will be lost." Fern scratched the dragon's sides and added in a small whisper, "And me."

How to satisfy two souls with very different causes of concern? Or were they? Fern had long maintained that another hand took her father's life. What if the same reason had stirred Mr Plummer?

Her thoughts took a darker turn as she toed off her boots and walked in her stockings across the kitchen floor. A large hand broke through the shimmering mist in her mind.

"Here." George thrust a stuffed journal at her.

Fern took the bundle in her hands and stared at it. Loose

pages of mismatched paper were inserted behind the cover, and the whole thing was tied together with a piece of green ribbon.

"What is this?" She glanced at the older man, who had a lump of cheese and a loaf of bread spread before him on the table.

"My notes." George sliced a piece of cheese from the block and dropped it onto a doorstop-thick piece of bread.

"Of what?" Fern took the chair beside George and stole a slice of bread for herself.

"That's everything from when Rowan died. All the people I talked to, or wrote to for more information." He folded the bread around the cheese and practically unhinged his jaw to take a bite. He chewed with a satisfied glint in his eye.

George had done his own investigation. And never told her. She swallowed the lump forming in her throat. Oh, right, it was a chunk of bread.

"Does Ambrose know you are eating the last of the walnut loaf and his favourite cheese?" Fern murmured as she placed the journal on the table and snuck a wedge of cheese to nestle inside her slice of bread. With one hand, she munched on the rolled cheese, while the other tugged at the ribbon and opened the journal.

Page after page was filled with George's neat script, only interrupted by quick sketches of anything he must have deemed relevant. Like the desk where they found her father. Tears misted her vision as she stared at the cup of tea, slightly askew on its saucer. Beside him, his open journal. Close by, a writing set with a quill not quite replaced in its holder.

"Why didn't you tell me you had done all this?" Fern struggled to believe that while her father's lifelong friend thought Rowan took his own life, he had nonetheless searched for answers. Or had his inquiry led him to that conclusion?

"I didn't see the point until now. We're not going to lose you. There might be something there that helps." He spoke in snatches as he cut the remaining bit of cheese into three. Keeping two for himself, he passed the last bit to Fern on the tip of his knife.

Fern wiped her eyes with the heel of her palm. "Thank you, George. I will study it tonight. But first, I need to go see Doctor Dodd. Did you know that Mr Plummer was working at the abbey in the days before his death?"

George shook his head but remained silent since he was munching on the last of Ambrose's favourite loaf and sharp cheese. Fern could foresee an argument in the future if both items were not replenished in the larder. She made a mental note to stop at the bakery after visiting the doctor and the general store to see what cheeses they had available.

"I wonder if his death might have been caused by the horrible concoction they brewed at the abbey. Smoke poisoned a handful of villagers, but what if he bathed in the pulp or ate it? Perhaps he served himself a bowl full of the stuff, thinking it was porridge, and that caused what looked like a heart attack." Fern could tell a thrip infestation from powdery mildew, but human diseases were outside of her field of expertise. While she cultivated beautiful and deadly plants that could kill, that was purely for their botanical value and not because of any desire to have anything more than a theoretical knowledge of poisoning.

That line of thought got her wondering if the wood from the rare subspecies of kelmsgale was poisonous. That would certainly explain the effect the smoke had on the village. It would have to be the subject of her next research paper once she finished the one about the *Helix mortifera*.

Holding the journal about her father's demise to her chest, she hurried to her study and placed it on her desk next to the other notebook. She rested one hand on each cover. "I will find the answer, Father. I promise."

Having made her vow, she grabbed her satchel, kissed George's cheek on her way out, and headed off for the doctor. Fern walked down the bustling main street of Drake's Bend on her way to the surgery. Before she delved into an older possible murder, she had to prevent an impending one. In the baker's shop, she purchased the dense loaf with traces of walnut that her uncles enjoyed. The general store had a small piece of sharp cheese that, after being wrapped in waxed cloth so it didn't leech its odour to the rest of the contents, was nestled in her satchel.

As she continued on her way, Fern gathered her thoughts with each step. Spirits didn't leave their eternal peace and return to the realm of the living for no reason. With all their ancestors waiting on the other side, no one was so lonely that they had to snatch their family members before their time. Particularly when, as the Moray sisters explained to her, time moved differently for the deceased. Years were but a moment —although she didn't want to ask how they knew that! There would be a cause. She just hadn't found it yet. But a tickle at the base of her skull whispered she was *finally* on the right path.

The doctor lived on the western side of the river, in a cottage between the Drake's Rest tavern and where the main street ended. Its location made it easier to find medical help in an emergency. There was no gate, and the garden was delineated by a spill of lavender that brushed against the clothing of passersby.

From a wooden post at the end of the path hung a sign with 'Doctor Dodd' painted in faded black letters. Technically, their doctor hadn't finished her medical degree and wasn't supposed to call herself that. But she was far more qualified than others with an official piece of paper. The university administration had taken a dim view of things when they discovered their star student was actually a woman in male clothing. Fern thought it said volumes about the quality of medical knowledge being taught if the crusty old lecturers and other students thought a pair of trousers was what denoted male or female.

Joe Dodd had gone to university with Fern's father, George, and Ambrose. When the latter heard of the scandal at the medical school, Ambrose had immediately suggested Drake's Bend as a place to stay while she determined her next course of action. Twenty-five years later, the good doctor was a beloved fixture of their village. With her forward-thinking approach, they enjoyed a better level of care than other villages with either no doctor at all, or ones who clung to the idea of bleeding and leeches to cure everything from a headache to a severed limb.

The door to the cottage was open, indicating the doctor

was within and available to see anyone in need. Muffled voices came from the parlour used as a consulting and treatment room. Fern popped her head through the partially open door to find Doctor Dodd conferring with a young woman.

The doctor had close-cropped dark hair that was silvering over her ears and a rounded face with kind, brown eyes. She wore a waistcoat over her plain cotton shirt, the sleeves rolled to her elbows as she worked. She glanced up at Fern and waved. "We are nearly done here, Fern. I'd love a cup of tea if you don't mind?"

Fern nodded and carried on to the kitchen at the rear of the cottage, where a rectangular window looked out onto a wildly neglected rear garden that ran into the embrace of the surrounding forest. There was a beauty to the self-seeded tomatoes and pumpkins that scrambled among the wildflowers blown from other gardens. Not that the doctor needed to maintain a vegetable patch, as the village ensured a hot meal was thrust into the medical person's hands at least once a day. Others took care of the little cottage to keep it clean and tidy.

After coaxing the range back into life, Fern filled the kettle from the barrel of water kept by the back door and then set it to boil. Once puffs of steam were bursting from the spout like an indignant Squib, she poured off a little to warm the teapot before searching in the cupboard for the tea caddy.

By the time the doctor strode through the door and dropped into a chair, Fern had the tea made. She poured a large mug (there were no delicate little cups here), sweetened it with a bit of honey, and pushed it across the table.

"Busy day?" Fern enquired as she sipped her mug of the strong brew.

Doctor Dodd ran a hand through hair that was kept far shorter than Fern's curling locks. "Late night. Another villager came into the world, but it was a dastardly difficult breech birth. The wee mite refused to be turned and wanted to enter the world feet first. There was a fair bit of cussing involved, but thankfully, mother and her daughter are doing well this morning."

"They are lucky to have you." Fern marvelled at women who battled Mother Nature to bring forth life. So many mothers and babes were lost in the process. Doctor Dodd had spent years learning beside old, skilled midwives, who were disdained by *male* physicians.

"I do what I can. A woman's lot is a harsh one in a man's world, and we should support each other, not make the path harder." They exchanged a long look, each well aware of the price they paid to be true to themselves.

For Fern, trousers were a convenience when working in gardens. To Doctor Dodd, male attire enabled her to be at ease in her skin.

"But I am sure you aren't here to discuss the ignorance of men." A warm smile lit the doctor's brown eyes.

Fern traced a fingertip around the rim of her mug. "No, I need to talk to you about Richard Plummer. Our restless spirit. Can you tell me about the night he died?"

"Ah. I thought you might ask, and I found my journal from that year and re-read my entry about it." She rose from the table and fetched a worn journal from a dresser by the window. Flipping through the pages of tight, neat script, she stopped at a faded cloth bookmark. "I was here that evening. His oldest came and fetched me, saying his father was having trouble breathing. By the time I arrived at their home, there was little I could do. It seemed he had been feeling ill all day with a tightness in his chest and waves of dizziness. His wife sent the lad for me when his breathing became worse."

"Do you think he could have been poisoned, like the villagers were recently?" The more Fern mulled the idea over, the more it seemed the most likely reason why the quiet man had reached out to the spectral orchid. He might be seeking justice.

The doctor's head snapped up. "What makes you say that? There were no blue tinges on his hands or fingers."

"I discovered today that he had taken work at the abbey in the days leading up to his death. That got me to thinking whether he might have swallowed some of the pulp, and it might have worked differently from the smoke." Fern sipped her tea. Now she said it out loud to the doctor, doubts started to creep into her mind.

Did the timing work?

Lord Drakeman had said that the tree shavings and dragon blood had to be simmered together for some weeks as the first step in brewing the dragon silk. If they were correct in their estimates of when the dragonet was slain and the tree felled, was there enough time for the first batch to have been created? If not, could another plant have been responsible?

"There are some poisons that present as a heart attack, as you know." The doctor leaned back in her chair and crossed her arms as she considered the possibility that her diagnosis might have been incorrect.

"There are far too many, sadly. Yew, oleander, lily of the valley, monkshood, or foxglove. But most of them are fast-acting and cause sudden death. I doubt he would have had time to make it home if he ingested one at the abbey." Fern's mind wandered the path of her garden, where beautiful blooms hid a deadly touch.

"Remembering that night, his heart simply gave up. He had lost consciousness by the time I got there, and all we could do was watch him slip away." Doctor Dodd held out her hands as though water poured through her fingers. Then she turned them over, and short nails rapped on the wood as she scanned her memory. "The plants you mentioned all induce severe chest pain, irregular heart rhythm, confusion, nausea, and shortness of breath. All symptoms of a heart attack. But collapse is usually sudden and follows quickly after the poison is administered. Unless someone closer to home was adding tiny doses to his food over a period of time."

The idea of someone going to the time and effort of poisoning the unobtrusive man just didn't sit right with Fern. "Poison is favoured by women," she murmured to her drink. She tried to add the moniker of *murderer* to that of the image of Mrs Plummer.

No, it didn't seem right. Nor was there any rumour of Mr Plummer ever raising his hand to his wife. Something that was never tolerated in the village. The men were quick to address such behaviour when it surfaced among them.

"I never had to tend Mrs Plummer for walking into a doorknob or falling down some stairs." Doctor Dobb followed Fern's line of thought.

Neither could Fern imagine his daughter poisoning her

father, even if they had access to the plants required. From what she had learned, there were no wronged women or any secrets about the man that would provoke such fatal anger. She let out a sigh.

Fern held the mug of tea to her chest as she imagined the night Mr Plummer's soul had let go of his physical form, no matter how the doctor tried to urge it to remain. "Sometimes, no matter how much we want a person to stay, that decision is beyond our control."

The doctor had eased her mother's last hours, administering poppy syrup to take away her pain as they said goodbye.

"I would challenge the gods themselves to save those under my care." The older woman's head dropped as she stared at a tendril of steam swirling in her mug.

"You do all you can. None of us expects more than that." Magic had its limits. The Moray sisters brewed potions and salves that soothed complaints, but no one possessed enough magic to drive away Death himself.

Doctor Dodd huffed and raised tired eyes to Fern. "I will not stop seeking a cure for all ailments while I walk this earth. Galvanism may yet provide the answers we seek. Although I'll not call down lightning where it might set fire to my neighbours' homes."

"If it was indeed natural causes that took Mr Plummer and there was nothing unusual about his death, I am no closer to finding why his spirit has returned." Worry for the man's widow was consuming Fern. The woman fell deeper into the embrace of fatigue and struggled to rise from her bed, only to snooze in a chair in the sun. The spirit would have to be banished and his quest, whatever it was, left unfinished.

Doctor Dodd tapped her journal. "There was one small detail...but it may be nothing. Mr Plummer collapsed on his bed fully clothed, and his family were undressing him when I arrived at their home. When I examined him, I noticed a bloodstain on his trousers but no such injury on his body." She pushed out her chair to point to a spot on her dark grey trousers. "Here. Above the knee."

"Are you sure it was blood?" It could have been a blob of jam from the man's midday meal.

A smile softened the tired lines on the doctor's face. "I have some familiarity with it."

That was the second time Fern had asked such a question and received such a response.

CHAPTER 20

FERN CONSIDERED where a blood stain might have come from. "Did he have a cut anywhere else?" The blood could have been from an injury elsewhere. More than once, Fern had jabbed herself with something sharp and had pressed a cloth to a cut.

"Not that I found on him. And I checked every inch of his skin. Whoever the blood belonged to, it wasn't Mr Plummer." She shrugged and took a long slurp from her drink.

Most likely, one of the other men had cut himself, and Mr Plummer had tended the wound. "Thank you, Doctor Dodd. I am not sure it helps, but I will take whatever possibilities I can grasp hold of at this point."

Fern left the doctor's cottage, nodding to the family waiting in the parlour with a visibly ill child, and struck out for the Plummer cottage. Time slid through her hands like grains of sand. She would need to visit the witches. While it would exhaust the old women, it was better to perform the ritual to banish Mr Plummer before he worked loose his wife's soul.

A knot of anxiety spiralled inside Fern as she rapped on the widow's door. When no one answered after a few minutes, and with concern turning into a rampaging beast inside her, Fern let herself in and approached the parlour. "Mrs Plummer?"

"Here," came a rasped reply. Mrs Plummer sat in an armchair before the fire, a blanket draped over her knees even though it was a warm day outside. "Forgive me, Miss Oakby. I must have fallen asleep."

If possible, the widow looked worse than the last time Fern had seen her. The lines around her eyes were more deeply etched, her shoulders slumped, and her complexion was drained of its colour.

"I am sorry to bother you, Mrs Plummer." Fern bit her tongue before she blurted out, *You look terrible, and I'm scared that we'll be attending your funeral sooner than expected.*

"I know everyone is trying." The older woman gestured to the chair beside her.

Fern dropped to the patterned brocade and clutched her satchel on her lap. "I went out to the Putnam farm today. Why did you not mention your husband had taken work at the abbey just before he died?"

The widow shook her head, and her eyes narrowed in confusion. "The abbey? But Dick worked the land for the Putnams."

"Yes, he did. But Mr Putnam said he left a sennight or so

before he passed. Are you sure he didn't say anything to you?" Fern leaned forward, needing to be closer to hear the older woman's whispered words.

"Silly man. He never said a word. We had been worried about making ends meet. But he brought home more than usual that week. I didn't question why." Her eyelids fluttered closed.

Fern tucked away the issue of money woes as another possible problem. "I have spoken to Doctor Dodd. It might be that the root of the problem lies in your husband's last day. She made a comment, and, well...it is going to sound silly, and the answer is probably no..."

"Just ask it, Miss Oakby, so that I might go back to sleep." Mrs Plummer's eyelids drooped even though dusk was still a few hours away.

No one needed to tell Fern twice to speak her mind. "The doctor said there was an odd stain on your husband's trousers. But that he didn't have any cuts or wounds. I don't suppose...is there any chance at all...that you kept his trousers?" Clothing was never thrown out as long as it still had wear in it. That was wasteful. The items might have been passed to one of the sons or someone in need in the village.

A wan smile touched the other woman's lips. When she opened her eyes, clarity had returned and washed away a little of the tiredness. "You will think me silly. But I still have his clothes. When I miss him terribly, I like to touch his shirt. It still smells of him, you see. Sweaty and a bit horrid, but for a few breaths, I can imagine he is still here."

Fern held her silence, not knowing what to say. The Plummers might have been an unremarkable couple, but they obviously cared for each other deeply. She shouldn't judge relationships by their outward appearance. It never occurred to Fern that the widow loved her husband so much that she sniffed the shirt he had been wearing when he died. Mr Plummer seemed so...ordinary. But everyone deserved an extraordinary love, and that took a different form for each person.

The widow rose and shuffled to the next room. Through the open doorway, Fern caught a glimpse of her opening a cupboard and reaching in for a neatly folded stack of clothes. Hugging the items to her chest, she returned to the parlour.

"I should have passed them on to John, but I wanted to keep them for a little longer." Her hands hesitated as she held them out.

"I only require the trousers. You may keep his shirt." Fern didn't want to ask if the widow also inhaled the lingering odours of the trousers. That seemed a little too personal.

She unfolded the item and examined the fabric at the knees. "Yes, here it is." A dark patch. Smaller than her hand and, just like the doctor had said, it appeared made of drops and splatters. "Could I take these with me, please? I will return them, but I need to seek another opinion about what might have caused this mark."

"Of course. If it helps soothe him back to sleep." A brief smile crossed her lips, and then she continued on past Fern back to the armchair. Still clutching the shirt to her chest.

Leaving the exhausted woman to the quiet of the house, Fern slipped out the front door. She tucked the trousers into her satchel and considered what to do next.

"Millie." Fern needed to talk through the ideas colliding

in her head, and a cup of tea would help to make sense of them. The decision was made. She headed for Scribbles.

When Fern pushed inside the bookstore, the low murmur of conversation greeted her. A group of women was clustered along the stacks, discussing which books to acquire. Millie sat at her desk with a frown on her face as she peered at her customers. The displeasure turned into a smile when she spotted Fern.

Squib bounced up and down from his perch on Millie's shoulder and trilled with a questioning note.

"Hello, Millie. I am sorry, Squib, but I left Riddy at Nemython House." Fern didn't have to speak dragon to understand him.

The pixie dragon stopped his hopping, narrowed his gaze, and huffed at Fern. There were days she was rather glad he wasn't a large species of dragon, as she suspected she would have been eaten or incinerated for displeasing him.

"They won't leave, and it is past closing time," Millie whispered and gestured with her head to the lingering customers.

"I shall deal with them if you could ask Alice for a pot of tea, please?" Fern replied.

"Deal." Millie perked up at having an assistant to help, and she hopped down from the tall stool—nearly dislodging Squib in the process.

Fern straightened her shoulders and approached the group. The three women seemed to be playing pass the parcel with a book.

"Hello, ladies. It's past time to leave, and Mrs Carlisle is waiting to lock up. Let me take that—" as Fern reached for the book, the woman holding it blushed and shoved it back onto the shelf without looking.

"No need. We have changed our minds," she said and grabbed her friends by the hands, hurrying them out the door.

Curiosity aroused, Fern waited until the door had closed behind them before she searched the shelf for where the book had been jammed. Pulling the slim volume free, she read the title and then the opening page before chortling to herself. The book was a particularly saucy romance. Obviously, the women had been trying to pluck up the courage to purchase the novel.

"Perhaps they will be braver tomorrow," Fern muttered as she found the correct spot for the book with the other romance stories.

She wandered the rows of books to ensure no one else was hiding with a story they couldn't put down. Then Fern locked the front door and flipped the sign to CLOSED.

Millie joined her in the conservatory, the tiled floor soaking up the last of the afternoon sun. It was pleasantly warm, and Fern dropped to her favourite chair. Tiredness tugged at her limbs, and part of her longed to stretch out in bed and pull the blankets over her head.

"Is Mr Plummer still wandering the cemetery?" Millie asked as she puffed up a cushion before settling into her chair.

"Yes. And my father is roaming the halls of Nemython." She recalled the journal that George had placed in her hands. The answer to settle her father would be among the pages. All they needed were fresh eyes on events of that day.

Millie leaned forward and placed her hands over Fern's.

"I will not lose you so early in our friendship. We will discover the fiend who poisoned your father. After we have chased Mr Plummer back to his grave."

When Alice brought the tea tray, she cast a concerned look at Fern. "Ma told me that Mr Oakby has returned." The maid held the tray to her chest as though it were a shield against the returned dead.

"There is nothing to worry about, Alice. He will soon return to Mother." Fern tried to reassure the younger woman, but she feared the smile on her lips didn't quite reach her eyes.

"Since Mr Plummer is now supping on his wife's soul, let us banish him first. What secrets do we have left to reveal?" Millie poured tea into a mug and placed it in Fern's hands. Then she picked up her favourite cup and saucer.

"Only one. He left his regular employment to work at the abbey just days before he died." Fern sipped the tea and let the warmth flow through her body.

"Oh! Do you think he participated in their nefarious activities?" Millie's eyes were wide over the rim of her cup.

Fern thought of the bloodstained trousers. "I am beginning to wonder if that might be why he returned. Especially since we have now discovered what they were brewing up on that hill."

Perhaps the noxious smoke had doused the spirit in guilt and made him reach from beyond the grave.

"He died a year ago, did he not? Isn't that when you think the tree was cut down and...you know...the other thing happened?" Millie whispered the last part of the sentence, not wanting to say out loud what happened to the dragonet.

Squib followed the conversation with interest. From the sunny spot where he lounged, he kept one eye open and fixed on his mistress.

"If he did..." Fern struggled to think of the mild-mannered man having anything to do with what happened at the quiet spot beside the river. "I don't see what we can do about it."

"If he is channelling guilt through the spectral orchid, then he will be seeking forgiveness. Although how one forgives such an act, I do not know." Millie glanced at her tiny dragon companion.

Silently, Fern agreed with her friend. How could such a slaughter ever be forgiven? "I had better discover if that is the true cause first."

"How—is there a way to ask him?" Millie asked.

"Lord Drakeman." Fern didn't have to say anything else. The name alone conjured the image of his laboratory and the bubbling containers and ancient books.

Millie's mouth made a rounded O shape, and her eyes sparkled.

"Do not say a word about me kissing him," Fern said before the writer's imagination charged off with her again.

Her friend stared up at the corner of the room and deliberately ignored Fern's gaze. After a pleasant tea, she couldn't put it off any longer. She hurried home and saddled her horse as quickly and gently as she could. At the Hall, her rap at the door went unanswered until the third attempt.

Quint flung the door open and glared at her. "What?! I was busy."

"Trimming your furry palms? His lordship told me about

the unfortunate...incident." Fern waved to the black leather gloves covering his hands. Today, there was no sign of the pink trim.

The butler growled. "If I find you had..."

"Shouldn't you be talking to your boss? He's the one who mixes who-knows-what concoctions in his laboratory. He told me he thought something might have reacted with silver polish." That was only a teeny white lie. Fern had raised the idea, and the earl simply hadn't dismissed it outright.

Quint's eyes narrowed further until they were mere slits. He bore a remarkable resemblance to a disbelieving Squib when he did that. If he huffed, the impersonation would be near perfect.

"Where is he, please? In or out?" She couldn't manage a grin today. Her stomach rumbled, and her limbs grew heavier by the minute.

"Out." Then he slammed the door.

Was that a flash of pink she saw?

Fern walked the mare across the meadow to the earth-enclosed building and found a spot with lush clover to tether the horse. She hesitated before she knocked on the door. A chilling theory had formed in her mind after talking to Millie, and she desperately wanted to be wrong. But people might die if she didn't find out.

Making up her mind, she knocked and waited.

After some shuffling from within and a muffled curse, the bolt slid back, and the door opened. Lord Drakeman arched an eyebrow but stood aside to allow her to enter. The door making an ominous thud as it shut behind her.

Fern approached the square table under the skylight with the slow, steady steps of a funeral procession, skirting around a broken flask and what appeared to be golden tendrils that spread from underneath a cupboard. The alchemist said nothing, but he kicked aside a tendril that recoiled and shot back under the cabinet.

The silence was unusual for him. Normally, he would hurry her along or yell at her to get out. His behaviour had certainly changed for the better over the last few weeks, since Eurydice had started visiting the Hall.

And since Fern had kissed him.

Waving that image from her mind (but it did make her curl her toes inside her boots), Fern reached into her satchel and pulled out the folded clothing. She held onto the item and wet her lips. "You told me that you had a way of telling that the blood of the slain dragon was found in the pulpy mix brewed at the abbey."

Her fingers curled into the rough fabric. *I'm wrong. I have to be.*

He stared at the trousers and then at her. Curiosity simmered in both the dragon and human eyes. "Yes. Dragon blood is unique. The easiest way to explain it is that it wants to be with itself. A sample will reach for another sample if they both originated from the same body."

"Like magnets?" Fern had seen how one lump of metal would wriggle along a bench to attach itself to another.

"Yes. It is similar to a magnetic attraction." With his arms crossed, he waited for her to explain further.

Magnetic attraction. She glanced at him from under

lowered lashes. Was that what made her want to stand next to him? To lean a fraction closer until the warmth of his larger frame touched hers? To discover if the dragon-scale scar ran over his torso?

"I have learned that Mr Plummer was working for the abbey when he died. These are the trousers he wore that day. There is a stain. Doctor Dodd thought it looked like blood. Given the timing of his demise…I wondered if…" She couldn't finish the sentence. *Did Mr Plummer slaughter a dragonet?*

That inscrutable dragon gaze pierced her soul and plucked the question from her brain. "I can try."

He held out his hands. Fern unfolded the trousers and laid them out on the table to indicate the mark above the right knee.

He leaned over them, his tilted face close to the rough woollen fabric as he used his dragon gaze. "It's not much, but it may be sufficient."

Fern nodded. Any answer would direct what she did next. If it were jam from his toast on that final day, she wouldn't waste any more time trying to resolve Mr Plummer's unfinished business. His soul would be banished. It was a horrid thing to do since no one knew for sure what happened to an expunged spirit, and some speculated they were shredded and spent an eternity in agony. But it was a necessary thing to save his family in the living realm.

"Thank you," she managed to whisper.

Lord Drakeman gathered up the trousers with the stain exposed and approached a workbench. He selected scissors and a clean beaker before returning to the table.

As Fern turned to leave, he wrapped his fingers around her arm. "We will learn the truth."

That silver gaze cut through her, but this time, instead of feeling exposed, a warm connection rippled between them. Along with a slight magnetic pull.

CHAPTER 21

THERE WAS little Fern could do until she heard the results of Lord Drakeman's tests. So she turned her attention from one spectre to another. The next day, she devoured George's notebook, with its meticulous recording of her father's last days. But she had failed to find any clue as to who might have wanted to harm Rowan Oakby.

She sat at her desk with her head resting on her hands. George's notebook sat to one side. Open before her at its last pages was her father's journal. Or what should have been the last pages. If she stared at the jagged remains hard enough, perhaps she might be able to conjure what had been on those torn sheets.

Over five years ago, Rowan had gone to Oxford for research. He had needed access to old manuscripts and volumes of botanical lore kept at the university library. Such trips were not uncommon, particularly when he was planning an expedition and wanted to learn as much as possible about a plant he intended to find. Before his death, he and

Fern had discussed a trip together to find the rare *Crystal-lophoenix nivalis,* or snow Phoenix flower.

"What was worth your life?" she whispered to her father's spirit.

His spirit had come back, so why didn't he offer any guidance?

Heaving a sigh, she pushed the journal away and turned her mind from one mystery to another. Unfolding the map, she studied the location of the kelmsgale trees. The trees were much on her mind with the discovery that Mr Plummer may have been present the day a previously unknown variety of one was felled. "Why aren't you here?"

She kept running into questions with no answers.

"What's missing?" George poked his head into the little study.

"A tree." Fern turned in her chair and waved the map at him. "Between here and Warrington Manor used to stand a rare form of kelmsgale—the *Sorbus celmsgeul beatha.* A tree that, when combined with dragon's blood, makes dragon silk. A tree that I didn't even know existed until recently. But Father must have done. I don't understand why he left it off his map, even though it was a subspecies." She shook the map a little harder, hoping the answer would slide off and pool on the rug.

"So it's a rare tree?" George asked.

"Exceedingly so. And its wood can make something... dangerous called dragon silk." Fern couldn't call the silk marvellous, not when the production required the death of dragons.

"So it's something best hidden." He leaned on the door-jamb, his broad body filling the open space.

Fern hadn't considered it that way. "Possibly, he left it off for that reason. But why not tell *me*?" She sucked in an urge to pout. They had been so close and shared everything. Why had he not told her of the unusual tree?

George stepped into the study and crossed to her desk. He picked up the map and held it to the light streaming in through the window. "What would some men do to acquire this dragon silk?"

Fern sucked in a sharp breath. To possess a fountain of youth in the form of a luxurious garment? People had been killed for far less. "They would kill for it."

George put the map back down and drew a silver flint tin from his pocket. Grabbing a candle in a holder from the shelf, he lit the wick. Then he held the map near the open flame.

"No!" Fern cried out and lunged for the map. "You can't burn it. Please." It wasn't just a map of the trees that released magical motes, it was a piece of her father. He had laboured over every line of the drawings.

"I'll not destroy it. Look." George held the map too close to the naked flame for Fern's liking with one hand, while he pointed with a meaty finger at a spot a few inches above Drake's Bend.

As Fern watched, the faint outline of a tree appeared. Above it, written in a familiar hand, a single word—*beatha*.

Her tired brain struggled to make sense of what she saw. The rare variant had been there all along. But unseen. "How is that possible?"

George chuckled. "When we were lads, we used to play a

game, pretending we were spies for the crown. Rowan and I used to leave secret messages for each other stuffed in a tree hollow. We wrote with lemon juice so the page looked blank if it fell into enemy hands. The words are revealed when held to a flame."

He handed the map back to Fern, the tree still visible in a brownish sort of ink. "The tree was there all along."

Ideas spun in her head. Her father had correctly identified the rare tree and then kept its existence a secret. Fern could only think of one reason why. He had known that possessing such knowledge was dangerous. But when had he stumbled upon a reference to the tree? Lord Drakeman had thought his family had the only book showing the rare alchemic process involved in making the fabric.

A spark flared in her brain and cleared away the fog. "Oxford." She breathed out the word.

Turning to George, she explained further. "I don't think Father was researching the snow Phoenix in the oldest parts of their library. What if he had found the grimoire that mentioned the *beatha* kelmsgale? Once he knew of such a tree, he would have been driven to find any remaining in the country."

Her theory meant there had to be two books of dark alchemy that told of what foul things could be done with dragon blood. Or three. Since Sir Luxton had another such book to know how to brew the pulp and what arcane runes and spells were needed on the spinning machines to turn it into fibre.

A finger rapped on the inside of her skull. She was overlooking something rather obvious and distasteful. What if the book her father found and the one in Sir Luxton's possession were the *same* ancient grimoire?

"Oh, Father. Were you working for Sir Luxton to find the trees he needed?" The words tasted like ashes over her tongue.

"Rowan wouldn't work for him—the man's a rat. Some of us value more than coin," George bit out.

He was right. Her parents had always placed people and community above financial gain. There wasn't a purse of gold large enough to convince her father to abandon his ethics to condone chopping down such rare specimens. But his thirst for knowledge would certainly have been ignited at the intellectual challenge of finding them.

Others might then have taken that knowledge from him.

By force.

Her gaze dropped to the journal with its missing pages. "That's what he was working on. And what cost him his life. *Sorbus celmsgeul beatha.* Perhaps Father had heard a whisper about the variant and decided to see if there truly was such a tree. Somehow, Sir Luxton had learned about the grimoire and its horrid alchemic process for dragon silk. From your association at university, he would have known Father was the best chance he had to discover if any such trees remained. We will never know what conversation might have taken place between them. Perhaps Father refused to hand over his research about where it stood, knowing what they meant to do with the specimen."

George huffed. "Rowan defended that tree with his life."

Rowan leaves and dragon's breath are the key to life and death. The old rhyme drifted through Fern's mind. The words were now forever tinged with sadness at the darker meaning they hid. Three lives lost—human, dragon, and tree —in the pursuit of vanity and an exotic fabric that would extend life for a few wealthy individuals.

"All for nothing. They took what they needed, anyway. The torn pages must have been his notes about the trees' possible locations." Fern traced a finger over the ragged stubs of paper. Her father had a fondness for cyphers, and she could imagine that it took people employed by Sir Luxton a few years to crack the code and point to their prey.

A large hand dropped onto her shoulder. "He has shown you the reason at last. Let Rowan's spirit return to Delfie now."

Fern's vision blurred as tears burned in her eyes. Picking up the battered journal, she held it to her heart. "We might know why, but we don't know who." One question might have been answered, but a dozen more sprouted in its place.

She turned to stare up at George and blinked away the tears as resolve returned to her limbs. "We can't let them get away with it."

At last, others would know her father's life had been stolen from him. But justice demanded that the killer be made to account for their crime. Fern just had to figure out who. Most likely a Luxton henchman. Did the hand that ended her father's life also take that of the dragon?

A sudden chill washed down her spine, and she bit her fist to stop from crying out. Had mild-mannered and likeable Mr Plummer also slain her father? That could be the reason that both spirits now rose from their graves.

George pulled her out of her chair and into a bear hug.

Fern wrapped her arms around his broad torso as far as she could reach, and her tears soaked the rough cotton of his work shirt.

"Please, George. I have to know," she whispered.

"We'll do what we can." He patted her back as though she were a child once more. "If I find them, I'll string them up myself. But there will be no justice without proof."

Fern pulled back from the large man and used the heel of her palm to wipe her eyes. A tiny grin tugged at her lips. "Are you forgetting how stubborn I can be? Someone in Luxton's employ put the poison in Father's tea. They can't hide forever."

Possibly, they already floated around the cemetery looking for forgiveness so they could return to their eternal slumber. If Mr Plummer had anything to do with her father's death, Fern would ask the witches to craft a banishment revenge that would see his soul spend eternity wrapped around a forever-growing cactus.

George squeezed her shoulder. "If anyone can uncover the truth, it's you. Ambrose and I will do whatever we can."

"What have you dragged me into now?" Ambrose's voice came from the hall. No doubt his curiosity had been aroused by the whispered conversation in the study.

"We have a murderer to find. What ears do you have in Luxton's circle?" George said, letting Fern go.

"Luxton murdered Rowan?" Ambrose's eyebrows shot up, and he glanced from his partner to his niece.

George huffed. "Doubt it. He'd never dirty his hands. Or have the guts. But one of his cronies would."

"George found *Sorbus celmsgeul beatha* drawn in invisible ink on Father's map. I believe he had been trying to find the tree and somehow got tangled up with Luxton. Then they killed him when he refused to hand over his notes with the location." She refolded the map and tucked it into the front of the journal, satisfied that she had at last uncovered the truth of the matter.

Ambrose shuddered. "That all makes a horrible sort of sense. Luxton knew Rowan from when we were all eager students. Who better to find a mythical tree than an old chum who became a renowned botanist? But Rowan would never have condoned chopping the thing down."

"And possibly, it might have been Mr Plummer. He started working for Sir Luxton at the abbey just before he died and had an odd stain on his trousers that Doctor Dodd believes is blood." The words rushed from Fern as she told her uncles everything else she had learned.

George stared at her and blinked.

Ambrose let out a squawk. "Dick? You think *Dick* did away with Rowan?" A slight note of hysteria tinged his words.

"It's only a vague idea, but it seems rather coincidental that both spirits returned at the same time, don't you think?" Fern fiddled with a pencil to give her hands something to do.

"If Dick were bound that tight to Luxton that he murdered for him, he would have left his job at Putnam Fields five years ago." George pointed out the rather significant flaw in Fern's theory.

"We will know more soon enough. Lord Drakeman is going to determine if it was dragon blood on Mr Plummer's trousers." In Fern's mind, if a man could draw a blade across a dragon's throat, the same hand could drop poison into a teacup.

George headed for the door, pausing to touch his partner on the shoulder. "Rowan has got his message through. Fern is out of danger now."

"Good. As much as we love Rowan, we would prefer to keep Fern with us for many years yet." Ambrose hurried forward to give her a hug and smoothed some hair away from her forehead.

Fern had found it comforting to know her father's spirit lingered in the house. But his spirit had dwelt in their realm for long enough. Exhaustion nibbled at Fern's limbs as the spectre slowly drew off her essence to maintain itself. "The flower will wither, and the petals will fall and turn to black tears now his task is done." A silent prayer formed in her head as she recalled the unexpected problems in settling Mr Plummer. *Please let this have been Father's unresolved task.*

"But ours has just begun. I shall quietly spread the word among our associates and find a mole inside Luxton's household." Ambrose tapped his chin as he considered whom to write to.

That night, Fern climbed into bed clutching her father's notebook with its torn pages. Tucked safely behind the cover, the map of kelmsgale trees with a lone rare specimen inked with lemon juice. If she drifted off with all the questions for her father in her mind, would his spirit answer them during the night?

IN THE MORNING, Fern awoke without the notebook. At some point, she had tucked it under her pillow. Or at least she hoped she did it, and not that her father's soul had poltergeist tendencies. The first thing she did was stumble into the parlour and stare at the orchid.

"No," she whispered. The beautiful flower was as luminescent as ever, with no speck of decay.

Finding the tree on the map was not enough to satisfy her father's ghost.

Ambrose and George were silent when she told them the news. But the men had arisen before her and would have already seen the pristine bloom.

Seated at the table in the kitchen, Fern used her spoon to create eddies in her porridge as thoughts swirled through her mind. At times, only a single word went around and around. Why?

Why didn't her father tell her about the *beatha* trees?

Why didn't he mention his association with Sir Luxton?

Why didn't he trust her enough?

The last question made her heart ache, and a rap at the door startled her. Grateful for the distraction, Fern rose from her chair to lift the heavy iron latch. Denis Fawcett stood on the other side of the aged oak door.

"Morning, Miss Oakby. Letter for you from his lordship." He held out the folded sheet of paper.

"Thank you, Denis. If it's a summons, please tell Lord Drakeman I will be along shortly." She took the letter from him.

The groom touched the brim of his cap and strode back through the garden to the stables.

Fern walked slowly to the table and stared at the note, her name written in the neat hand. Picking up a knife, she slit the dragon seal on the back and unfolded the sheet.

The tests are done.

Will discuss at your earliest convenience

Lord D

"A polite summons from his lordship." She told her uncles. Breakfast had formed a heavy lump in her stomach, but she ignored it.

Mrs Plummer was now confined to her bed, sleeping most of the day as she slipped away. If today did not reveal the reason for her husband's unrest, he would be forcibly evicted from their realm. Nor was Mr Plummer the only spectre who reached for a family member. While her spectral orchid had only been in bloom for a few days, every morning saw Fern wake as exhausted as when she lay her head down.

She had trouble dragging herself from bed but blamed Mr Plummer. Worrying about the cause of his restlessness kept her awake at night. Surely that was the only reason for her being so tired, and not her father's spirit trying to usher her through Death's door. It should have been easy to soothe her father—he needed people to know he had been murdered. But the orchid stubbornly clung to its petals.

If she had to find the person responsible...well...there simply wasn't enough time. Concern for George, Ambrose, and the Bentleys drove her on. As much as she loved him, she would not let her father siphon the soul from anyone in their forged family that she loved fiercely.

He had to be banished, no matter that it would splinter her heart all over again.

CHAPTER 22

FERN LEFT the note on the table, pushed aside her bowl with its cooling contents, and drained the last of her coffee. Not that it had any impact on her weary brain. Eurydice was awake and snuffling around the garden. Fern left her dragon companion peering into George's workshop. He was up early, too, and sawdust was drifting through the open door.

The quiet ride out to the Hall eased a little of the turmoil in Fern's mind. As horse and rider walked along the shady, treelined road, Fern dropped the reins and closed her eyes. She drew one deep breath of air into her lungs after another and let her heartbeat slow to the rhythm of the horse's hooves.

When the mare halted at the gate, her thoughts were a little clearer. Today, the gate was open wide enough to admit a horse and rider, but the mare was used to Fern dismounting to push them apart. Or did she worry she wouldn't make it through the gap? The horse was fond of her feed and could put on weight in the blink of an eye if given access to too much green grass.

"Come on, girl. You can fit." Fern nudged the mare forward with a gentle tap of her heel.

They paused again at the end of the driveway to regard the silent house. Since she had been summoned early, Fern suspected the earl would be found in his laboratory and not having his breakfast in some enormous and lonely dining room. There was a thought that hadn't struck her until now— how solitary his existence must be. He had no extended family or friends to fill the rooms with chatter. No other nobles visited, nor did he host house parties. There was no one to share his excitement about an interesting passage he read in a book, or a discovery in his laboratory.

Apart from Quint and whatever other staff roamed the halls, like shadows flitting between trees.

A twinge of sympathy wound its way through her.

"He did it to himself, cutting himself off from all society," Fern muttered as she nudged the horse towards the meadow. "Come on, girl, there's plenty of clover by the laboratory."

One of the mare's ears flicked back as she listened to her rider, and she lengthened her stride. Fern slid to the ground before the squat, stone building and looped the reins around a low-hanging branch. The mare shoved her nose into the middle of a pink flowering clover and seemed content with the world.

Fern rapped on the metal-studded door. "It's me. Miss Oakby," she called out.

She barely had time to rock back and forth on her heels before the bolt slid across and the door opened.

"Good morning." Lord Drakeman nodded as he stood

aside to allow her entry, one hand curled around the wood near the top.

Nerves erupted under her skin as she crossed the threshold. Part of her dreaded what she would shortly hear. Part of her was relieved that, whatever the answer, Mr Plummer would soon be back where he was supposed to be. Her pace slowed a little as she drew level with the earl, shooting a glance at his larger frame and the forearm extended to hold the door above her head.

He wasn't such a bad person once you dug under the rude surface. Rather like a potato, you had to brush aside the foliage and dig down to find the tuber beneath. And scrub the dirt off. Her thoughts made her swallow a chuckle. Even if there was a kind heart within his stony exterior, she doubted he would want to know she compared him to a potato. Or would it depend on what variety? Pink Eye, Early Shaw, or Lumper?

Definitely not Pink Eye. If he were a potato, he would be a brand-new variety. The Silver Eye.

The door slammed, and she jumped. The alchemist strode to one side of the square table, and she took the other. Thick stone walls kept the laboratory cooler despite the summer warmth. The shelves were lined with brass instruments, jars of curious liquids, and strange objects (or were they appendages?) floated in preserving fluid.

"Was it blood?" she blurted out, dragging her curiosity back to the reason for her visit.

"Yes." Lord Drakeman leaned both hands on the worktable. The sleeves on his dark-blue shirt were rolled to the elbows, the sides of his grey waistcoat hung unbuttoned, and a singular intensity flared in his mismatched eyes. He gestured to the things laid out on the table before them. Mr Plummer's trousers were now missing a square of cloth as large as her palm, cut from above the knee. An open notebook revealing hurried entries lay open. A wooden stand held three delicate glass vials. Each contained a soft lilac liquid that reminded Fern of lavender flowers.

The stain was blood and not a blob of jam. Dare she ask if it was human or from another creature?

He gestured to the containers with their slender necks as though the glass maker had pinched them while still molten. "These contain extracted samples. One from the fabric, one from the pulp mixture, and one from the skeleton you found. What do you notice about them?"

She wasn't prepared for an exam. Fern leaned her elbows on the table and pulled the stand closer. She studied each vial in turn. Apart from an etched symbol on each, which appeared to be part of the glass and most likely a way to distinguish the contents of them, she couldn't discern any difference.

"They all look the same to me," she admitted.

He crossed his arms. "Exactly. The samples have harmonised, indicating that all three originate from the same source. Or the same dragon."

Oh...bother. It was dragon blood. Her stomach plunged. Everyone described Mr Plummer as a quiet, unassuming, and good man. And yet, he did such a terrible thing.

"He did it. He...killed that poor, sick dragonet." Fern bowed her head as she tried to imagine what the creature must have gone through in those last few moments. Did it think the men were there to help it, and hope had surged within its chest until a knife was drawn from behind Mr Plummer's back?

"No. I don't believe he did it." Lord Drakeman shuffled through the pages of his notebook to a double spread with a drawing in thick blue ink. He rotated the book for Fern to see.

Across two pages was the odd stain and blotches the dragon's blood had left on Mr Plummer's trousers. She stared at it. Was it some sort of magical stain that contained the name of who did the deed? "I don't understand what this means? How could he have the dragon's blood on his trousers but not be responsible for its death?"

Lord Drakeman moved around the table to stand next to Fern, and she swayed on her feet towards him, soaking up his warmth like a heat-loving clematis planted by a stone wall.

With one fingertip, he tapped the pattern on the paper. "Stains can tell us what happened. Look at the angle and concentration. It suggests a very specific position. Arterial blood flows fast and sprays outwards, even in a sick hatchling. It would have left a trail of small droplets and not a larger and slower patch like this."

Fern stared up at him. *How does he know such things?* An image shimmered in her brain, and she scrubbed it away before it could form. It was a rhetorical question. She really didn't want to know *how* he knew what happened when a knife was drawn across a throat.

Taking her silence as understanding, he continued with his explanation. "These drops were made by a slower volume of blood. I suspect they came from underneath his knee, rather than above it."

Fern's brain was fuddled as she tried to imagine how blood flowed from under a bent leg. She hated to admit she didn't understand, but some things were far beyond her experience to figure out—even if she had the inclination to learn more about blood patterns. "I still don't understand how you can tell this from a stain and what it tells you about who ended the dragon's life?"

Lord Drakeman cupped his hands and held them before him. "I suspect Mr Plummer knelt on the ground, holding a bowl by his leg. Some of the contents splashed onto him. Your restless spirit caught the blood; he did not spill it."

Fern's breath caught. The slight difference meant everything. The man went from being the executioner to an accomplice. Willing or coerced? She couldn't say.

"He didn't kill the dragon," she whispered. At least now she could face his widow and wouldn't have to lie about what unsettling truth had kept her husband from eternal rest.

"He was not responsible. But he was present." The alchemist spoke in a low tone that made shivers erupt across Fern's shoulders.

She sank onto the stool, imagining the shame Mr Plummer had carried home that day. "What he participated in caused his death."

Doctor Dodd said that Mr Plummer had been having chest problems for a few days. The fatal tightness in his chest and struggle to breathe had come from his guilt at being complicit in the demise of a rare and marvellous creature.

The mild-mannered man had played a horrid part in something he couldn't prevent nor speak of while living.

Fern needed to think, and that required her feet to move. Hopping off the stool, she paced beside the table. Shame had combined with a weakened heart and taken Mr Plummer's life before he could divulge his terrible secret. What could she do with that unvoiced confession? Settling a spirit required a ceremony to acknowledge their return and the business they had needed to air.

"How?" she muttered. How to acknowledge the heinous thing Mr Plummer had participated in and send his soul back without condoning what he did? To her, killing a dragon was unpardonable. But was it her decision to make?

If the spirit was to be offered forgiveness, it could only come from a dragon. That meant asking Eurydice and Squib.

While thoughts and ideas swirled in her mind, Fern stretched her arms up over her head to ease stiff muscles. Something went pop in her shoulders. What she wouldn't give for a soak in a steaming hot bath. Slowly, she rotated her neck to stretch a particularly cramped tendon when strong fingers gripped her shoulders and then dug into the tight muscle.

Part of her brain went *eep!* at the unexpected contact, but before she could duck away, another treacherous part of her brain let out a long-held sigh. "Oh, that is good."

Lord Drakeman attended to a knot with a firm press of his thumbs. This was no gentle poking that tickled more than relieved an ache, but a prolonged, deep pressure that made the rigid fibres yield. "You seem stuck on a particularly... knotty...problem," his voice whispered over her left ear.

Fern let out a groan that possibly sounded rather more pleased than she had intended. "I shall have to remove both myself and Riddy from the Hall permanently. Your attempts at jokes are getting worse."

"I am simply out of practice." He finished massaging her shoulders, but his hands remained in place.

The tiredness that nibbled at Fern's limbs made it harder for her brain to function. This, in turn, made it harder to sort out the turmoil his closeness stirred up within her. "Lord Drakeman..."

"Seth." He spoke the name in a quiet tone as his thumb moved upwards to stroke the side of her face.

"Seth?" Who was that? Mr Plummer's name was Richard. Or could it be Quint's real name?

"My name is Seth. I would like you to use it. If it pleases you." His voice lowered to a murmur as his lips brushed her skin.

When he trailed spidery kisses up her neck, she wasn't able to call him anything except *oompf.*

"I thought we had agreed to keep things on a professional basis." She stayed still, like a deer trapped by the gaze of the predator, and tried to determine if he would move on if she failed to react.

"I made no such promise." His mouth moved higher to taste her jawline.

"That's cheating." But oh...it felt so good. Her toes curled in her boots. Ever since the winter thaw, her body had thrummed with a building need. A longing that she normally sated with a summer dalliance during the kelmsgale festival. She risked her job if she gave in to her craving for his touch, and she didn't want to jeopardise that. But if his mood had softened, it gave her the opportunity to raise another matter that bothered her.

"The conservatory is taking all my time, and I won't be able to clean out the pool before winter. Which is such a shame. I was hoping you would let me swim there with Riddy when the weather cooled." Did her words conjure the image of her splashing around in the heated water, wearing just a chemise? Or nothing at all. That might have been a rather forward suggestion to make, but if it worked...

"You want to use the pool?" he drew the words out slowly and moved away a fraction.

"Yes. It would help Riddy's body grow stronger. She is becoming far too large for the bathhouse. And the pool there is shallow." Fern had already considered the stone building the villagers used and estimated that the doorway would be too narrow for the dragon by winter, given her current rate of growth. "There are young lads in the village who would be eager for the work in return for the chance to swim there, too. Nor would you have to see them. I can supervise their work, and I am sure Quint would also keep them in line."

Lord Drakeman scratched at his chin and, with his face half turned, only his dragon eye regarded her. Let him peer at her true self. He would discern no lies or deception in her words.

"If I could use the pool at the end of the day, it would save my housekeeper from boiling water for my bath. Nor do I like smelling of old sweat." She confessed the entirety of her self-interest in the project, just in case he did spy a teeny tendril of it within her.

"Five lads. No more. They may use the pool five times, once they are done. One time for each of them. Quint is to be advised when they are here so that I might avoid them, and their pay is to come from yours." Only now did he walk away and tap at an experiment whose flame blue spluttered as though about to extinguish itself.

Fern considered arguing about the terms of payment, but she would simply add the wages for the lads to her monthly invoice. "Very well. Your terms are acceptable. I will have George suggest the most reliable young men from among those who need work."

"Another bargain struck between us. I wonder what we shall agree upon next?" He arched one dark eyebrow, and an amused glint entered his all-seeing gaze.

If he thought for one second that she was going to ask him for a kiss...well, he was mistaken.

For today.

"Thank you, Lord Drakeman. I think I have enough now to deal with Mr Plummer, and I will advise Quint when we have lads ready to clean the pool." Fern spun and headed out the door, needing the refreshing breeze cutting across the meadow after the heady atmosphere of the laboratory.

CHAPTER 23

FERN UNTIED HER MARE, who had chewed a section of clover down to the roots, and rode for Scribbles.

"Riddy won't forgive me for the number of visits to Squib she has missed." She needed to take the dragon with her more often but didn't want to confine herself to either walking or having to take the cart.

The dragon grew every day and now stood as tall as a wolfhound. How long before she was as large as the cob who pulled the cart? Not that Fern thought she would fit into the cart if her body were as big as a horse.

She left her equine at the forge and walked back over the bridge, waving to Alice, who spied her from the kitchen window. By the time she walked through the front door, the maid was carrying the tea tray to the conservatory.

"No Riddy again today?" Millie looked up from her work and peered through the window.

"No. I fear she will never forgive me. She does enjoy her visits with Squib." Fern leaned on the waist-high desk and glanced at the scattered papers. Her brain was too occupied, and tired, to make sense of whatever tale the writer composed. She just hoped it was another instalment about the lady highwayman.

It seemed the pixie dragon also wouldn't forgive Fern. He sat on the edge of the desk, narrowed his gaze, and huffed short bursts at her.

Fern caught a page that fluttered close to the edge with the heated puff of air. "Will I be forgiven, Squib, if I tell you of an important task that only you and Riddy can perform?"

He huffed, but took a hop towards her. She took that as permission to tell him of her plan.

"I need you and Riddy to send a soul back to its grave. But only if you can find it in your hearts to forgive someone who was there when one of your kind was slain." Fern dared a glance at the pixie dragon.

Squib's eyes narrowed further until they were mere slits in his papery face.

"It takes a very kind-hearted and magnanimous dragon to offer forgiveness to one who, in our eyes, isn't truly deserving of it." Millie pressed a kiss to the top of the little dragon's head.

Squib emitted a long-suffering sigh and waddled over to Fern's hand. He thrust his head under her fingers and arched his neck. This was an indication that she was to stroke his head and possibly heap more adoring words onto him, while he considered whether he was in a forgiving mood or not.

Fern did as instructed and wondered if the story Millie wrote on his hide was one about a Roman emperor, given how the pixie dragon behaved.

With a ceremony in mind for Mr Plummer, they then had to wait until twilight, or the gloaming, for what needed to be done. Words of forgiveness would carry better across the veil when it was at its thinnest. Contrary to what some stories would have you believe, that wasn't at midnight. Rather, it was when day succumbed to night and during the act of one world surrendering to another.

With some hours to wait, Fern used the time as best she could. First, she fetched Eurydice and explained the task she hoped the dragons would perform as they travelled to the cottage to visit with Squib. Once the two dragons were happily sitting in the sun by the river, chatting in their lyrical language, Fern promptly left to see the Moray sisters.

Her step seemed heavier as she trod the path to the sisters' front door. They were inside today, which was unusual. It normally took a fierce wind or driving rain to send them scurrying back indoors, such was their love of nature and all her moods.

The rap on the door was answered with a muffled, "Come in, Fern!" from Nona.

Fern pushed the silvered wood open and toed off her boots. The three women were huddled around the kitchen table. An array of books, many older than the sisters, was spread across the surface.

"It must be this one," Decima said, tapping a sage-green cover with one hand.

Morda rested her hand over the tome and shook her head. "It's not the right one."

Nona muttered and plucked another book from the chaos to place under her sister's touch.

"What are you three up to?" Fern asked as she approached the group.

"There is a spell we may need, but we have not cast it for many decades." Nona picked up one of the discarded books and ran a fingertip down the spine.

Fern touched Morda's shoulder before taking the empty seat beside her.

"We can't recall which grimoire it is in. Not that Nona thinks we should brew it even if we find it." Decima glanced at her older sister. Her lips sucked in a scowl.

"It's too dangerous." Nona made a shushing motion at her sister.

Decima huffed and placed Morda's hand on another worn cover with a frayed edge. "It's necessary."

"It is not for us to make the choice for another." Morda grinned and used both hands to feel the title of the book before her. "Ah, here you are, my old friend," she crooned to the ancient book.

"You're not planning to poison an abusive husband, are you?" Fern was well-versed in how a little something in a violent man's meal or drink could remedy an awful situation for women with no other recourse. Not that she sold poisons to such desperate people. She only supplied the dried leaves and flowers to apothecaries and witches.

"Not today," Decima said in a bright tone.

Morda turned her milky gaze to Fern. "We worry for those who are touched by wandering souls. You have a dark path to walk."

"Sometimes the dark paths are far more interesting," Fern murmured. For some reason, the seer's words reminded her of a midnight adventure when she scaled a fallen wall with a gruff alchemist whose touch caused a maelstrom within her.

"Cup of tea?" Nona asked everyone after she had made a tidy pile of discarded books.

Fern sat in silence as the two older sisters made tea. Her eyes were unfocused as she stared at the book before Morda. The silver lettering of the title swirled around one another like dance partners.

"What news of Dick Plummer?" Morda tugged on Fern's hand and brought her thoughts into focus.

"He was there when the men killed the dragonet. He went home and died that very night." Fern thanked Nona as she placed a steaming mug before her.

"Guilt is a heavy burden to carry." Nona returned to her chair.

Decima carried over a jar crammed with shortbread and placed a creamy coloured square by each mug. "His heart had been struggling for months. Add the burden of witnessing such a thing, and no wonder it gave out on him."

"How do you forgive the unforgivable? For surely that is why his spirit cannot rest." Fern asked the question into the fragrant steam tickling her nose.

"Each soul pays for their choices made. It is not for us to add to their burden once they have passed," Morda said, then she chewed on her piece of shortbread.

Fern bit into her biscuit and let the buttery goodness dissolve over her tongue. While she wanted to pout and refuse Mr Plummer forgiveness for not stopping the man who used the blade, would it serve any purpose now? Who knew what torment awaited him on the other side? Perhaps the spectre of the slain dragon would peck out his eyes for all of eternity. If she looked at the situation from a different angle, forgiveness in their world might hasten any punishment in the next realm.

"I have asked Eurydice and Squib to forgive him on behalf of dragonkind. If they can." If the dragons could not cooperate, then Mr Plummer's ghost would be forcibly sent back. It seemed rude to expect the dragons to forgive one of their kind being slain, even if the Moray sisters could promise a horrible and torturous revenge in the next realm.

Morda extended her hand across the table, and Decima plucked another piece of shortbread from the jar and placed it on the deeply lined palm. "The young dragon will see the truth in his heart," the youngest crone said.

Fern wondered if the dragon-eye ability to see a person's true face and their soul worked on the dead. She would simply have to trust that everything would go as planned. Then she could focus on her own wandering spirit problem.

Conversation between the women was muted as they finished their tea. As Fern laced her boots back on her feet, Decima stood nearby.

"Could you spare us a lunanavis stamen, if you have one? It will be needed for the potion." Her old eyes were tight with worry.

The stamens of the rare plant had sold easily for a ridiculous sum. Fern had kept one for herself, but she didn't even hesitate to offer it to the Moray sisters. Whatever the witches intended to brew that had caused dissent among them, it must be a dangerous thing indeed to need such an ingredient.

"I have one left. But there will be no more until next

spring." Fern tried to sound stern and like a mother rationing out sweet biscuits to a child.

Decima took her hand and squeezed. "You have a kind heart, and it will be repaid one day."

Fern kissed the elderly woman's cheek. "I don't need repayment. I quite enjoy the chaos you lot bring to my life."

She left the cottage to the comforting cackle of the witches laughing.

Later that afternoon, as the sun dallied about snuggling under its horizon blanket, Fern once more steered the reliable cob towards Scribbles. Millie must have been waiting at the window, as she hurried out as soon as the horse and cart halted. Eurydice flapped her wings in excitement as Squib shot out the opening door and hurtled towards her.

Millie was draped in an inky-blue cloak with a volumi-nous hood, and she carried an unlit lantern. Fern had changed into her mother's old silk gown, with its ethereal floaty layers, and wrapped a woollen coat around herself to keep off the chill of descending night.

The writer's eyes burned with excitement as she climbed onto the cart beside Fern. "Do you think we will see him? Will there be a ghostly screech as he is dragged back by Death to whatever awaits him?"

"Events aren't usually that dramatic." Fern had to disap-point her friend.

A little of the light diminished in Millie's gaze.

Oh, dear. She hadn't meant to extinguish her friend's excitement. "But I've never involved dragons before. So who knows, there might be screaming banshees this time."

"Oh! Perhaps Riddy will shoot flames at the ghost and

burn him into oblivion?" Millie perked up as she thought of other things that might happen.

"That doesn't sound pleasant for Mr Plummer's family. I wouldn't want that to happen to my father's ghost." Besides, Fern didn't know if Eurydice could snort fire. She hadn't seen anything that indicated such an ability. Squib was huffing heated air from the very first day of his existence.

By the time they turned into the tree-covered tunnel that led to the graveyard, the eerie stillness of twilight was settling over the forest. Birds rushed to find their roosts for the night before owls and other predators stretched their wings to find their breakfast. Fern left the horse to snooze under a spreading elm, and the little group made their way through the scattering of wildflowers.

As birds settled above, a hush lay over the cemetery, broken only by the soft rustle of the leaves, the crunch of a twig underfoot, and the whisper of breath from a dragon's nostrils. Twilight spilt across the sky like ink diluted in water, staining the clouds in pale bruises of violet and grey. The last rays of sun caught on the lichen-carved stones, turning the names of the dead into soft gold.

They reached Mr Plummer's grave. Fern stood with Millie beside her. Eurydice lay curled on Fern's other side, the dragon's eyes half-lidded and her tail twitching with unease. Squib flew from Millie's shoulder to perch on the rounded top of the gravestone.

"I have written something." Millie drew a folded piece of paper from the inside pocket of her cloak. As she unfolded it, the parchment fluttered slightly in the breeze. She drew a breath and began to read.

"Once, there was a man who held a bowl.

It overflowed with despair and regret.

His hands shook.

He wept at his decision.

The weight of the bowl would never leave him.

Long after it was taken from his grasp.

The burden of it pressed on his heart.

Even after it ceased to beat."

Fern thought it was an evocative piece. Simple, and it spoke of the magnitude of what Mr Plummer had participated in, without casting shame or offering forgiveness.

As Millie's voice faded, the air thickened. The forest around them seemed to listen and hold its breath.

"It is up to you now, Riddy and Squib. You must look into your hearts and offer any solace you can for the tortured soul. But only if you think he deserves a mercy that wasn't shown to another of your kind." Fern dropped one hand to the dragon's head.

Moments passed, and the silence flowed around them like honey. When Fern was wondering if both dragons would leave Mr Plummer's soul caught between two realms, Eurydice moved.

The dragon stepped onto the grass that covered the grave. She lowered her head to the ground, nostrils flaring, as she breathed out a thin stream of shimmering heat—not fire, but something older. And colder. It swirled like breath on winter glass. Where it touched the air, it shaped a sigil above the grave of a closed dragon's eye with a single tear poised to fall from the corner.

"Oh," Millie breathed out in wonder. "How did she do that?"

Fern stared, amazed, but had no answer. The eye Eurydice made was comprised of tiny silver specks that hung in the air, like the spirit mist she used to find the soul that had touched the spectral orchid. Then, one minuscule dot at a time, it dissolved and drifted to the headstone and Squib.

The little pixie dragon spread his wings. The last gleam of twilight and the luminescent dust painted his hide in violet sparks. Then he arched his neck and began to sing.

Not words—but a melodious bird song. It was high and thin at first, like the cry of something lost in a cavern. Eurydice joined in with a deeper tone. Her voice was rich and full. Fern thought it could have been an ancient lullaby a mother used to soothe a child long before language and words were first uttered. The dragons' voices intertwined, one melody climbing while the other fell, weaving sorrow and grace into sound.

Tears misted in Fern's eyes, and she realised the dragons didn't sing a lullaby to send Mr Plummer back to sleep.

It was a release—the sound of letting go.

CHAPTER 24

As Eurydice sang, more of the shimmering air twisted through each cry and clung to the grass like mist on a chill morning. Then it rose and fashioned a shape above the grave. This time, instead of forming an eye, the silvery motes clung together in a recognisable outline...that of a head and torso. Mr Plummer's spirit flickered above his grave. His face contorted by fear, and his mouth open wide in a cry. But when he turned to the singing dragons, his features eased into wonder, and his mouth relaxed into a faint smile.

Eurydice stepped closer to the hovering spectre, tilting her head to the side. She extended one claw and etched a symbol into the soil. A spiral that curled inwards, then out again.

Squib flapped his wings and flew up into the air to hover above his friend, his body coated in faintly glowing violet motes. He sang one final note—a pure, piercing cry that cracked through the hush of dusk.

The air stilled.

Then ghostly Mr Plummer bowed his head.

A single silver tear—not water, not spirit, but something in between—slipped from his spectral eye and fell to the grave. The droplet retained its shape and glistened like a pearl.

Eurydice lowered her head and touched her snout to the tear.

The moment stretched. Breathless.

Then Mr Plummer's form began to dissolve. Not like smoke, but like dew touched by the rising sun. Silver light rose from the ground and curled into the shape of wings that enclosed the spirit...then they both vanished.

Eurydice stepped back to Fern's side and leaned against her thigh, a slight tremble of exhaustion running through her body. Squib flew to Millie and burrowed under the warmth of her cloak's hood.

Fern, throat tight, whispered, "He's gone."

Millie nodded. With one hand, she stroked her small dragon companion. "And forgiven. Do the spirits always appear like that and then melt away?"

Fern shook her head, still struggling to understand what she saw. "No. That's why it can take some time to find the right reason for the soul's return, as there is never any visible sign that what we do has worked. Apart from looking at the orchid the next day. But until now, I never knew any dragons to ask for help. They did this. Somehow." She knelt down and wrapped her arms around Eurydice's neck. "You are extraordinary," she murmured against warm scales.

A long tongue licked the side of Fern's face, and Eurydice butted her head gently against Fern's cheek.

"What will you tell Mrs Plummer?" Millie asked.

Fern stared at the grave in the descending dark. "I think the whole truth can stay between us. I shall tell her a part of it. That her husband had changed employment to work at Sibylcrest, and he retained guilt for not telling her. A weight that pressed on his spirit and was made worse by recent events and the sickness that spread from the abbey."

Millie tucked her sheet of paper back into a pocket and tugged her hood up over her head. "Oh, that sounds believable. Not as exciting as a hidden life as a highwayman, though."

Fern placed a hand on the cool stone at the head of Mr Plummer's grave. "No. But quiet lives can still contain surprising twists."

THE NEXT MORNING, Fern rode out to the cemetery and checked on the spectral orchid with a small amount of trepidation. If the ceremony hadn't worked, she was out of ideas. She let out a sigh to find the petals had withered and fallen to the ground. She plucked them from the loamy soil around the plant and placed them in a clean piece of cloth. The previous white of the blooms was now stained a deep brown as though they had been dropped into a strong cup of coffee. Over time, they would darken to the black of a starless sky and harden into a substance like obsidian.

Wrapping the remains of the flower with care, she tucked the parcel into a pocket. Lifting her horse's head from the long grass, Fern climbed back into the saddle and headed for the Plummer household. Her knock at the door was answered without much of a wait at all. Mrs Plummer's eyes were clearer today, and the lines around them shallower.

"Is it done?" she said, her hands burrowing into the fabric of her apron.

"Yes. Your husband is at peace now." Or possibly not, if his soul had to make amends for his part in the dragon's death and was doomed to an eternity of punishment. But Fern would keep that bit to herself.

Mrs Plummer stepped aside for Fern to join her in the parlour. "What was bothering my Dick?"

Fern had rehearsed what to say in her head to ensure it sounded plausible without giving away the entirety of what the widow's husband had done. "It was his work. I discovered that he had left the Putnam farm to work at Sibylcrest not long before he died. Mr Putnam said they offered him a high wage. Most likely, your husband was saving for a surprise, perhaps to help your daughter and grandchild, but he never got the chance to tell you. Then the sickness was spread by the smoke coming from the abbey, and his soul felt some guilt about what happened and that he had some responsibility for those who fell ill."

"Work?" Mrs Plummer sat in the armchair in the sun. "He was a silly man to worry about not telling me. But I can see how he might have thought he was responsible for that awful smoke in some way."

"Mrs Carlisle and I took it upon ourselves to have a small ceremony for Mr Plummer last night, letting your husband know that he wasn't in any way responsible for what was emitted from the chimneys at the abbey, and no one in the village blames him." Fern dipped a hand into her satchel and removed the cloth-wrapped parcel. She held it out to the widow and drew back one side of the cloth. "The petals have fallen. You can put a hole in them before they harden, if you wish to turn them into a necklace."

Mrs Plummer took the small bundle as though it were full of precious gems. She stared at the browning remains of the bloom. "I can't believe he left the Putnams and didn't tell me. But knowing what I do of Dick, he wouldn't have wanted others to know he worked for that noble fellow and not a local man."

"Yes, I am sure that was part of it. I am surprised it wasn't the potatoes, though. He did seem rather proud of his vegetable patch." Fern changed the subject. Mrs Plummer spent some time regaling her with tales of the nights Mr Plummer leapt from bed to protect the tender potato shoots from a late frost. An entirely sensible precaution in Fern's view, and one she had done herself on occasion when she had failed to place straw around the emerging tendrils.

After a pleasant hour with the widow, Fern left to turn her mind to how to settle her father's soul. On her way through the kitchen at Nemython House, she had poured the remains of George's pot of coffee into a mug and carried it with her. Needing the warmth from the sunlight pouring into the parlour, she collected two notebooks and the map from her study and settled at her mother's little writing desk. Placed under the window, it had a view of the pretty front garden and was where her mother used to answer her corre-spondence.

Some hours later, papers were strewn across the desk, but Fern was no closer to an answer. She rose to her feet to stretch muscles cramped from holding a position for too long. How she wished she could have asked Lord Drakeman to lay his hands on her to ease the tightness.

The spectral orchid sat on its plinth out of the direct light, but where it could still bask in the warmth.

"What more do you want from me, Father?" Fern stared at the bloom, its delicate petals responding to the slight stir of the air around it and heightening its resemblance to a spider that had dropped from the moon. There wasn't any hint of a splotch of darkness on it, and not a single petal wobbled as though about to fall to the ground.

George had found the hidden tree on the map. Fern made the connection to the horrid plans of Sir Luxton. What more was she supposed to do?

"It could take months or years to find the hand responsible. I vow to you that I will do everything I can. But I need time." Her hands curled into fists, nails biting into her palms, and she wanted to cry in frustration.

George had been thorough in trying to find an answer to what had happened on that day. There were drawings of the desk, teacup, and even Rowan's final pose. The notebook contained pages of what sounded like interrogations of anyone he could lay a heavy hand on in the surrounding area. The widow who had rented the rooms to Fern's father, which had their own entrance, was questioned at length. As were scholars at the university. Even patrons from the coffee shop across the street and a terrified child running an errand for their mother.

Or that was how Fern imagined the youngster in her mind, when he replied to George's questions with "I didn't see nutin', gov." Under the transcription of the brief conversation was the description *boy, ten or younger, scrawny, sharp glint in his eye.*

Page after page revealed her uncle's methodical investigation. Yet nobody saw anything. Rowan occasionally had a coffee with members of the faculty at the coffee shop, but he was never seen in anyone else's company. No one had been seen entering or leaving his rented apartment. No one bore him any ill will. The lack of any evidence to the contrary was what had convinced George that the weight of Rowan's grief over losing Delphine had finally swept him away.

"It was as though a wraith slipped in through a window and added the poison to your tea." Fern returned to the desk to select the drawing of the cup in question, sitting askew on its saucer as though it had been dropped with careless haste. One thought kept running through her mind, weaving everything together into a strong, metal rope of certainty—everything is connected.

She placed the drawing back on the pile of papers and sat on the chair. With elbows on the desk, she rested her head in her hands. Weariness filled her. As though she were an empty vessel and cold sand was poured into her. It settled in her feet first. Each step took more effort to lift. Now her legs were packed with the damp sand and dragged below her torso. If she dared to jump into the river for a swim, would she sink to the bottom?

On thinking about the spectral orchid, how it worked was rather self-defeating. It drained the life from the closest relative—the one person who was most likely to know why the spirit had awoken. But once the fatigue settled into your bones and mind, how were you supposed to figure out the reason before your essence was siphoned away?

"It's cheating," she muttered to the notebook. "The touch of a beloved one should give you mental clarity and insight so you can solve the mystery." She would consult both the alchemist and the witches if there was a way to alter the touch of the orchid.

The situation seemed hopeless, but she refused to give up. What she needed were reinforcements. Luckily, it was Sunday, which meant Millie and Alice, along with Squib, were expected for dinner. Fern gathered up all the papers and the notebook and carried them through to the dining room. She laid them out and then fetched her father's journal, the map of kelmsgale trees, and fresh paper and pencils.

Then she ventured into the kitchen, a dangerous mission when Mrs Bentley was preparing the Sunday meal for both households.

"Whatever are you up to?" Mrs Bentley asked from her spot at the bench. Lucy helped her peel vegetables for the evening meal.

Fern stopped out of lunging distance of the long knife. "I need help to figure out what happened to Father, and I plan to enlist everyone before dinner." The meal time was still a good couple of hours away, and they would need something to sustain their endeavours until then. "Could I trouble you for tea, coffee, and something to nibble?"

"Lucy can put the kettle on, if you can set out the tray. I have my hands full here." Mrs Bentley waved the blade.

"Of course." Fern set out the tray with cups, mugs, and plates while Lucy warmed the teapot.

By the time everyone gathered, a summer rain had set in outside. Fat droplets smashed against the panes and slid down, leaving silver trails. Fern herded her family along the hallway. Eurydice sulked in the stables, as she couldn't be included.

"What are we looking for?" Millie asked after she had been ushered into the cosy dining room. Before taking a seat, she plucked a drawing from those laid out and held it up to study.

"Anything that might hint at who killed my father. I think we can safely say that Mr Plummer was not a mild-mannered assassin, given his eternal guilt at merely being present when a dragonet died." Fern poured tea for her friend and dropped in a slice of lemon before passing it across the table.

Lucy had carried through a pot of tea, one of coffee, and a plate of scones to fuel their task. Squib navigated around the scattered papers and finally settled with his back against the teapot, warming his hide against the porcelain.

George found a large sheet of paper and on it wrote dates and times as they reviewed every scrap of information. Next, he set out a map of Oxford and pushed in a pin where Rowan had taken rooms. Soon, they had a path drawn of what her father had done and where he went in his last few days. Millie used a deep red ink to draw arrows to the names of people whom he spoke to. A blue trail was drawn over a map, showing his known movements.

After two hours, the pots were empty and the plate of scones had been reduced to crumbs, and several more sheets of paper were added to the pile. But they were no closer to an answer. Squib strolled across the map, following in Rowan Oakby's footsteps and stopping on the square that marked his rooms and final location.

"We have gone over and over those last few days and... nothing. What are we missing?" Fern leaned back in her chair and turned to watch the droplets hitting the window.

The thrum of rain outside was accompanied by the soft clang of copper pots as Mrs Bentley and her youngest put the finishing touches to dinner in the kitchen.

The familiar sounds of the household routine were broken by Millie. "The beginning." Her voice was tentative.

"What do you mean, dear?" Ambrose smiled at her in an encouraging fashion.

Millie gestured to the paper mountain of notes. "What we have here is the culmination of a story. But where are its origins? What called Mr Oakby to Oxford in the first place?"

Fern stared at her friend with her jaw slack, while her tired mind struggled to recall the weeks and days before her father had announced his trip.

"Have I said something wrong?" Millie shrank into herself.

"No! On the contrary. You are a genius." Fern jumped to her feet as excitement fizzed under her skin and revived her senses. "We have been looking at this all wrong. As you rightly suggest, Father didn't go off on a whim. He knew exactly what he was looking for in the archives at Oxford."

"Someone wrote to him," George said when Ambrose's frown deepened.

Ambrose's eyes widened, and then he stood and gestured

to the ceiling. "There's an old chest. Up there. After Rowan passed, I stowed away all of his old correspondence."

Fern dared to grasp a tiny tendril of hope—the answer she sought might have been gathering dust in the attic the whole time.

CHAPTER 25

GEORGE WAVED Millie and Fern away when they tried to rush to the door. "We can't all fit up the attic stairs. I'll fetch it."

To keep their hands busy, instead, the pair cleared the table of empty cups and carried them through to the kitchen. Returning to the dining room, they made neat piles of the papers and journals on the sideboard. Mrs Bentley had gestured to the dinner about to be served, so they needed room to eat on the oval walnut table.

They had wrestled the room into order, and steaming plates of dinner were waiting when George returned, carrying a tin trunk about a foot long and eight inches deep.

He placed it on the floor before the window and then stepped back, letting Fern lift the brass latch to reveal the contents. A cloud of dust wafted upwards, and Squib, who had been leaning over it from his perch on the hanging candelabra, sneezed and flapped his wings, which sent him and the light fitting rocking backwards.

Within were bundles of letters, their ribbons sun-bleached and with folds as brittle as moth wings. Piles of invoices, florid invitations, and the heavy cream of society notepaper. Tiny, folded notes, no more than three inches square and that would fit into the palm of Fern's hand, were scented with lavender.

"Those are from Mother." Fern picked one up and inhaled the aroma that still lingered, despite the passage of years. "She always wrote one and tucked it into Father's luggage when he travelled."

Those private moments between the couple were reverently placed to one side. For the rest, they carried them to the table and worked through a delicious dinner of pie and vegetables. Ambrose read addresses. George scanned senders and dates. Millie scrutinised handwriting, looking for a slash of a pen that spoke of a conspiracy. Fern skimmed the contents for anything odd.

Halfway through the trunk, Millie halted and held up a particular letter. "This is different from the others. The paper is an expensive sort, and there is a...deliberateness about the penmanship."

A thick ivory sheet lay in her hand. A deep-blue stain remained where a wax seal had been prised off. The script inside was slanted like goose tracks through snow—precise, impatient, and with a rich navy ink that possessed a faint shimmer.

Fern's voice wavered as she took the letter from Millie's outstretched hand and read:

"Mr Oakby—

Further to our previous correspondence..."

Here she stopped to glance at her companions, but the shake of heads told her that no other letter in the chest matched the one in her hands.

"—*Have you ever considered the hypothesis that the so-called mythical flora recorded in Barlett's 1572 catalogue were not inventions at all but records of extinct or exceedingly rare specimens? The veil of myth might be nothing but a clever disguise for things not meant for the average man. Take, for example, the rumours of...*"

She had to pause again, skimming ahead as her heart beat faster. "*—rumours of another variety of kelmsgale that has hitherto been unknown to your colleagues in the Botanical Society.*"

George blew out a whistle. "Someone dropped a rather large hint into Rowan's lap and ignited his curiosity."

"What botanist could resist if there is the smallest chance that a mythical compendium actually contains rare specimens waiting to be rediscovered?" Ambrose leaned in to peer at the letter over Fern's shoulder. "Who is our mystery correspondent who set your father on a path to Oxford?"

Fern held up the page. The correspondence ended abruptly at an exposed edge where the bottom third of the sheet had been ripped away. "Whatever name there was is gone. I wonder if there was information that Father needed to direct his search. Although I don't know why he tore it off and didn't take the entire letter."

Or perhaps he left a clue, in case he never returned.

Throughout dinner, they continued their examination of every letter, invoice, and card. By the time Mrs Bentley carried through the cheese and coffee, the entire contents of the chest had passed through everyone's hands without revealing any further clues.

Fern stared at the torn sheet of paper. Did the hand that held the quill also tip the poison into her father's tea? She scratched in her mind, trying to think of ways to figure that out. "We need handwriting samples from everyone associated with Sir Luxton. I have a theory that this will match one. Do we have ears in his household yet?" She turned to Ambrose.

"My sources are trying, but he's rather a suspicious fellow. It's almost as if he has something to hide. We have someone who may be suitable, but it is taking time." Ambrose reached out and squeezed Fern's hand.

She sucked in her lip and told herself that she would not cry, no matter how tired and frustrated she became on the inside. "I need those samples as soon as possible. Please, Ambrose."

"You're not getting them anytime soon," George said, and he rose from his chair.

The shadows in the room elongated as he walked the length of the table and stopped in front of the door. A chill whispered down Fern's spine as the atmosphere in the room became heavier. George crossed his arms and blocked the exit.

Fern eyed the window. Why did people think doors were the only way into and out of a room?

"We might..." she started, glancing at her uncle for help.

"We are running out of time," he murmured. "As much as we loved Rowan, we have no intention of losing you."

"You won't lose me. We will find the answer...it is in here, and we are a step closer with tonight's discovery. I am sure of it. All we need is a little time." She gestured to the stack of papers on the sideboard and the letter by her plate.

"Which we don't have." George narrowed his gaze. Then his eyes softened. "We're not giving up on finding the answer, Fern. But if this letter isn't enough to send Rowan back to the other side, we won't let him drain you to death."

"Please, Fern." Millie's eyes were round with concern, and her voice a mere rasp. Squib flew to her and trilled in agreement. The pixie dragon glared at Fern for daring to cause his mistress distress.

A tired sigh heaved through Fern. They were right. Of course. Today marked six days. If the petals hadn't fallen from the orchid when she awoke tomorrow, she would only have the same number of days as she did fingers on one hand. She screwed up her eyes to stop the tears that burned. "I know, but..."

"We have spoken to the witches. They have brewed the necessary potion." Ambrose rested a hand on her shoulder. Lightly. As though not wanting to add to her burden.

"But if we do that, Father will be banished, never able to reach out again. Nor do we know what it will do to his soul on the other side. What if he is separated from Mother forever, torn apart, or something equally awful happens to him?" A tear leaked from one corner of her eye, and she wiped it away.

George strode across the room and lifted her from the chair in a bear hug. "Rowan would do it to save you."

After squeezing, he released her to Ambrose, and she was folded into a softer embrace.

"I can't, Uncle Ambrose. Please don't make me." Her voice turned to a whisper, and the tears flowed freely.

Ambrose stroked her hair. "We will wait as long as we can, dear child. But even the clue we found this evening still does not answer the question of who was responsible. And you are fading before our eyes much quicker than we anticipated. It must be done before we cannot sever the connection."

Fern nodded, unable to talk as sobs heaved through her. She had failed, and her father might be lost for eternity once they banished his spirit back to the other side. The bloom would wither, but there would be no obsidian tears. Only a brown, foul-smelling mush would be left.

"I'll do it. Tomorrow. I promise. If you'll give Father one more day. Perhaps he wanted us to find the letter, and the petals will fall from the orchid now." *Give me one more day of his presence within these walls* was her unspoken plea.

"Of course, Fern. Let us see what tomorrow brings. Why don't you walk Millie home and clear your mind?" Ambrose rubbed her back and let her go.

She pulled a handkerchief from a pocket and wiped her eyes before blowing her nose.

Once the fabric was shoved back away, Millie laced her fingers with Fern's. "Let's have a quiet stroll."

Alice was still visiting with her mother and younger sister and said she would follow later since her older brother had offered to escort her back to the bookstore. Outside, Squib sat on Millie's shoulder, and Eurydice joined them to pad at Fern's side.

In silence, they walked along the driveway and out onto

the road. An owl hooted in the trees, and leaves rustled as it flew close to the foliage on its evening hunt.

"This isn't an end to your quest, Fern. Only an obstacle to overcome. We will discover who murdered your father. Together." Millie leaned in close and rested her head on Fern's shoulder for a moment.

"Thank you." This wasn't how she wanted events to unfold when one of her parents touched the orchid. But Millie was right. They had a direction now, and the search for those responsible would continue—whether or not her father's spirit roamed the halls of their home.

Fern tipped her head back. The night sky was unobscured by clouds, and stars twinkled like diamonds thrown against velvet. What would it be like to drift among the stars? Would it be warm, like floating in a bath, or were stars cold like precious gems? "It's so beautiful out here."

"And quiet," Millie added. "I think the whole time I was in London, I could barely hear myself think. There is a clarity in Drake's Bend that has soothed my mind like a gently rocking boat at sea."

"I am glad to hear it. Does that mean there will be a new instalment in the tale of the roguish highwaywoman?" She bumped her friend with her shoulder.

With the sombre mood broken, they chatted for the rest of their walk, and once at Scribbles, Fern waited until Millie had lit a lamp before she turned to head back to Nemython House. Eurydice appeared to have no difficulty in managing their walk in the dark. It eased a little of the pain in Fern's heart to see how much the creature had improved over the last few weeks.

"You will be too big for a stall by the end of the year," she said to the growing dragon.

After seeing her companion settled in the straw and with her favourite blanket pulled over her wings, Fern sought her own bed. This time, she fell into a dreamless sleep as soon as her cheek touched the pillow.

THE FIRST THING Fern did in the morning was rush downstairs to the spectral orchid. The plant stubbornly clung to its perfectly white bloom.

"I think, Father, you have a somewhat unrealistic expectation of how much I can achieve in a few days," she said to the spirit that lingered just out of her vision. Or had her father watched from the other side and thought five years was ample for her to fully investigate, and this was him giving her the final push? The problem was that it would be a *final* touch from her father if she failed in her task.

She picked at her breakfast and tried to ignore the worried glances her uncles exchanged. "I'll go see the Moray sisters after breakfast," she muttered to no one in particular.

"Will we hold the ceremony here or at the cemetery?" Ambrose asked. "Indoors or outdoors affects what I wear."

Fern wondered if the Ladies' Handbook provided guidelines on what a young woman should wear when banishing a soul. She thought dark colours would be most appropriate, or mourning wear. "I will ask the sisters. It might need to be where the orchid is flowering."

There was much she wanted to ask the sisters when she collected the brew to banish a soul, like what would happen to her father. Would he be reunited with her mother, or did something awful happen to spirits who failed to have their business resolved?

After clearing her dishes, Fern grabbed an old coat from a hook and shrugged it on as she walked through the garden. Eurydice called out to her and waddled over from where she had been lounging under a tree.

"I'm going to see the Moray sisters, but I might be a while. Do you want to come?" Kneeling down, Fern rubbed her cheek against the dragon's. The contact helped soothe the grief battering her insides.

The dragon trilled and fell into step beside Fern. Across the river and along the road, they found the three old women all seated outside, as though they had been waiting for her to pay a visit. Which Fern supposed they had since George and Ambrose had asked them for the spirit eviction potion to sever the connection to the spectral orchid.

All three had their faces set in tight lines, as though they had argued recently.

"Hello," Fern called out. "You all have a sombre air for such a beautiful day." She took Morda's hand and helped the seer to her feet.

"Death is a serious business," Nona muttered as she led the way inside.

Eurydice didn't fit through the cottage's narrower door, a sign of her continued growth. Instead, she curled up in the morning sun on the doorstep, like a rather large cat. Her placement also meant Fern couldn't leave without her, as she would trip over the slumbering creature.

"You know why I'm here. George said he asked you to brew what is needed." Fern's feet dragged as she approached the embers of the fire that heated their stove. She rubbed at her arms, not realising how chilled her flesh was until she moved inside and away from the caress of the sun.

"We prepared another way." Decima glanced at her older sister.

"No," Nona's refusal came quickly and firmly.

Fern sank into her favourite cushion on the floor. Despite the fact she had only risen from her bed an hour or two ago, she wanted to curl into the softness like a puppy and drift back to sleep, warmed by the fire.

"It does not matter if you agree or not. Either way, she is lost." Morda gestured at their visitor.

Some old argument spun around the room, and Fern had the distinct feeling she was at the centre of it. She pushed off the squishy pillow and sat up. Her tired brain lagging a few minutes behind in the conversation. "What do you mean, another way?"

"Before we banish Rowan back to the spirit realm, there is a way to seek an answer from him." Decima approached Nona with a determined set to her shoulders.

That idea swept away some of Fern's fatigue. Her mind perked up at the prospect of her father being able to answer questions. Or just one rather important one. "Would it give Father a voice?"

"It's too dangerous." Nona crossed her arms and glared at

her younger siblings. Normally, they respected her leadership, but dissent had been sown in their ranks.

"We must show her the path. It is her choice if she walks it or not, not ours," Morda spoke with a firm tone and smacked her fist into her other palm.

"You are outvoted this time, Nona. And part of you must agree, for you helped us prepare the spell." Decima softened and laid a hand on her sister's arm.

"Very well. But she must know of the dangers before her." Nona turned her sharp gaze to Fern.

"What exactly are you expecting me to do?" How much would she risk to speak to her father again?

Almost everything.

CHAPTER 26

Decima moved to sit on a chair beside Fern. "There is a potion that will work somewhat like the spectral mist. While the mist creates a shadow of the spirit in our realm, this brew will allow you to become one in their realm."

To be a shadow...in the spirit realm? Fern tried to imagine what that would be like.

Nona stabbed a finger into the air. "Except if you dwell too long, you won't be able to return. Like a shadow at noon, you will disappear from our world."

That did seem risky. But she didn't need a long conversation with her father. All she needed was enough time to ask *who murdered you?* And for him to shout a name in response.

"That's why you needed the stamen of the lunanavis." Now Decima's request for the valuable ingredient made sense.

The middle sister nodded, her eyes bright. "We have made the potion. All you have to do is wait for the gloaming and use it. If you dare."

"The choice is yours, Fern. You do not have to walk the shadow path to their realm, for there is another way." Nona held out a bottle with a golden hue. "This will sever his connection to this world and send him back to his eternal slumber, without any harm to you."

Fern could imagine George scowling at her from a corner. She knew what her uncles would choose—the option that posed the least danger to her. But what if she spent years trying to match the handwriting on the letter to someone in Sir Luxton's circle and never found the answer she sought?

The idea of her father's killer never being brought to justice sat like a block of ice inside her. While instinct shouted that someone in Sir Luxton's employ had sent the letter to her father, she had no way of discovering who had committed the fatal act. The sisters offered her an opportunity to guide her search that might never occur again. Besides, she wouldn't need to be a shadow in the spirit realm for terribly long.

Decision made, she met Morda's milky, all-seeing gaze. "What do I need to do?"

The three women huddled around Fern and explained the steps she had to follow. Nona scowled her disapproval the entire time and issued dire warnings if she lingered too long in the realm not yet meant for her. Even Decima gripped her hands tightly as she handed over the bottle.

"We would prefer you to come back to us," she whispered.

Before she left, Fern took both of Morda's hands in her own and waited. At this point, the seer usually uttered something cryptic and scary-sounding. Instead, she grinned and stroked Fern's cheek. "It is time to fly."

Fern kissed her wrinkled cheek and kept her silence. The poor thing was far gone if she couldn't tell the difference between Fern and Eurydice. But the words gave her hope. Her friend would fly. Soon.

Outside, Eurydice shook herself like a dog awaking from a snooze, and she chirped in a questioning tone.

"I have to return home and lie to my uncles." She tucked the bottle and a bowl into her satchel.

She hoped she would encounter Ambrose because if he were distracted, he wouldn't press her too much. George could spot an untruth at a hundred paces and would drag the true story from her.

Eurydice watched the fish in the pond while Fern popped inside. Her uncle by blood was in the parlour, working on a story at the small writing desk.

"What did our witches have to say?" he asked, with only a quick glance over his shoulder.

"It will be more effective if the three of them do the cere-mony. I am going back tonight with Riddy to watch. They thought after nightfall would be the best time for it." Fern hated deceiving her uncle, but if they knew what was in her satchel, it would be confiscated for her safety.

Better to ask forgiveness than permission, she reasoned. Tomorrow, she would confess what she had done. "Decima said something about everyone having to be naked under the moon for the banishment to work quicker."

Ambrose shuddered at whatever image those words conjured in his mind. "Yes, well...umm...to ensure Rowan's soul is reunited with Delfie, perhaps it is best we leave the sisters to weave their witchy motes without any men present."

Fern swallowed a smile. Her plan would work. "I'm going to visit Millie and thought I would have supper with her to keep myself occupied until then."

That part was true. There was nothing she could do until twilight, and the bookstore and her friend would keep her mind from dwelling on what might happen. She had considered not telling Millie what she intended to do, but that was one deception too far for Fern. Besides, she was fairly certain the writer would fully endorse her journey to the spirit realm. The biggest problem would be stopping Millie from trying to join her.

Outside, Eurydice paced in the garden as though the creature sensed what Fern intended to do that night. She butted her head against Fern's thigh, as if saying they were in this together.

Fern rested her free hand on the dragon's head. "I don't think I could do this without you."

They took the cart into the village. As Eurydice grew stronger, Fern waned, and she wasn't sure that she could manage the distance. At Scribbles, the dragon wedged her body in the kitchen doorway and called out for Squib. Alice startled at the unexpected visitor and nearly dropped the warm loaf in her hands. Fern waited until the dragon companions were happily chatting in the sunshine before apologising to the maid and then slipping through to the main room.

"Fern!" Millie called from along a stack, where she had an armload of books. "Did the petals fall from the orchid?"

"No. It seems my father's spirit is not satisfied yet." She leaned on the bookcase for support as weariness dragged at her body.

"He will be banished, then?" Millie's hand paused mid-task, a book dangling a mere inch before the shelf.

"Only if my other plan doesn't work."

One book was shoved into the waiting slot, and the other books in Millie's arms were deposited on a stool. The writer took Fern's hand and tugged her towards the conservatory and then into an armchair. "Tell me everything."

After explaining what she would do to an enraptured audience (as Fern had suspected, Millie was excited about the prospect of venturing into the spirit realm and terribly disappointed she'd not be going), Fern moved to the chaise and stretched out on the cushioned length. "I'm just going to have a wee snooze. Can you keep an eye on Eurydice, please?"

"Of course." Millie tucked a woollen blanket over Fern and crept away.

A HAND SHOOK Fern's shoulder, and she tried to swat it away.

"Dusk is approaching, and you've been asleep all day," Millie said, close to Fern's ear.

She sat up, her mind foggy, and her thoughts slowed.

"Dusk?" Impossible. It had been mid-morning when she curled up in the sun. How could she have slept the day away?

The world came into focus, and two violet eyes stared at her without blinking. Squib balanced on Millie's shoulder and puffed cool air in Fern's face.

"Thank you, Squib," she murmured and rubbed his head. She had to act before her body could no longer be roused from the spectral-induced slumber. "The horse..."

"I went to the forge before I roused you. Benjamin is bringing him over now." Millie's eyes wrinkled in concern as Fern leaned on the arm of the chaise to rise.

By the time Fern grabbed her satchel and they left the bookstore, the blacksmith was standing on the lawn holding the reins of the placid cob. He arched a worried eyebrow as Fern leaned a little too heavily upon Millie for support.

"I am taking her home," Millie said as Fern climbed onto the seat.

Benjamin nodded and, with his usual taciturn silence, helped Eurydice into the back. Once their little party was settled, Fern took up the reins. She managed a smile and a wave to reassure the blacksmith before they set off. The well-trained horse knew the road, and Fern had to do little once she turned his nose in the right direction. They didn't talk on the short journey north, both women wrapped in their own thoughts. Even the dragons held their tongues.

At the cemetery, an eerie quiet blanketed the meadow. While not a place that saw much in the way of loud conversation, birds and the rustling of leaves made a constant murmur of activity, especially with the advent of dusk. This afternoon, Nature held her breath. Watching.

They left the cart by the tunnel of trees, with the reins looped around the brake and the horse content to snooze in the shade. The group walked to the stone-carved tree that marked a spot at the forest's edge. Fern touched her parents' gravestone and then sat on the grass to one side. Eurydice sank to the ground and turned wide silver eyes to her.

"What shall we do?" Millie asked, knitting her fingers together to keep them still.

"Watch over me, please." *And raise the alarm if I don't come back* was the unspoken request.

Millie and Squib sat on the other side of the grave. Fern drew forth a metal bowl and settled it in the grass, adjusting the container until it sat level. Then she pushed a little weight through her hands into the bottom to make sure it had a supportive depression. She might also have been playing a little for time, as butterflies had erupted in her stomach at the enormity of what she was about to do. Drawing the bottle from her satchel next, she held the bottle in both hands. The sisters told her to wait until a soft golden light swept over the cemetery and then edged into a deeper amber as the gloaming approached.

"Now or never." Fern unstopped the bottle and poured the entire contents into the wide and shallow container.

It flowed almost transparent with the faintest blue tinge against the tin of the bowl. Just before the bottle was emptied, the silver lunanavis stamen emerged and plopped into the liquid. Fern put the bottle to one side and watched as the stamen drifted a little this way and then that before settling in the exact middle with one end pointing at her.

She had read of spells that could be cast with the rare

ingredient. One told that it would point to what your heart desired most. There were echoes of that in her instructions from the witches. Gripping the bowl on either side, Fern closed her eyes and leaned over the surface. A tang rose from the liquid, sharp like lemon and a salt-laden ocean breeze, and it teased out old memories of a family trip to the seaside.

In her mind, she pictured her father as she had last seen him. Excited for his stay in Oxford and to research the medieval manuscripts in the library. She recalled the warmth of his hug as he reassured her that he would only be gone for ten days at the most. Not a lifetime.

Tears burned with the wave of grief that flowed through her. Only now did she open her eyes and stare at the bowl. Her face bent over the surface as instructed. The needle-like stamen began a slow rotation.

Then, before Fern could wonder if it would point to where her father's spirit hovered, the piece of dried flower... dissolved. It bled into the liquid like a swirl of silver, creating a tightly drawn spiral with each revolution until nothing of it remained. This was the point the sisters had told her to wait for, couched in the slightly cryptic terms of *when the transformation was complete* and that *she'd know it when it happened.*

"Now." She breathed out the single word. Cupping her hands together, Fern scooped up the silvery, mercury-like substance, lowered her head closer, and washed it over her face.

The instant the moonlight-filled liquid touched her skin, it was as though Fern had drawn a velvet bag over her head. The world disappeared, and she let out a gasp of fright.

"Riddy!" A slight panic entered her voice as utter darkness enclosed her.

The dragon butted her head under Fern's elbow. A human hand, Millie, gripped her forearm. Fern's breathing eased as the panic subsided. Her friends were with her, and she was not alone.

Second by second, her vision adjusted. Night embraced her, but one with no stars or moon above. The trees were pale-grey skeletons that seemed to waver in and out as though they exhaled. Something in her chest tugged. Fern rubbed at the point but could see nothing. She assumed this was the guiding thread that would lead her to her father. When the sisters told her of the spell, she had assumed, wrongly, that the stamen would float in the bowl forming a compass, and she had only to follow where it pointed.

She rose to her feet, and the world lurched underneath her. Millie was a ghostly shadow plucked from a gothic novel. Squib had become a bright violet spark on her shoulder. Eurydice glowed like a polished pearl with flickers of mossy green and pale blue. The dragon trilled and flapped her wings, her gaze tracking Fern's movement.

"I'll not be long," Fern promised.

Then she took a few steps. The tugging pulled her first one way, and then another if she veered off course. She kept her hands out in front of her, not wanting to walk into a gravestone or tree. Her footsteps kept a rhythm with her heartbeat. Shapes flowed around her, some flying or darting through the air. Others were massive, the size of elephants, as they disappeared at the corner of her eye.

In her mind, Fern held tight to the image of her father to

navigate by her desire to find him. How far had she gone? Her feet moved, and the ghostly trees rearranged themselves, but she had no sense of crossing the meadow or reaching the road through the tunnel.

"Father?" she called out.

Was this what a spirit experienced in the human realm? A feeling of being lost in the dark, yet driven forwards by a connection to a living person. With each step, a chill swept over her. First, it settled on her skin, then seeped deeper to reach her bones. When her jaw began to ache from the cold, the first tendril of fear wound through her. What if she didn't find him and searched for too long? With no moon or stars or any way to judge the passage of time, how did she know when to return?

In hindsight, she should have asked how time moved for the dead. It could be like the Fae realm, and a few moments were days in her world. She tried to shake off the idea before the fear paralysed her.

"Father!" Fern shouted, louder this time. He had been dead for five years, after all.

"Fern." A familiar voice whispered the single word in answer to her cry.

CHAPTER 27

FERN NEARLY SOBBED in relief as the thread connected to her chest snapped tight, like a thrown anchor that sank into solid rock. In front of her and between two broad ghostly trees, a black curtain shimmered. Only the slight glint from whatever ethereal fabric made it even hinted that it was there —stretched between trunks.

"Father? Is it really you?" She reached out a hand but didn't touch the veil made of inky night.

"Fern," he whispered again.

"I didn't come this far to not be brave," she muttered to herself. Then, with arms outstretched, she pushed on the curtain. Her hands were immersed in something like water, but thicker. It flowed over her skin, and she became... translucent.

Before she could doubt her actions, Fern drew a breath (was she even breathing here?) and shoved her whole body through the odd drape that separated the living from the dead.

Like plunging into frigid water, shock hit her lungs. Fern gasped, but no noise left her lips. Gritting her teeth, she pressed onwards and stepped through the shimmering mist. A sob broke free as before her stood an achingly familiar shape who beckoned her towards him.

Her father's form flickered like candlelight in a draft before he backed away, pointing frantically behind her. His mouth moved in urgent, soundless words she couldn't decipher. The thread in her chest, now a visible red strand like unwound wool that ran in two directions, hummed in warning.

Fern spun around as the ground beneath her spectral feet dissolved. What had seemed like solid earth moments before now revealed itself as a writhing mass of shadow-serpents. Their forms constantly shifted between liquid darkness and writhing coils. She stumbled backwards, but there was nowhere to go. The serpents rose around her like a tide. Eyeless heads seeking. Always seeking.

One brushed against her translucent ankle and immediately began to spiral around her leg. Wherever it touched, a pulling sensation tugged at spectral Fern. As though the creatures tried to drain something essential from her very core. The red thread grew brighter and frantic in its pulsing. With horror, Fern realised the serpents were drawn to it—to the very lifeline that tethered her to the living world.

"No, no, no. This is bad," she whispered, but no sound emerged.

She tried to run, but her ghostly feet slid a few inches above the undulating ground. More serpents wound around her waist, reaching for the thread that marked her as an intruder in the realm of the dead.

"I'm sorry, Riddy." Fern gritted her teeth as panic threatened to overwhelm.

Then came a screech like an angry bird of prey. It sliced through the endless night and struck the serpents like a physical blow. They let go of Fern with angry hisses and recoiled, creating a narrow path free of their intertwined bodies.

She didn't hesitate. Fern plunged forward, letting the tendril of red guide her. Behind her, the serpents regrouped and blocked the path. Not that she wanted to go that way. She strained to see anything up ahead. A faint glow turned into the sparkle of moonlight on water and formed a gently arching bridge made of glass that spanned the chasm.

Now, Fern hesitated. The glass structure looked insubstantial and unable to take her weight. Nor did it have any means of support to keep it suspended over the black void below. Peering into the dark, Fern could just make out the flickering shape of her father. He seemed further away now, as though he continued to retreat as she advanced. The thread keeping a constant tension.

Drawing a breath (did she even need to breathe as a shadow in the underworld?), she placed one foot on the bridge. A high-pitched ring shot up through her body and made her bones ache. Each step elicited a different, soundless tone that reverberated through every part of her. With growing dread, she wondered if the bridge was summoning something in the impenetrable depths below.

From the chasm rose a shadow that was blacker than black. Only its movement made it visible. It flowed under the bridge, and fingers like tree trunks wrapped around the fragile sides. The thread in her chest stretched taut, and her connection to the living world strained to the point of snapping.

Fern paused, glanced down through the walkway, and gasped. An image shimmered below her from five years ago. That younger version of Fern sobbed over the fresh soil of her father's grave. Every tear shed since his death, the years of sorrow, had weighted her form. An ear-splitting crack came from under her feet. Spider web fractures radiated out from where she stood as the ache inside her that longed for her parents became a physical thing that tried to pull her into the abyss.

How easy it would be to fall into sadness.

"Not grief. Joy." She fought one with the other. Recalling happy moments with her father in the garden at first light. Laughter-filled days. Memories of the three of them.

The fractures stopped. The shadow hands shook the bridge, and it swayed.

"Time to move." Fern kicked herself into action and drew her gaze away from the woman who would mourn for eternity in the inky void.

Wrapping herself in memories of her father's love, she kept walking. Step by precarious step, she made her way across the swinging bridge. At last, she reached the other side and stepped onto the edge of a cliff. Before her clustered a grove of tall, silver trees. Their luminous forms reminded her of *Betula jacquemontii*, with its dazzling white bark. Beneath the largest tree stood her father.

Tears spilt down her cheeks as she reached out to touch

him, but her hand passed through his torso. Only then did she remember the warning from the sisters. She would be a shadow in their world, just as a spirit was but an echo in theirs. She had risked so much but couldn't touch her father. Balling her hands into fists, she let out a short, sharp burst of frustrated anger.

Rowan held up one hand, motioning for her to be patient. The same gesture he used when they had crouched in the garden, waiting for a rabbit to venture out from under a shrub.

His mouth shaped a word, and it reached Fern's ears after a few seconds' delay. "Time."

She understood. Sand tumbled through her hourglass. While part of her wanted to stay with her father and move deeper into the celestial forest to find her mother, an odd, empty pang shot through her. If she stayed, she would miss her uncles, Millie, Eurydice, and Squib. Not to mention all the other inhabitants of Drake's Bend. Was she really ready to let go of her life?

No. She wouldn't stay, but she needed an answer.

Only here, standing (or slightly hovering) before her father, did she voice the secret worry that resided deep inside her. "Please tell me that you were killed, and you didn't choose to leave me behind?"

In size, she shrank until she was merely a child, pleading not to be abandoned by her parents. She understood the fierce love they shared and the gaping hole the death of Delphine left inside her father. But couldn't he have waited a little longer before joining her?

A shake of his head. No. He didn't go willingly.

A sob of relief tore through Fern. She had always known it but had wavered in that belief even after they found the letter with its tantalising hint of a mythical tree. "Who? Please, Father, tell me who."

He reached out, his hands on either side of her face. While she couldn't touch him or feel flesh, her heart warmed, and the beat eased as though her father had wrapped her in a comforting embrace.

The void around Fern shifted into shades of lighter grey, as though she watched a shadow play. Her father sat at a desk in the small townhouse he had taken in Oxford while doing his research. The light was dim at the room's only window, and a lantern burned on the corner of his desk. Before him lay open the battered notebook. Beside him, a thick book, and he followed a line of text with his left hand. With his right, he appeared to be transcribing something from the old volume into his journal.

He tapped a symbol and let out a whoop as he threw his fist up into the air. "I have found it. *Beatha*. The legends are true."

Fern heard his voice in her mind—clear and firm in his excitement.

Dipping the quill into the inkpot, he scribbled across the page with a feverish energy. Line after line of scrawled analysis. Then he grabbed another pen and a small vial of something yellow. His hand slowed as he sketched a tree on a familiar map. He blew on the brown outline until it faded away. Quickly, he folded up the map and tucked it back into the front of the journal.

Footsteps approached as he drew a familiar tree over the

open page at the back of the journal. His hand stilled. "Your hypothesis was right. It exists."

A tea tray was placed on the corner of the desk, holding a pot and two cups. A chill ran along her limbs. There had only been one cup when her father was discovered. Yet he had not been alone that day. The person remained out of view. A shadow that stood too close to the other shadows cast in the room, and Fern couldn't make out the figure.

"Move into the light," she urged the other person, but the words came out as only puffs of mist.

"A cup of tea. To celebrate your discovery." The voice was quiet and not one she recognised.

Man or woman?

It could have been either. The tone was light but sure. Fern strained all her senses to remember every clue as the scene continued to unfold around her.

"Yes, yes." Rowan waved at the other person. His attention fixed on his work. "All this time it had been so close," he muttered. With a flourish, he added to the drawing.

A cup of tea slid towards his elbow, and absentmindedly, he picked it up and took quick gulps, draining it as though parched.

"No!" Fern yelled. Her throat was tight as tears burned in her spectral eyes. She stretched out a hand, wishing she could move through time and fling the poisoned cup from his hand.

Then he stilled. He stared at the empty contents. "What...?" The cup clattered to the saucer, missing the centre and balancing on one side. "Why...?"

The questions went unanswered. An eternity seemed to

stretch before Fern. Then Rowan slumped over the desk. One hand rose, fingers quivering before falling back down.

The shadow moved to one side and took the notebook. Holding the last few pages together, they ripped them from the book before closing it and setting it under Rowan's elbow.

"A pleasure doing business with you." The shadow folded the papers in half. As they did so, for a brief moment, the hands came into view. A woman's hands. With a distinctive ring on her right hand—a square-cut sapphire in a brilliant blue.

The scene dissolved into the ground, and the all-encompassing night embraced Fern once more.

"Who was she?" she shouted at her father.

But he didn't reply. Instead, he gestured behind her.

Turning, Fern found the glistening bridge had disappeared, swallowed by the monstrous shadow that reached from the void. Darkness raced towards her. She had run out of time.

How she wanted to stay. But couldn't. Her heart tore in two, each jagged part hot with pain. There was so much more she wanted to do before she joined her parents. The blackness approached, and she swayed towards it.

Do not jump unless you can fly. Morda's prophecy echoed in her mind.

"I can't fly," Fern sobbed in fear as she stared at the bottomless space nibbling at her toes. Where had the bridge gone?

"Jump. I will catch you," a voice said. One she didn't recognise but, at the same time, she instinctively trusted.

With one last look at the shimmering form of her father, Fern jumped.

Fear punched up through her as she fell, and fell...

Then, with a thump, there was something solid underneath her. Warmth and love surrounded her. Fern wrapped her arms around a neck and held on tight as they glided across a black velvet ocean.

A WEIGHT PRESSED on Fern's chest, and her lungs struggled to expand as they needed. Cracking one eye open, Eurydice peered at her from only a few inches away. The dragon lay with her head stretched across Fern's torso, and each exhale puffed warmed air over her face. Something solid held her, and she hadn't felt so safe...for a very long time.

"We thought we had lost you," Lord Drakeman rasped.

Where had he come from? Fern tilted her head back to find another dragon eye regarding her. She lay in his arms under the spreading boughs of the trees that sheltered her parents' grave.

"How...I didn't know how to get back. I fell." Her mind was a jumble of images and thoughts.

"Riddy fetched me and led me here. Then she dipped her face in that bowl and stretched across you. I thought you had both gone." His roughened voice caught on the words, and his arms tightened around Fern.

"Riddy fetched you?" Fern glanced around. Where had Millie and Squib gone?

He swallowed, and she found the action of his Adam's apple fascinating from her position. Only then did she notice he wore no cravat or coat, and his waistcoat hung unbuttoned. "She flew and landed on the roof of my laboratory. It's lucky the glass is extra thick, or she would have broken through jumping up and down."

Fern sat up further and gathered the dragon's head in her arms. "You flew? I knew you could." Happy tears rolled down her cheeks, and she rested her face against a warm, scaled one. Realising the young dragon had finally flown made another connection in Fern's overwhelmed mind. "It was you. You caught me."

She didn't know how. She only knew with a certainty deep in her heart that Eurydice had journeyed to the other realm, caught her falling soul, and carried her safely back to the world of the living. "How?"

"All dragons have inherent magic, but it appears that this one has a particular affinity for the spectral realm. Since she has bonded to you, she was able to find you and bring you back. I have read of it in the old journals but never believed it was possible. Until now." The alchemist stretched out a hand as though he intended to pat Eurydice but curled his fingers into his palm before he touched her green and grey hide.

The dragon made a soft cooing noise and closed the gap to press her face into his hand. Instead of withdrawing, he caressed her head, and Eurydice made a happy gurgling sound. A rare smile touched Lord Drakeman's lips. Apparently, all Fern had to do was risk her life and scare her dragon by travelling to the realm of the dead to see the drake man remember how his family were bound to serve dragons. He even seemed to be enjoying the contact.

Thinking of enjoyable things...

"I would like you to kiss me now," Fern said when the moment ended and the drake man stopped petting the dragon.

Fern liked being in his embrace and had little inclination to move. Or at least not until her worried family appeared.

"Would you?" His smile widened.

"Yes. You said you wouldn't kiss me again unless I specifically asked you. So consider this an official request. But I'll not ask twice. The festival is only a few days away. I can certainly find another..."

She didn't get to finish the sentence. Lord Drakeman claimed her lips in a kiss that made her entirely forget what she had been about to say.

Fern slid her hands into his hair, catching the short locks between her fingers as she lifted up to seek more. He was a very good kisser. Perhaps he had many books on the subject in his library. Or etchings in the dim recesses of his laboratory.

"Seth," he murmured as he kissed along her jaw.

"Who?" So much had happened in a short amount of time, and it was all crammed in Fern's head, like the cupboard at the end of the hall no one wanted to open lest it all leap out. As a result, she struggled to make any sense of the events.

"That's my name. Remember? I would like you to use it."

"That seems wholly inappropriate for an employee, Lord Drakeman." Fern tilted her chin and tried to look snooty.

Something that was difficult to achieve while reclining in his arms and grinning from being most thoroughly kissed.

He quirked one eyebrow, and she marvelled at how humour made his dragon eye sparkle like sunlight on water. "So you'll not use my given name?"

"I shall only use that name when I want you to kiss me." Fern pretended to consider the idea, but it was a token protest. Despite the potential risks in embarking upon any sort of *affair* with his lordship, she had decided to embrace the unsettling and decidedly wonderful effect the alchemist had upon her. She wasn't made of stone, after all, and enjoyed the earthy pleasures. She would simply have to exercise caution to ensure no one she cared about was adversely impacted.

His name rolled across her tongue, and mischief gleamed inside her as she said, most deliberately, "Seth."

CHAPTER 28

SETH LOWERED HIS HEAD. Fern quite enjoyed having a secret code word to use when she needed kissing. She suspected the word would get regular usage.

"Fern!" Millie shouted.

They sprang apart, or rather, *Seth* helped her sit up so she wasn't draped over his lap.

The cob came cantering through the tunnel, pulling the bouncing cart laden with her family. Millie held a swaying lantern while George urged the little horse on. A quick snap of the reins and the horse planted its feet and halted by the trees. Only now, as the lantern swung in circles, did Fern notice another horse standing by the trees. The earl must have galloped to the cemetery after Eurydice raised the alarm.

Jumping down, Millie ran ahead of Ambrose and George. Squib flew, emitting short, sharp trills as he veered straight for Fern.

"You're alive!" Millie screeched and flung herself at Fern,

ignoring Lord Drakeman, who ended up being half-hugged at the same time.

"Millie said you had become a ghost." Ambrose wrung his hands, and George took up the abandoned lantern to cast them all in bright yellow light.

"I said you wouldn't have been so bloody stupid." George frowned at her.

"I did what I had to and, as you can see, I am fine." Fern took Millie's hands and rose on unsteady feet.

Lord Drakeman stood and remained by the tree-shaped headstone.

Ambrose hugged Fern tightly, and George encircled them both with strong arms.

"How could you?" Ambrose asked and lightly tapped Fern's shoulder in reproach.

"I had to try. Father was murdered by a woman with an unusual sapphire ring. And I'm going to find her." Fern escaped her uncle's embrace.

"You saw him?" Millie pressed closer while one hand scrambled for a pocket.

Fern laughed. "I will tell you everything. But right now, I have a splitting headache and desperately need a cup of tea. It's not easy traversing the spirit realm." She turned to Lord Drakeman, who was about to retreat into the shadows. "You will join us, won't you, Lord Drakeman? We all want to hear how Riddy flew to fetch you."

Gasps came from Millie and Ambrose. George grunted in surprise. Eurydice trilled and flapped a few feet off the ground.

Seth, because she could only think of him by that name

now, turned to stare at the hovering dragon, and a snort came from the stallion tied to a nearby tree. For the length of a pause between heartbeats, Fern thought he would refuse.

He glanced at her, and the wicked smile still lingered on his lips. "I thank you, Miss Oakby, for the invitation. I would be delighted to join you and tell my tale."

Only now did she consider exactly how much of what transpired he would tell her family.

Ambrose helped Millie into the cart before climbing next to her and taking the reins. Fern declined Lord Drakeman's offer to ride before him, bareback, on the snorting stallion. The idea of being pressed and jiggled against his chest for the short journey to Nemython House made her skin heat in uncomfortable ways. Instead, she sat in the back of the cramped cart with George. Eurydice, having discovered she could fly, appeared not to want to touch the ground ever again. She circled the cemetery, further alarming the fractious stallion, and shot upwards with a few strong upbeats once they moved through the tunnel.

Back at Nemython House, Ambrose bundled them all into the parlour, except the dragons—Eurydice was exhausted and Squib chose to curl up with his friend in the stables. George stopped in the kitchen to ask Mrs Bentley to kindly brew tea and coffee. By the time he entered the room, his life partner was already pouring out generous fingers of whisky. Fern curled up on a sofa with Millie. A quick glance at the orchid confirmed that, at last, her father was satisfied. The petals browned at the edges like leaves succumbing to autumn. By morning, they would have fallen to the marble top of the plinth.

Fern began the story, telling of how she pushed through the eerie veil to become a shadow in the realm of the dead and the terrible things that had reached for her from the thick darkness. Then she narrated the vision her father shared and the distinctive ring on the hand that had placed the teacup by Rowan's elbow.

"Jewellery can be as unique as a signature. It will not take my eyes and ears in London long to find the piece—and its owner," Ambrose said. His eyes were bright at finally having an active role to play in hunting the killer.

Then Lord Drakeman told of how Eurydice had landed on his glass roof and jumped up and down until he raced outside. She flew overhead, calling out in alarm as he ran across the meadow, grabbed his horse from the stables, and galloped down the long driveway.

At Fern's side, the young dragon had dipped her face into the silver bowl and lay down across her friend.

"How amazing," Millie gasped. "To think she flew to find you and caught your soul as you tumbled through nothingness." The writer had her little notebook in hand, and she was scribbling the ideas spiralling in her mind.

"You said Riddy had an affinity for the spirit realm. What does that mean?" Fern asked Seth.

"Some dragons have stronger magic in particular areas. The scales of the dragon I used in the potion to heal the villagers, for example, were given by a healer dragon. Their scales make any spells or potions to heal or mend people stronger and more effective." Seth lounged in an armchair, one foot crossed over his knee, and the whisky tumbler balanced on his booted ankle. Mrs Bentley had let *him* inside with muddy boots on, but she had been too busy staring at the earl to remember to admonish him for leaving dirty footprints. "Eurydice, perhaps rather fitting given her name, has magic that is attuned to spirits and the dead."

"That would explain her behaviour when we used the mist at the cemetery to find Mr Plummer. She seemed to know which direction it would lead us in before the silver dust had formed." Fern's wonder of the young dragon grew.

"And how she settled Mr Plummer's spirit. But Squib joined in with that. Do you think he can also see ghosts?" Millie had paused in her writing.

Fern shrugged and glanced at Seth. "Do pixie dragons also have magic?"

He scratched at his jaw and the dark shadow that clung to his chin. "I would have to consult the old journals. Pixie dragons are rare, and I can't recollect my father saying if any had ever lived at the wyvernry or been studied."

"Perhaps Squib has your ability to create with words, Millie?" Fern suggested.

Millie's mouth made a silent O. "Do you think so? Why, that would be simply marvellous."

The group talked until the whisky decanter, and then the tea and coffee pots, were drained. George stood and told the earl it was time for him to leave so that Fern could get some rest. Seth squared his shoulders, but instead of arguing, he agreed and wished them all a good evening.

Fern hugged Millie in the kitchen and left her friend in the care of George, who would escort her and Squib back to their home. Then she climbed the stairs and sought her bed. This time, as she drifted off to sleep, she recalled the phantom touch of her father as he had placed his hands on either side of her face in the land of the dead.

Two days later, the evening of the kelmsgale festival arrived. The summer weather complied and delivered a cloudless sky, a lingering warmth, and the barest hint of a breeze to stop dancers from becoming too overheated. The musicians set up on a wooden platform in front of the Drake's Rest, which meant they were kept supplied with beer to ensure they continued playing. Dancers swirled on the grass in the middle of the green. Children ran around laughing and waving ribbons on sticks. Stalls were dotted around the outside edge, selling marvellous sweet treats, bright trinkets, or offering games and entertainments.

On a whim, Fern had used some of her earnings from her work at Wyndham Hall to buy the floaty, light-green dress that had been in the modiste's window for months. With its embroidered leaves and vines spiralling around the skirt, she felt like a dryad dancing among the trees. Dryad? That recalled the words of the sisters after she had touched the soul of the whisperwoods. No, she still couldn't believe it. There was no such thing as dryads. She did possess a green thumb, though, and would content herself with that.

Millie looked radiant in a blue gown that bordered on violet and, with her dark hair, made her look like a Fae princess. The two women sat on a pile of cushions scattered on the grass under the kelmsgale. Above their heads, the kelmsgale flowers, with their cream cupped blooms like a *magnolia grandiflora*. The light breeze lifted the magical pollen, and it drifted around the village green.

The three Moray sisters sat on a long bench placed under the kelmsgale, the hard seat padded with cushions and blankets.

A gasp of wonder came from Millie, and she held out a hand. As though a sparrow perched on her fingers, she brought it closer to her face to peer at something. "Oh, it's so beautiful." Wonder filled her voice.

Fern frowned. There was nothing there. "I don't see anything."

"It's a mote. Like a tiny, glowing firefly. And slightly warm, too." She turned her hand over.

A cackle came from Morda. "The blinkers are gone from the writer's eyes."

"You can see motes?" Fern had to stop herself from pouting. Why did Millie suddenly have the gift after only a few months of living in the village?

"I used to as a child. Bertie said it was silly, and Father disapproved. Then as I got older, I just...stopped seeing them." She stood and gently carried the speck to the Moray sisters, who sat nearby with a stack of glass jars.

"Thank you, my dear," Nona said as she brushed the magical dust into a jar and screwed the lid back on.

Two children who also had the gift to see motes helped the old women. They raced around the green, plucking at the invisible specks. When they had a handful, they thrust their fist into the container before shoving a hand over the top to stop them escaping.

"You will have to join the children when they have classes with Nona," Fern said as she hummed along to the music.

"Classes?" Millie's gaze tracked another, unseen to most people, glowing mote.

"You must learn how to mould magic. You are truly one of us now," Decima said, and she winked at Fern.

Fern was happy for her friend. She just hoped the old witches didn't teach Millie how to use motes to bring more stories to life.

"Speaking of learning things. I remember you once told me that the earl's man, Quint, is a local. What family does he belong to?" Fern hoped the enjoyable evening would loosen the witches' lips.

"He's a Payne!" Morda cackled.

"He's a pain all right. But who are his family?" Fern tried again.

Decima laughed and spelled out the surname. "P. A. Y. N. E."

Fern burst into laughter. "Never was a name better suited to a person." She vaguely knew the family but didn't have much to do with them.

"Could I have the pleasure of this dance, Miss Oakby?" A familiar voice sent a ripple down Fern's spine.

Turning, Seth stood near them. He wore a cream linen shirt and a tweed waistcoat like the other men present. Yet even without a noble's regular evening wear of top hat and swallow-tailed coat, there was something about his bearing that marked him as different. And it wasn't the scaled scar and gleaming silver eye, either.

A wave of chatter washed around the green at finding their lord amongst them after a long absence. People looked, and children, as always, were curious. But there were no shouted comments, and no one harboured any cruel intent. Regardless of rank, he was one of them. There were polite smiles and nods of heads, as though seeing the earl in the village was a regular occurrence. That Fern could remember, he hadn't been spotted for years and was last seen at the kelmsgale festival when he had been a lad.

A dragon at Wyndham Hall has been good for its lord.

"Of course, Lord Drakeman." Fern placed her hand on his outstretched one for balance as she rose to her feet.

"Will you be all right, Millie?" If the noise became too much for her friend, she would sit out the dancing to keep her company.

The writer waved her away. "Music and laughter outside don't crush me like the same noise in a crowded ballroom. Besides, I want to see how many motes I can find. They are becoming easier to spot now that I have decided to see them again. Go, enjoy your dance."

The musicians struck up a quick country tune, and Seth spun Fern around. She laughed, and her heart lightened. Then a sight made her stop so suddenly they nearly collided with another couple.

"Good grief. Is that Quint?"

The butler stood with a group of men by the tavern, all with tankards of ale in their hands, as they swapped rowdy tales. "And he appears to be...laughing."

She shook her head, sure that her eyes were playing tricks

on her. She had drunk two ales herself, and it had obviously addled her brain.

"He's quite the entertaining storyteller if you get him in the right mood." Seth's hand at her waist guided her back into place before they collided with anyone else.

"You brewed something in your laboratory, didn't you, and dosed him with it?" That could be the only explanation for the surly man attending the festival and laughing, instead of sitting in a dim room polishing his knives.

He donned a serious expression. "Quite possibly."

"You will have to tell me his first name, now that I have discovered he is a Payne." That was the last bit of information she needed.

He huffed. "If you know that much, you will be able to dig it up. But I must swear you to secrecy."

"I promise I shall not breathe a word of it."

He glanced at the group of men as they roared in good humour.

"Butram," he whispered in her ear.

Fern snorted and nearly choked on a surge of hysterical laughter.

Butram Payne.

Quint was, quite literally, a pain in the butt.

With a monumental effort, she managed to school her features and hide the glee at having a true name in her arsenal for future use. Then her gaze stopped at another set of familiar features. "Is that Moyles?"

Lord Warrington's gardener stood beside Quint and was drinking an ale.

"You were correct, he is tolerable. Quint also said that

hiring him would stop you from making his ears bleed with complaints about all the work I make you do." Seth's full lips quirked in good humour.

"Oh...take that, Lord Warrington." Now she actually wanted to see Millie's brother again so she could drop a hint that she had been responsible for him losing the capable gardener. She had a strong suspicion that the arrogant noble would explode with outrage. She met her dance partner's gaze. "The last few weeks have wrought quite a change over you, my lord."

"It was time I remembered my responsibility to this village. And it's people. We will find where Luxton has taken the dragon silk and who killed your father." He held her a little tighter.

Tears burned in her eyes as she recalled the last thing her father saw, and she blinked them away. The path she walked to find a killer was a dangerous one. But she was not alone. Family, by blood and friendship, surrounded her.

"Will you be able to stand another dance or two? I think you will be compelled to dance with Nona, and Millie would love to examine you up close. If you could tolerate it, Seth?" Only now did she worry about what he saw among the happy faces. The lies, grief, and weariness in their hearts were all exposed to his dragon gaze.

"I shall simply focus on the one face I find imminently tolerable." His lips grazed her ear as he lowered his head closer to hers. "I shall start a tally of the kisses you owe me. That is one."

The man didn't know her at all if he thought telling her

he was keeping count would be a deterrent. "As you wish, Seth."

Two, he mouthed.

A tingle ran along her veins. Her mother used to caution her to be careful what she wished for. She had wished for a summer romance and found an unexpected one. Rather like throwing a line into the water, hoping for a minnow, she had instead caught a shark.

Or a dragon.

What would she do with him now?

"Seth, Seth, Seth, Seth..." she murmured in time to the music.

Hunger flared in his mercurial eye, and Fern curled her toes. This was going to be the *best* evening.

FERN's botanical adventures continue in...

THE BLIGHTED REEDS

The river remembers—and it wants its story told.

When Fern Oakby is summoned to the quiet village of Witherby, she expects a stubborn botanical nuisance. Instead, she finds a river strangled by unnatural reeds, a mill ground to a halt, and villagers who no longer dare to go near the water. At dusk, the reeds begin to sing...and something beneath the surface stirs.

As Fern and Millie investigate, they uncover an old tragedy, a drowned child, and a grief that has taken root and grown monstrous. The child's tale has been rewritten so many times that the truth has sunk beneath the surface, warping the magic that once flowed through the river.

With Millie's gift for uncovering hidden stories, the two women must confront a sorrow that refuses to rest—because something in the water is waking, and it remembers exactly who was lost.

To save Witherby, Fern and Millie must untangle a twisted tale before it claims another life. If they cannot rewrite the ending, the river will go on taking...and it might drown them all.

BUY The Blighted Reeds at:

https://tillywallace.com/books/leaf-and-scale/the-blighted-reeds/

ALSO BY TILLY WALLACE

For the most complete and up to date list of books, please visit the
website: https://tillywallace.com/books/

Available series:

Tournament of Shadows

Manner and Monsters

Highland Wolves

Grace Designs Mysteries

Magic of Wyldefen

Leaf and Scale

ABOUT THE AUTHOR

 Tilly drinks entirely too much coffee and is obsessed with hats. In her spare time she writes whimsical historical fantasy novels, set in a bygone time where magic is real. If you love found family and comfort reads, come and escape reality in her tales.

Email: tilly@tillywallace.com
Web: https://www.tillywallace.com
STORE: https://www.tillywallacebooks.com

If you would like to support Tilly for as little as a coffee a month, members of the *Gaslamp Parlour* read early chapters of her current work and exclusive stories, vote on story ideas. You can find more information at: https://www.patreon.com/TillyWallace

patreon.com/TillyWallace
facebook.com/tillywallaceauthor
instagram.com/tillywallaceauthor

www.ingramcontent.com/pod-product-compliance
Lightning Source LLC
Chambersburg PA
CBHW030602120726
47904CB00006B/1738